ENTHRALLED

VIKING LORE, BOOK 1

EMMA PRINCE

BOOKS BY EMMA PRINCE

Viking Lore Series:

Enthralled (Viking Lore, Book 1)

Shieldmaiden's Revenge (Viking Lore, Book 2)

The Bride Prize (Viking Lore Novella, Book 2.5)

Desire's Hostage (Viking Lore, Book 3)

Thor's Wolf (Viking Lore, Book 3.5)—a Kindle Worlds novella

Highland Bodyguards Series:

The Lady's Protector (Book 1)

Heart's Thief (Book 2)

A Warrior's Pledge (Book 3)

Claimed by the Bounty Hunter (Book 4)

A Highland Betrothal (Novella, Book 4.5)

The Promise of a Highlander (Book 5)

The Bastard Laird's Bride (Book 6—Reid Mackenzie's story) coming Fall 2017!

The Sinclair Brothers Trilogy:

Highlander's Ransom (Book 1)

Highlander's Redemption (Book 2)

Highlander's Return (Bonus Novella, Book 2.5)

Highlander's Reckoning (Book 3)

Other Books:

Wish upon a Winter Solstice (A Highland Holiday Novella)

ENTHRALLED

VIKING LORE, BOOK 1

~

By
Emma Prince

For Scott. Always.

1

---

806 A.D.
North Sea

"Lower the sail!" Eirik bellowed. For a moment, he feared the wind had snatched his voice, but then he saw the black outlines of his crew rise from the deck and move on uncertain feet toward the halyard lines.

The ocean surged beneath the ship, threatening to topple some of the men overboard. Somehow, they all managed to keep their feet, and a moment after they reached the rigging, Eirik could see the inky shadow of the sail slowly lower toward the deck.

Eirik tightened his already white-knuckled grip on the tiller. They should have brought down the sail at the first sign of rain, but this cursed storm had broken upon them so quickly that he'd barely had time to bark out a few orders before the seas turned rough and the rain and wind hit them full force.

Even now that the sodden wool sail was almost down, the sea still threatened to overpower his grip on the tiller, which would send the ship careening off course.

"To oars! To oars!" Eirik shouted into the wind. A flash of lightning illuminated the wave-battered deck as the crew scrambled to thread the long wooden oars through the oar holes below the gunwales.

Another flash of lightning revealed Alaric's drenched figure lurching toward Eirik.

"Give up on staying the course we charted, Eirik!" Alaric yelled when he reached the tiller. "And you'd best give the men their coins!"

Dread sliced through Eirik, far colder than the wind and rain that lashed him. Every last member of the crew was hunkered over an oar, pulling with the might of Thor. If they were going to die in this storm, at least they should have a gift to give to Ran, the sea god's wife.

Eirik gave Alaric a single nod before letting the tiller go. Instantly, the tiller swayed wildly. They were now at the sea's mercy.

Alaric stumbled toward the rowing men. Eirik followed, feet wide to absorb the ocean's violent rolling. As he passed each rower, he reached into the leather pouch at his belt.

"For Ran," Eirik said to each man as he passed out gold coins.

"Ja, for Aegir's wife!" some of the men responded, nodding solemnly through the rain at their captain.

When every sailor had a gold coin to give Ran to appease her and ease their journey to Valhalla, Eirik took up an oar across from Alaric. If the gods decided that it was his time to die, at least Eirik would go down fighting alongside his closest friend and this worthy crew.

Only a tiny twinge of regret shadowed his vision of entering Valhalla with his ship, his friend, and his crew. He would never get to see the lands to the west if Aegir and Ran claimed him and his men this day.

He dug his oar deep into the roiling sea. By Thor, he could not die just yet. He had to live to set eyes on these fabled lands to the west.

It wasn't until the last raindrop had fallen that the crew of the Drakkar stood and cheered to the gods for surviving the storm. For Eirik's part, he kissed the gold coin he'd kept for himself and tossed it into the sea. It was both an acknowledgment and an offering to Ran and Aegir.

Eirik gave orders to withdraw the oars and unfurl their red and white striped sail once more. Then he took a firm hold on the tiller and pointed them southeast. Based on the sun's position, they had been blown farther north than they'd intended to travel, but land still should lie ahead of them.

"Did any of you girls piss your pants?"

Eirik cringed internally. He recognized the voice immediately. His cousin Grimar seemed determined to make enemies within the crew.

"One storm and you're all cowering like women!"

Grimar came into Eirik's line of sight as he ducked around the mast and sauntered toward the stern.

"Say that again, *boy*."

Muttering a curse, Eirik waved for one of the nearby men to take the tiller from him. Before he could reach Grimar or Madrena, he heard the hiss of metal being unsheathed.

"Madrena, Grimar, hold!" Eirik bellowed as he reached his cousin and Alaric's twin sister. Alaric had beaten him to Madrena's side, however, and looked ready to cut Grimar down if his sister didn't.

"I'm sick of this dog filling the air with his stench," Madrena snapped, her eyes locked on Grimar. Due to the close quarters on Drakkar's deck, her bow and sword remained over her shoulders, but she had her seax drawn and pointed toward Grimar's throat. A sunbeam glinted off the blade.

"And I'm sick of this sow taking up space on a ship where a *man*, a *real warrior*, is needed," Grimar shot back, his own seax in hand. He held the blade lazily, though, as if to further insult Madrena by treating her drawn dagger as naught more than child's play.

"Enough, both of you!" Eirik bit out. The tension had been thick the entire voyage—by the gods, it had been thick long before they'd set sail a sennight ago—but now it was dangerously close to boiling over outright. "Madrena, to the stern. Grimar, the bow."

"'Tis for the best," Grimar muttered under his breath. "Run along to my cousin for protection, *girl*. Spread your legs for him, and he might even make you captain."

Alaric caught Madrena's wrist just as she lunged toward Grimar's neck, seax flashing. She let out a shriek of rage and frustration as her brother prevented her from landing her blow. Grimar's pale blue eyes flashed in surprise for the briefest moment, but then he chuckled and strolled toward the bow.

Alaric wrenched the blade free from Madrena's hand, but Eirik could see that the fight had gone out of her.

"He's not worth the effort it would take you for you to clean and re-sharpen your seax, sister," Alaric said quietly as he guided Madrena toward the stern.

"Tell me again why your swine cousin is on this voyage, Eirik," Madrena hissed when she, Alaric, and Eirik reached the tiller.

Eirik let out a breath and motioned for his man to move out of the way so that he could reclaim the tiller. He didn't need anyone else poking their noses into the discontent that brewed on his ship.

"You know as well as I," Eirik said flatly to Madrena. She rolled her pale gray eyes at him.

"Just because he's kin—"

"Ja, and Jarl Gunvald's son. What did you expect me to do? Let you kill him for his offense?" Eirik lowered his voice further so that he would be sure only Alaric and Madrena could hear him. "The Jarl is the one who decides where we raid, when we raid—and if we raid at all. It took me three years just to convince him to let us travel westward instead of staying in the safe waters of our neighboring fjords or crossing to Jutland."

Madrena flipped the blond braids trailing down her

back and waved dismissively. By the gods, she was as hot-tempered as her brother. Yet at least she was not like his cousin, whom they called the Raven for his black temperament. Eirik would trust his life to both Alaric and Madrena, his kinship with Grimar be cursed.

"But he practically accused me of incest. Lying with you would be like lying with my blood brother," Madrena said lowly, the fires of anger still simmering in her eyes.

"Leave it, Madrena," Alaric said. "Everyone can see that Grimar is just trying to cause trouble. He's testing you." The last applied to Madrena, but Alaric's eyes flickered to Eirik.

"I need to rid myself of Grimar's filth," Madrena said tartly. She stalked to the gunwale and leaned over, scooping up handfuls of seawater and splashing them over her face. Only a fool or a blind man would question Madrena's worthiness to be on this voyage. Grimar was neither. Eirik felt himself sinking into a foul mood.

Alaric must have sensed the weight settling over Eirik, for he said lightly, "Regale me again with the tales you heard about this land to the west we sail toward. Can the stories be believed? Will this all be worth a fortnight in close quarters with your cousin?"

Alaric's quirked mouth and raised eyebrow softened the underlying questions that Eirik had been mulling over himself for months—nei, years.

"If the monks I visited are to be believed—and I think they are—we will encounter unguarded treasure beyond anything we have thus far encountered in our raids."

The rumors had started almost fifteen summers ago, when Eirik was no longer a boy, but not quite a man. They spoke of a land to the west which was rich and ripe for the taking. Unprotected places of worship sat all along the coastline, filled with treasures unimaginable— gold, silver, jewels, and more. By the time Eirik was old enough to go on raids against neighboring Jarls' lands, he knew that some day he would have to see this land for himself.

But in the last few years, change brewed in the air. The Jarls across the Skagerrak Straight in Jutland had begun to consolidate their authority under one all-powerful King. Jutland's King was bent on taking these westerly lands—with their treasures, rich farmland, and soft climate—for himself. Though Dalgaard, Eirik's village on the north side of the Straight, was large and prosperous, it would easily be swallowed up by competing powers unless men like Eirik did something.

As if sensing his thoughts, Alaric interjected. "And you believe that if Dalgaard can claim its share of this new land's wealth, we will no longer be bound to the endless in-fighting with our neighbors?"

"Ja, claim this land's wealth—and perhaps more. Think of it, Alaric. Jutland's King is rumored to be leaving settlements in the west and south over the winter. How great will his power grow if he gains control of this new land as well as all of Jutland?"

"When will his appetite for land and power be sated?" Alaric said lowly, rubbing the golden-brown stubble on his jawline. A somber silence settled over the two men for a long moment.

"But how can you believe the stories?" Alaric said incredulously, once again lightening the mood. "Unguarded piles of gold? Weakling men who can't even wield weapons? Those monks were probably trying to send us all to our deaths!"

"The same tales keep spreading through the North-lands—there must be at least a seed of truth to them, nei?"

Alaric still looked skeptical. "And you think our future lies in this foreign land?"

Eirik believed it so much that he had traveled several days northeast to visit a village where two monks from Lindisfarne, a holy place they called a monastery, were enslaved as thralls. The monks had been reluctant to talk to him at first, but Eirik had been persistent. He had practically begged them—him, son and nephew to Jarls, and they, thralls—to teach him their language and a bit about their religion.

Eirik had spent nearly a year in that village to the northeast of Dalgaard, eventually winning over the enthralled monks and learning all he could. He hadn't even had his uncle's permission to embark westward at the time. He had wagered everything on his conviction and knowledge, hoping that they would be enough to convince Jarl Gunvald that the future of Dalgaard lay to the west.

"Ja, I do, brother," Eirik said with a wry grin. "But I suppose we won't know until we get there."

"Land!"

The shout from the bow jerked both Alaric and Eirik's heads up.

"Land, straight ahead!" Haakon, one of Eirik's most trusted seamen, was leaning over the curved prow of the Drakkar, squinting into the thin mist that settled over the water around them.

Just then, Eirik saw a foggy shape emerge from the mist. His chest tightened. Land. Despite the storm, despite being blown off course to the north, they had found it, the storied lands to the west.

A bellow went up from the crew. Several drew their weapons and brandished them at the large landmass that was taking shape before them, at the sky, and at the sea.

As the ship drew closer to the shore, Eirik handed over the tiller to Alaric and strode to the bow.

"Quiet!" he barked over his shoulder. "Your noise will carry across the water."

Despite his admonishment, he clenched his fists impatiently as the land in front of them slowly emerged through the mist. He longed to leap over the gunwale, sword in one hand, ax in the other, and place his feet on solid ground. But he couldn't be sure yet that this was the stretch of coastline they were aiming for.

Just then, the land in front of them solidified and darkened, but another landmass eased out of the mist behind it. This was just an island off the larger mainland, then. The sharply rising island grew more distinct as they drew nearer. Eirik could now make out some sort of structure perched on top of the hump rising from the sea.

Eirik squinted as the structure emerged from the mist. He could make out the arched stonework and bell tower the monks had described as indicative of a Christian holy house. But as they got nearer still, he noticed that some of the stones and archways were crumbling and the bell remained silent. Surely their red and white striped sail would be visible to the inhabitants of this island monastery?

A thought flitted across Eirik's mind, quick as an owl's wing. Could this be Lindisfarne itself? The monks had described an island monastery in the north of these lands, in a kingdom they called Northumbria. All the wooden buildings had been burned in that initial raid, they'd said, and even some of the stonework had been destroyed.

Mayhap they sailed still farther north than they intended, Eirik realized. The monks had told him tales of the complete destruction of Lindisfarne some thirteen summers ago. As such, Lindisfarne was not his destination. Over the months of talking with the monks about their religion and country, he'd learned that many such monasteries dotted the coastline, removed from villages—and armies that could have protected them.

"Steer south!" Eirik called to Alaric through the eerie silence created by the dampening fog. Or perhaps it was being in the presence of the desolate and deserted monastery. Eirik had heard the boasts of the Vikings who had captured and enthralled the Christian monks. They'd found the monastery completely unguarded and yet had cut the monks down like so many babes in their cradles. Some of the monks, those who hadn't been saved as thralls, had even been taken onto the Vikings'

ships, only to be thrown over to drown for the Vikings'
amusement.

Eirik suppressed a sneer and a curse for such
Vikings. It was dishonorable to cut down a man who
didn't even have a weapon in his hand. Death could be
honorable, and sacrifice appeased the gods, but
slaughter—nei, those men, boasting about their easy
kills, would never find glory in the afterlife.

He felt the ship shift under him as Alaric turned the
tiller and pointed them southward. They'd have to keep
close enough to the shoreline of the mainland to avoid
going too far out to sea, yet far enough not to be readily
spotted. If Eirik was right, there would be more monasteries like Lindisfarne to the south—except he wanted
more than mere treasure. His village was counting on
him, counting on this voyage. He couldn't let
them down.

2

**Whitby Abbey
Kingdom of Northumbria**

L aurel bit off a curse as her foot made contact with the bucket and she heard the slosh of water behind her. So absorbed had she been in scrubbing the refectory floor that she hadn't noticed how close the bucket was.

Sighing, she crawled over to the widening puddle behind her and began working the stone floors with the boar-hair scrub brush. She'd need more water to finish cleaning the enormous refectory, but at least she could make use of the spill.

When the water had been spread evenly and the floors were clean beneath it, she scooped up the bucket and stood with a groan. Her back ached from so many hours hunched over, her hands and knees had long ago gone numb, and of course there was the constant scratch of her rough woolen dress.

Laurel had to suppress another foul thought as she crossed through the refectory and toward the kitchens. She had it better than some. Aye, she had to labor in the most menial tasks at the monastery. And aye, Abbess Hilda and the other nuns and monks who lived at Whitby Abbey never let her forget that she was an orphan, born in sin. But she got to eat twice a day, she slept with a roof over her head, and she had a straw-filled mattress to lay her weary body upon each night.

She crossed the kitchens, which were quiet at this time of night, and stepped through the back door toward the river. The cool grass tickled her ankles as she strode down the sloping hillside to where the River Esk flowed. The moon was nigh full and glinted off the slow-moving water.

She should be grateful. Why did she rankle so much at life in the Abbey? She had known naught else. She wasn't owed anything. She was no one.

And yet, was there naught else to life than back-breaking work from sun-up to sundown? Was there naught else than the feel of coarse wool against one's skin? Was there naught else than to feel like an outsider, a burden, that one's mere existence was a sin?

Laurel approached the river cautiously so as not to slip on its shoreline and tumble in. If she fell and drowned, no one would notice her absence until the morning. She shivered at the thought and carefully dipped the bucket into the river. 'Twould be enough to finish scrubbing the refectory floor, she thought with relief. She wouldn't have to come back to the dark, flowing waters tonight.

As she straightened and turned back toward the Abbey, a shadowy figure moved in front of her. A strangled noise of surprise came from her throat.

"Hush, girl, unless you want to wake everyone in the Abbey."

She recognized the voice, but instead of feeling relief, her stomach dropped in fear.

"Brother Egbert, what are you doing here?" she asked flatly.

"I was making the rounds, extinguishing the last of the candles, when I saw you," he said lowly, stepping toward her. She took a half step back and suddenly halted. She was already standing in the mud of the riverbank. Another step or two and she would be swept off to the North Sea, which she could hear even over the rush of the river behind her.

"Let me pass," she grated out.

"And waste the privacy and the moonlight?" he whispered. "I think not." He closed the distance between them and took her in a rough embrace. Laurel tried to scream, but his mouth crushed hers, muffling the sound. Panic rose in her throat. They were too far away from the monastery. The noise of the river and the ocean bordering the Abbey on the north and east sides would drown out her cries for help.

She swung the still-full bucket at Brother Egbert's head and heard the thunk of the wood connecting with his skull. The bucket's water splashed over both of them.

Brother Egbert groaned and tore his mouth from

hers, yet his grip on her arms tightened so that she was immobilized.

"Wicked girl," he hissed under his breath. He pressed her down to the muddy bank, using his body weight to pin her.

Laurel thrashed wildly, realizing that the monk intended to do more than steal a kiss or inconspicuously grope her in passing, as he had done for months now.

"You are a man of God!" she choked out. "Let me go!"

One of his hands released her arm to find the hem of her gown. "I am only a man. And you have been tempting me for years."

Laurel squeezed her eyes shut, nausea sweeping her. Then she realized one of her arms was free. She jerked her hand from underneath her and raked her nails down Brother Egbert's face. He howled in pain, falling to her side and clutching his face.

She scrambled to her feet and bolted uphill toward the Abbey. Though her simple leather boots were slathered with mud, she reached the top of the hill faster than she ever had. Behind her, she heard Brother Egbert curse her and make his way to the Abbey.

Laurel plowed through the kitchen and into the refectory, not knowing where she was going. Perhaps the nuns' quarters would be safer than her own straw mat in the corner. Just as she turned toward the wooden door that led to the nuns' side of the double monastery, the doors banged open on their own and light flooded the refectory.

"What in God's name is going on here, child?" Abbess Hilda boomed at her, candle held high.

"Abbess, I—"

"Abbess Hilda," Brother Egbert interjected, stepping into the refectory. "Thank the Lord you've stopped this little witch from escaping. She attacked me by the river."

The Abbess's cold, dark eyes took in the scene before her. Laurel glanced down to find herself a muddy, bedraggled mess. A quick look over her shoulder revealed Brother Egbert in little better condition. His brown robes weren't as muddy as her dress, but he had four angry red lines running the length of his face, which was wrinkled in a dark frown.

"What do you have to say for yourself, girl?" the Abbess asked calmly.

"I—I was getting more water to finish scrubbing the floor. It was Brother Egbert who attacked me at the river! He kissed me and tried to—tried to…"

Laurel swallowed. Abbess Hilda's eyes had widened for a moment, but then they narrowed with obvious suspicion.

Brother Egbert jumped into Laurel's faltering silence. "The girl is clearly lying—I have the marks to prove it." He gestured toward the red scratches on his cheek. Then he bowed his head in an overt attempt at piousness. "And if I have been tempted into impure thoughts about her…well, it must be the Devil testing me. After all, she is sin incarnate."

Abbess Hilda shifted her gaze back to Laurel, and she knew all was lost now.

"Come here, child." The Abbess's voice was quiet and flat.

Laurel approached slowly, her head held steady. She would not grovel for a wrong she hadn't committed—either for tempting Brother Egbert or the fact that she was born out of wedlock. When she halted in front of Abbess Hilda, the older woman's mouth turned down in a sneer at her audacity.

"Ever since the day your shame-filled parents abandoned you on the Abbey's doorstep, we have clothed you, fed you, and tried to guide you toward God's light."

Laurel had heard these admonitions before. Each time the Abbess or one of the nuns or monks who lived at Whitby started in about her sinful origin or her ingratitude, she had hunched a little more, bowed her head lower, shrinking inside herself.

Yet tonight, after scrubbing the refectory floor in the dark, being attacked by Brother Egbert, and having to stand before his lies and the Abbess's reproofs, she felt her spine harden. Her stomach turned to lead, her hands clenching at her sides.

"Yet despite our best efforts, you carry sin with you —you are willful, proud, slothful, and now you tempt a monk, a holy man devoted to God, to join you in your sin."

Abbess Hilda eyed her for another moment, no doubt taking in her level chin and rigid body. The Abbess sighed and gazed heavenward.

"Yet it is our duty to continue to set you on the right path. We cannot abandon you, as your parents so easily did. We must cleanse you of your sins."

At the word "cleanse," Laurel's strength evaporated. "Nay," she whispered.

"The chair," Abbess Hilda said calmly.

"Nay!" Laurel screamed. Her legs suddenly gave out underneath her, and she fell to the cold stones of the refectory floor.

"Brother Egbert, wake the Abbot and tell Sister Agnes to bring the chair to the refectory," Abbess Hilda went on, paying no attention to Laurel.

Laurel knew there was no point in begging not to be put in the chair. The Abbess rarely used this punishment, but when she did, she was unyielding to pleas for mercy. Laurel would rather take the switch than the chair—but the Abbess knew that.

Brother Egbert scuttled out of the refectory toward the monks' sleeping quarters. A few minutes later, Abbot Thomas emerged, looking rumpled and cantankerous. Then Laurel heard the scraping sound that was so often the opening to her nightmares. Sister Agnes appeared, dragging the heavy wooden chair behind her. The sister's eyes drooped from sleepiness, but she was ready as usual to help Abbess Hilda administer Laurel's punishment.

Laurel bit her lip to prevent from screaming out in terror. The Abbot and Abbess lifted her under the arms and dragged her toward the chair while Brother Egbert reemerged with several lengths of rope. Laurel was dropped into the chair and her wrists held against the chair's wooden arms. She didn't struggle, though it took every ounce of willpower not to. It would do little good. Both the Abbot and Abbess had a firm grip on her.

When her hands and feet had been lashed to the wood, the Abbot, Abbess, Brother Egbert, and Sister Agnes lifted her, chair and all, and began shuffling toward the kitchens. Laurel tried to control her breathing. Panicking would only make it worse, as she'd learned at a young age. Nevertheless, her heart hammered in her ears.

The group passed through the kitchens and out the back door, following the same path toward the River Esk that Laurel had taken earlier that night. She could hear the river flowing lazily below them as they made their way carefully down the grassy hillside. The North Sea sighed restlessly to her right.

With grunts of exertion, the group pivoted when they reached the riverbank so that her back was to the water. Brother Egbert tied two more lengths of rope to the chair's arms and handed one to Abbot Thomas.

"Laurel, child of sin, you must be purified of your wickedness," Abbess Hilda intoned. "Let the waters of the River Esk be like God's light, washing you clean and humbling you."

Brother Egbert leaned over and placed a hand on the chair's back, easing it backward. While his arm and the surrounding darkness blocked his face from the view of the others, he gave her a twisted sneer.

The chair tilted backward toward the river. Laurel grasped the chair's arms with sweating hands, taking huge gulps of air. Brother Egbert and Abbot Thomas each held the rope attached to the wooden arms. They began slowly, torturously, lowering her into the water.

Even in midsummer, the river was cold. It touched

her lower back first, causing her to buck and twist, but of course her bonds held fast. She turned her face to the side to be able to predict when the water would reach her head. It was a trick she'd learned as a girl to calm herself and avoid the shock of the water's cold, enveloping grasp. Despite the large moon overhead, the water around her was inky and depthless.

Now the water was at her shoulders, seeping up her braid and touching the nape of her neck. She took one last deep breath before the water swallowed her completely.

If she screamed now, she'd lose all her precious air, and who knew how long they planned to hold her like this? She counted to ten, then counted to ten again, then again. The water rushed around her head, clawing at her, trying to choke her.

Then suddenly she felt herself being jerked upward. She emerged with a gasp as Brother Egbert and Abbot Thomas pulled her up by the ropes.

"Again," Abbess Hilda said flatly after only a moment of blessed freedom from the swirling river.

Once again, Laurel was lowered into the river. She willed herself to remain conscious despite the lack of air and the strangling terror surging through her. When she broke the surface and could take several large gulps of precious air once again, she thought the worst was over. But the Abbess ordered for her to be plunged into the river again and again, more than she'd ever endured before.

Laurel's mind numbed to the repeated dunks. The water remained just as terrifying as it always had been

—or as terrifying as far back as Laurel's first such punishment from the Abbess. She couldn't swim, so deep water had naturally scared her, but it wasn't until the chair became the Abbess's worst punishment that Laurel had begun having nightmares about water strangling her, choking her, pushing her under its weight.

By the time Brother Egbert and Abbot Thomas hauled her up and the Abbess said a curt, "Enough," Laurel was shaking uncontrollably and seeing spots.

"Perhaps this time you will learn," Sister Agnes hissed as she leaned forward to loosen the ropes on Laurel's feet and hands. The older woman's face was puckered in a well-worn scowl.

"You will bring the chair back to the Abbey," Abbess Hilda said. "And then you will re-scrub the refectory floors to remove the mud you tracked all over them earlier."

Without another word, the Abbess, Abbot, Brother Egbert, and Sister Agnes turned their backs on her and began making their way up the hill toward the monastery. Laurel struggled to stand, her head spinning. Once she had her feet under her, she turned the chair around and grabbed it by its back. One dizzying step at a time, she began dragging the heavy wooden chair up the steep hill in front of her.

She had to stop every few steps to catch her breath and slow the spinning in her head. As she approached the top of the hill, she was surprised to see the shadowy figures of her tormenters standing close together. She halted behind them, listening.

"…Probably just a trick of the eye," Abbot Thomas was saying grumpily.

Just then, a cloud that was obscuring the moon scuttled away. Laurel followed the others' gazes toward the North Sea.

Sister Agnes shrieked at the sight before them. Laurel had to suppress a scream of her own.

Drifting toward the Abbey, illuminated by moonlight, was a ship. But it wasn't a fishing skiff from a nearby village. The blood-red striped sail, the curving serpentine prow—it was a Viking ship.

Laurel's stomach flew to her throat. She'd heard the rumors of the Northmen raiders who appeared from the sea, striking unprotected monasteries and vulnerable villages with deadly speed, and then retreating from whence they'd come. Abbess Hilda even used tales of the Northmen to frighten the nuns and monks at Whitby.

"And the prophet Jeremiah spake, 'Out of the north an evil shall break forth upon all inhabitants of the land,' for the day of judgement is at hand," Abbot Thomas breathed, his eyes riveted on the ship.

Abbess Hilda was the first to recover her wits. "Laurel, sound the bell. Sister Agnes, rouse the nuns. Brother Egbert, do the same for the monks. Abbot, gather everyone in the chapel. I'll lead us in prayer."

The others stumbled toward the kitchen doors, with Laurel following behind them. After the first few steps, her legs seemed to come alive again, despite the cold, sodden wool of her gown clinging to them. She moved through the kitchens and refectory toward the bell tower. She began shivering uncontrollably as she reached the bell tower's stairs yet forced herself to mount them.

Even with only the moonlight filtering through the open belfry, she'd rung the bell enough to be able to find the rope pulley. She jerked it down with all her might, sending the bell tilting. The bell's peal broke the night's silence. She gave another hard pull on the rope just to be sure the bell would continue to toll a warning to the monastery's inhabitants.

Though she didn't have time to waste, she peered over the belfry's open window at the beach below. The Viking ship had landed on the strip of sand below the cliffs atop which the monastery sat. The moon glinted dully off metal helms as warriors poured from the ship and onto the beach. Her chest seized. She sent up a prayer for all those in the Abbey.

Ripping her eyes from the terrifying sight, she forced her feet to move. She raced down the bell tower's stairs and made her way toward the chapel. She slipped through the wooden doors just as Sister Agnes and another nun were pushing them closed. Laurel helped the two women lift a large beam across the door to bar it.

Inside the chapel, the monks and nuns were in a panic. In the candlelight that softly illuminated the chapel's interior, the monks looked around with wild eyes and the nuns clung to each other, some crying.

"Silence!" Abbess Hilda barked at the altar. All eyes turned to her, the hush only broken by a few sniffles.

"Let us pray," the Abbess said with surprising calm.

The monks and nuns fell to their knees, Laurel following suit.

"*A furore normannorum liberu nos, Domine*," Abbess Hilda said. Abbot Thomas, who appeared by the Abbess's side, took up the chant, and soon the chapel was filled with the whispered prayer.

"From the fury of the Northmen deliver us, O Lord," Laurel echoed in Latin.

Suddenly a loud thud reverberated through the chapel. Several of the nuns broke the chanted prayer with shrieks of terror. The thud came again from right behind where Laurel knelt at the back of the nave. Abbess Hilda raised her calm voice over the murmurs and gasps, but a ripple of panic nevertheless was spreading throughout the kneeling monks and nuns.

The stones below Laurel's knees reverberated as the thudding persisted

"From the fury of the Northmen deliver us—"

The sound of splintering wood rent the air behind her. More screams rose in the chapel, and the Abbey's residents huddled toward the altar.

Before Laurel could crawl forward, the door to the chapel exploded in a shower of wood shards. She looked back over her shoulder, immobilized with fear.

A horde of Vikings poured through the chapel's splintered door. Their helms and weapons—swords, axes, knives, spears—shone in the candlelight. One giant warrior in the front of the swarm let out a bellow of glee as his eyes fell on Laurel.

The scream died in her throat.

3

It couldn't be so easy! Eirik had assumed that the Viking raiders who'd told tales of their attacks on Lindisfarne were embellishing at least a little. The monks he'd spent last winter with spoke of the atrocities committed against their helpless Brothers, but he'd believed they'd similarly exaggerated their stories. How could a place holding such treasures be so completely defenseless?

Yet here they were, inside the monastery's walls, with only a ringing bell, a stone wall, and a wooden door for resistance.

They'd had to sail for another day and a half south from what he'd suspected was the abandoned Lindisfarne monastery. But as the moon had risen tonight, they'd spotted a stone structure atop a hill, bordered on the north side by a river. The Drakkar had glided smoothly onto the sandy beach. He and his crew easily scaled the cliffs leading up to the monastery.

One of the men had to be boosted over the stone walls protecting the monastery, but soon enough he'd secured a rope to a tree within the wall, and one by one, Eirik and his crew had climbed over.

They followed the hushed sound of chanting to the building before which they now stood. Several men raised their axes, ready to set into the wooden door, but Eirik held up a hand.

"Follow my orders, and we'll share the plunder equally," Eirik said lowly. He looked at each member of his crew, lingering on Grimar.

Before they'd made landfall, he'd reminded his crew that there was no honor in shedding the blood of unarmed, unskilled men. Any man who chose to disrespect the gods with such actions would answer to Eirik. They'd nodded solemnly, each sailor looking Eirik straight in the eye—all except Grimar.

"What's the point of raiding if you can't take what you want—be it gold, blood, or women?" Grimar had said for all to hear. He was testing Eirik's authority again. Though Eirik was this voyage's captain, it was Grimar's father, Jarl Gunvald, who'd ordered the exploration and plunder of the land to the west.

Now, outside the wooden door, Grimar met Eirik's gaze with a smile that belied the animosity in his pale blue eyes, which glowed eerily in the moonlight.

"Begin," Eirik said. At once, his men set their axes to the door in unison, striking with battle-earned strength.

"You need to keep your dog of a cousin on a tighter leash," Madrena said quietly to him. "He has already overstepped his bounds."

Eirik didn't respond and instead kept his eyes on the door. He could hear screams coming from the other side. If this was what the monks called a chapel, it would be the likeliest place to find the riches they sought.

All at once, the axes burst through the wood and candlelight poured from the hole they'd made. With a shout, the men in the front surged forward into the building.

Screams of terror filled the air as Eirik and his crew stepped through the shattered door. Golden crosses and candle holders flickered in the candlelight. They'd done it. They'd made landfall in these western lands, stormed an unprotected holy house, and now would claim its treasures for Dalgaard.

As Eirik's eyes took in the scene within the chapel, however, he faltered. He recognized the men in simple brown robes with bald patches on their heads as monks. Yet there were also women here. They wore black robes much like the monks, their hair covered in black cloth. Something wasn't right.

Before Eirik could call the terrified group of men and women to order, he heard a piercing scream above the rest to his right.

Grimar was dragging a girl in a brown dress up from the floor. He threw her over his shoulder with a satisfied shout. Several of the men and women surrounding the girl tried to grab her feet and pull her back into their midst. With a growl, Grimar lashed out with his blade, slicing across the group indiscriminately.

As blood spouted from the group of men and women, the chapel erupted into chaos. They were like sheep who'd caught a whiff of slaughter. They clawed at each other in an attempt to get away from the Vikings standing in the doorway despite the fact that there was clearly no other way out. Even those who'd been wounded by Grimar's blade frantically crawled back.

"Hold!" Eirik bellowed at Grimar, striding toward him. "How dare you defy me?"

"They tried to take my property from me," Grimar panted, bloodlust firing his eyes. "I claim this girl as my thrall." He nudged his shoulder to indicate the thrashing girl he carried.

Eirik drew the sword he'd intended not to use this night and pointed it at Grimar's throat. "I gave strict orders that there would be no killing or raping," he breathed, trying to keep a hold on his temper.

"Nei, cousin, our mission was to plunder this land's treasures," Grimar replied. "I have not killed or raped. This girl is just another prize I now possess."

Eirik gritted his teeth, yet a growl of rage rose from this throat. He held his blade at his cousin's neck for another long moment, trying to order his thoughts. If he killed Grimar, he'd have to answer to the Jarl, and knowing Gunvald, the man would not let the death of his only son go without rebuke, kinship or nei. And Grimar did indeed have the right to claim a slave. Yet he shouldn't have shed blood, which directly flouted Eirik's order.

"We will continue this on the ship," Eirik bit out. Grimar smiled, but it was more of a sneer.

Eirik turned toward the huddled men and women at the back of the chapel. "If you cooperate," he said in their language, "no one—no one *else*—will be hurt." He shot a sharp gaze at Grimar again before returning his attention to the crowd.

The terrified mass of people hushed for a moment, presumably awed by the fact that he spoke their language. After a moment, an older woman at the rear of the group stood up slowly. "What do you want, heathen?" she asked in a loud voice.

"Give us your gold, your silver, and your jewels," Eirik responded, internally relieved that his training with the monks had paid off. He could understand their strange tongue, and they could apparently make sense of his speech as well.

His crew fanned out around him, moving to the walls and toward the back of the chapel. They stripped everything of value they found, to the horrified murmurs of the crowd of cowering men and women.

As Eirik watched, he noticed something else strange about this monastery. In addition to women, he also observed that everyone he laid his eyes on was old. The youngest he saw couldn't be less than fifty or so in years —all except the one whom Grimar had claimed, but Eirik hadn't gotten a good look at her yet.

His crew deposited the loot in the middle of the chapel.

"Is there aught else of value here?" Eirik asked the woman who'd first spoken.

"Nay," she said, glaring at him. "Take the Devil's child with you and be gone from here, heathens!"

Eirik narrowed his eyes at the woman's haughty

tone. By the gods, she acted as if they were inconveniencing her!

A yelp from behind him drew his attention before he could respond to the woman. To his surprise, the noise had come from Grimar. His cousin was holding his ear, blood streaming between his fingers. The girl he'd hoisted over his shoulder earlier now lay in a heap at his feet but was trying to scramble upright and away from Grimar.

With a curse, Grimar raised his bloodied hand from his mangled ear and struck the new thrall across the face. The girl went spinning, landing on the hard stone floors. Yet instead of cowering, she raised her head to look up with utter hatred at Grimar. Grimar's blood left a red handprint on her cheek.

To Eirik's complete surprise, the girl then lashed out with her foot, kicking at Grimar's shins. Grimar cursed again and raised his hand to hit the girl once more, but Eirik bolted between them.

"First you draw monks' blood, and now you'll beat your thrall to death," Eirik ground out. "You dishonor yourself in front of the gods."

"She bit me! Besides, she's mine to do with as I will!" Grimar shot back, though a look of uncertainty flitted across his face at the mention of the gods.

Eirik felt the eyes of the rest of his crew on him. They all knew how he felt about thralls. Though it was an accepted practice to have slaves in the Northlands, Eirik believed it was a sign of weakness to force others to do his work for him. What was the worth of a man who needed slaves to run his farm, tend his home, or warm his bed?

But Grimar was right. According to custom and law, a thrall was no more than an animal, to be put to whatever use its master saw fit. The thought of the blood-smeared, defiant little sprite being forced by Grimar turned Eirik's stomach, however.

Just then the old woman's words came back to him, and he turned to face the girl in question. She was on her feet and panting from fright, yet her eyes locked on him with a dark defiance.

He had guessed right that she was young, but more a woman than a girl, as he'd initially thought. Unlike the other women, she wore no head covering. The dark, thick braid that ran down her back looked to be damp. Despite her chestnut hair, however, her skin was as pale as fresh snow on the mountains surrounding Dalgaard. Most of the women back home were pale-skinned as well, but he'd never seen the combination of such rich hair with such fair skin.

Her eyes, which continued to bore into him, were as dark as her hair, almost black in the low candlelight, and seemingly depthless. Her lips were rosy and slightly parted, her breath coming fast. Eirik let his eyes travel further down her form, across her slim shoulders and over the shapeless brown woolen dress, which appeared wet like her hair. She was so small, so vulnerable looking, and yet something about her stirred him.

"Is this the one you call Devil's child?" he said over the girl's shoulder to the old woman. "How can a tiny girl have earned such a title?"

"She is the product of sin," the older woman replied. "Take her and be gone."

Eirik wasn't sure what the woman meant by sin, beyond what the monks had told him last winter about the Christians' strange views on what a person should and shouldn't do. Regardless, the girl was clearly an outsider here—she was at least thirty years younger than the youngest of the other women, she wore brown instead of black, and she stared back at him, her spine straight, while the others cowered.

"Girl," he said, turning back to her. "Is there aught else of value here?"

Her gaze swept over their pile of plunder in the middle of the floor. "Nay," she breathed, squeezing her eyes shut.

"She is the only one worth taking as a thrall," Grimar said from behind Eirik. He must have sensed that Eirik was preparing to go. "All the others look too old and frail to do any work. And the women look dry as autumn leaves."

Grimar spat on the floor, causing another ripple of distress from the crowd. He stooped to retrieve a bit of rope and stepped toward the girl.

Her gaze darted between Grimar and Eirik, unsure what was happening. To ease her fears, Eirik spoke quietly to her in her language. "You are coming with us. If you do not resist, no harm will come to you." He forced himself to speak what was likely a lie, given the fact that Grimar was her master now. Yet Eirik felt drawn to protect the small, fiery girl.

Her eyes widened and she tried to step back, but

Grimar snatched her wrists and bound them quickly, leaving an extra length of rope by which to pull her.

"Nay! I will not go with you!" the girl shrieked, her bluster and bravery from earlier ebbing into panic.

Eirik turned his back on her, unable to face those dark, searing eyes as she protested. He gave orders to gather their loot and move out. As he and his crew stepped through the shattered door and toward the wall they'd scaled, he heard the chant rise from the chapel once more. The girl's pleas and shouts mingled with the relieved prayers of the others.

The sky had turned from inky black to gray-blue as dawn approached. They made their way across the hilltop and down the sandy cliffs to the beach, where the Drakkar awaited them. The crew boarded with their loot wrapped in cloth and slung over their shoulders. As each one set foot on the planks of the ship, they cheered for the easy victory.

The last to board was Grimar, the girl trailing behind on the rope leash. In the yellowing light, Eirik saw her face go from frightened to downright terrified as her eyes took in the ship. Nei, it wasn't the ship her dark eyes were locked on, but the water surrounding it.

"Nay, I cannot! Not the ocean! Please have mercy! Do not make me go out onto the ocean!" she screamed, thrashing wildly despite her bonds.

"Is the girl mad?" Grimar asked Eirik, not understanding her words. He picked her up bodily and threw her over the ship's gunwale. She landed on her bottom onboard but immediately tried to leap off the ship.

Eirik lunged for her, wrapping her in his arms to

prevent her from escaping or hurting herself. She was so small that both arms wound completely around her body, yet she fought against him with all her might, babbling about the water.

"Are you sure you want to claim her, cousin?" Eirik said flatly to Grimar as his cousin vaulted himself onboard. Grimar eyed the thrashing girl warily, and Eirik internally felt a flood of satisfaction. Perhaps if he thought the girl was too much trouble, he'd not take her as a thrall.

But Grimar must have sensed Eirik's aim, for he pulled the girl from his arms and pinned her himself.

Standing slowly, Eirik instructed the crew to row them away from the shoreline. As they pulled away from the beach, the girl suddenly went still in Grimar's arms.

"See? She's already learning how to be a good thrall," Grimar said triumphantly.

But the breaking dawn illuminated something else on the girl's face. She was utterly paralyzed with terror, her eyes wide, her limbs shaking, and her breath shallow.

Eirik moved to the tiller uneasily, barking out orders to unfurl the sail. What had Grimar gotten them into?

4

The ship rocked upward on a sea swell again, and Laurel had to swallow hard not to lose the meager contents of her stomach. Nausea warred with fear as she clung to the ship's mast, which was the farthest point from the water she could find. Even still, she was only a few feet away on either side from the churning ocean.

But mayhap the sea's suffocating embrace would be a better alternative to staying on this ship surrounded by Viking barbarians. Risking taking her eyes from the horizon for a moment, she glanced around. Blessedly, the savage who'd been manhandling her was occupied with some ropes around the sail. The other one, the one who'd stepped between her and the Viking who'd struck her, was at the back of the ship, yet his eyes kept tugging toward her.

Laurel swiveled her head around to refocus on the horizon, yet even that small movement sent another wave of nausea through her. It was all too much. In less than a day, she'd been attacked by Brother Egbert, dunked in the chair, beset upon by a Viking seige, and now she was their captive—how could she possibly make sense of any of it?

And of course now she sat in a wooden vessel, no more than forty feet long and only ten feet wide, tossed like a toy at the mercy of the fathomless waters all around. She squeezed her eyes shut, but then immediately regretted it as the ship rolled lazily again.

"Try to eat something."

Despite her fatigue and numbness, she jumped at the deep voice right behind her. The barbarian from the ship's stern stepped in front of her, and despite her desire to cling to the mast, she felt herself cower away from him.

"It might help settle your stomach," he said, extending a chunk of flatbread toward her.

"You—you speak my language," she said cautiously. She eyed him, not taking the offered bread. She wouldn't have recognized him as the same man who'd stormed the Abbey last night, except for his bright blue eyes, which seemed to bore into her.

Of course, he was still enormous and foreboding, but he had removed the chainmail shirt he'd worn last night to reveal a simple belted tunic. And while his nasal helm had obscured most of his face and head when he'd burst into the chapel, now she saw that he had a mane of golden hair, held back on each side of his face with small braids.

His bronzed skin spoke of a life outdoors and on the

open seas. He didn't sport the thick beards that some of the other Viking men onboard did, yet the lower half of his face was covered in thick stubble slightly darker than his hair. His eyes, which had been fierce and unyielding last night, were now penetrating and—could a Viking barbarian be curious?

"Ya, I've learned a bit of it," he replied, but from what she'd already heard, he knew more than he was letting on.

He nudged the bread toward her once again. "Eat," he said, but this time it was more of a command.

Cautiously, she unwrapped one hand from the wooden mast and accepted the chunk of bread from him. She took a small bite and was surprised to find that it had the flavor of oats and honey, far more luxurious than anything they ate regularly at the Abbey.

"I have a few questions for you," he said, his eyes following the bread as she brought it to her mouth again for another bite.

She halted mid-chew. What could the barbarian possibly want to know from her? Did he expect her to cooperate with him in her own captivity? To betray her homeland and help him commit more raids?

His eyes narrowed slightly, and she realized her suspicion and wariness must be written on her face.

"Will you refuse to talk with me? For if you do, you'll not have answers to any of your own questions, girl," he said flatly.

Other than his words that they were taking her with them, she'd had no explanation about what was to become of her. She needed her own answers, and this was the only man who could give them.

Reluctantly, she nodded. "What do you want to know?"

He leaned back on his heels a bit, satisfied. "What was the name of the monastery?"

"Whitby Abbey," she replied, but then hesitated. "You know what a monastery is?"

He quirked a half-smile, and suddenly the hard lines of his face were transformed. She felt her eyes widen slightly, then quickly looked away. She had to admit that based on the stories the Abbess and the others at the monastery told, she was surprised that the Viking before her was more man than snarling dog.

"Ja, that is how I came to learn your language. You've heard of Lindisfarne?"

The air rushed from her lungs, all her surprise and curiosity about this man evaporating. "That was you? You were the one who attacked the holy island and razed Lindisfarne?"

The bile rose in the back of her throat, and she was sorely tempted to spit in the man's face. Stories of the horrors committed at Lindisfarne had spread quickly throughout Northumbria. Even though it was nigh fifteen years ago, the outrage over the Northmen's attack against a peaceful, holy place still ran hot. Laurel had heard the tales from the nuns at Whitby for almost as long as she could remember. Could the man in front of her, the one who'd protected her from one of his men, the one who'd left Whitby's residents unharmed, be the same man who'd slaughtered so many innocent monks?

A look of confusion flitted across his face. "Nei, I wasn't there. I only spoke with some of the men who were."

Why should she feel relieved that he hadn't done those horrible things at Lindisfarne? Mayhap it was only because she wasn't in the hands of those monsters. *But I don't know what this barbarian is capable of yet, either,* she thought with an internal shudder.

"I learned your language from some of the monks who were made thralls," he went on.

Something about that word tickled her brain. "Thrall. I've heard the other one say that word several times." She nodded her head inconspicuously toward the man who'd thrown her over his shoulder last night. "What does it mean?"

The golden-haired warrior's face darkened suddenly. "I'll explain in a moment." His bright blue eyes flickered to the other man, and if Laurel hadn't known they were shipmates, she'd have thought she saw rage in his look.

"Tell me more about this Whitby Abbey. Why were there women there? The Lindisfarne monks led me to believe that holy houses in your land are only for men."

"Nay, women can have holy houses, too—they're called convents. But Whitby is different. 'Tis a double monastery. It has a side for monks, with an Abbot as their leader, and a side for nuns, with an Abbess to guide them. But they all worship together."

He gave her a strange look as if she were talking gibberish. "But if they all stay behind the same walls and worship together, why do they not live together as men and women normally do instead of having separate sides?"

Laurel surprised herself by snorting softly in derision. "They aren't *supposed* to live as other men and women do, and yet the nuns used to get pregnant from time to time." She had never been able to voice her frustration at the hypocrisy of some claiming to lead a holy life. Even Brother Egbert's overt attacks had been blamed on her.

"Used to?"

"Aye, many years ago, pregnant nuns were such a problem that double monasteries were barred from admitting new monastics. That way, such places would fade and die out naturally."

"That explains their ages," the man said more to himself.

Laurel nodded. It had been a sad place to be a child. She'd been surrounded by the aging and dying, with no one to play with. Those who were left were clinging to an old tradition, and her presence was probably a constant reminder that their way of life, and they themselves, were fading away.

"But why were you among them? How did you come to be at the monastery?"

She sighed, letting her eyes drift to the horizon. "My parents abandoned me outside Whitby. From what little the nuns told me, I was born out of wedlock. They were kind to take me in." She spoke woodenly. She was tired of having to own her parents' sin and praise the nuns for their treatment of her.

He was silent for a moment, presumably sensing her

weariness. "Is Whitby part of Northumbria?" he eventually asked quietly.

"Aye, it is."

He nodded as if that was useful information, though Laurel wasn't sure how.

"What is your name, girl?"

The question brought her gaze back to him. The sky behind him was as vibrant as the pair of eyes that pinned her.

"Laurel," she breathed. She only had the one name. The nuns hadn't seen fit to give her either of her parents' family names since her birth wasn't blessed by God.

"Laurel." For some reason, her gaze was pulled to his lips as he tested the word on his tongue. "I am Eirik, son of Arud the Steady, captain of the Drakkar."

She blinked at the flood of information. He was the captain? Was that why he had the authority to stop the Viking who'd attacked her from hitting her again?

"And what is *his* name?" she asked, motioning again toward the cruel barbarian.

"He is Grimar the Raven, son of Jarl Gunvald. He is my cousin."

"Raven?" She looked over at Grimar. His pale blond hair was almost white in the blinding midday sun.

Eirik again seemed to tense slightly. "He is called the Raven for his temperament, not his hair."

Laurel swallowed uneasily. "And why does he keep calling me a...thrall?"

Eirik gave Grimar's back a hard look for a long

moment, but then he turned back to her, locking his bright eyes on her.

"Thrall means slave. Grimar has claimed you as his slave."

The ship rolled down the sloping backside of a wave, and Laurel felt the bread she'd just eaten rise in her throat.

She was a slave. A slave to a cruel, violent Northman.

She bolted to her feet and in two unsteady strides, she was clinging to the ship's gunwale. Her stomach seized and she vomited into the sea.

5

Eirik stood to go to Laurel's side as she leaned over the ship's gunwale and emptied her stomach. He stopped himself, though, clenching his fists in frustration. Instead he strode to Grimar's side. His cousin glanced at him casually, yet his voice was tight.

"Why were you speaking to my thrall, cousin?"

"Someone needed to explain things to her," Eirik bit out in response.

Grimar distractedly brought his hand to his right ear, where dried blood was crusted from where Laurel had bit him. "She'll learn soon enough."

Eirik felt his lips curl back in a snarl but remained silent. As he had suspected, his cousin would be cruel to the girl. Unlike other Vikings, thralls had no protection against being beaten, raped, or even killed.

"Why are you so interested in her?" Grimar said, facing him fully. He no longer feigned disinterest but looked at Eirik with open hostility.

"I'm not interested in her," Eirik shot back, yet even as he spoke the words, his eyes darted to her small, limp form as she dragged herself back over the gunwale and walked on shaky legs to the mast. In the bright midday sun, her hair shone a rich chestnut brown and her dark eyes glimmered with flecks of gold.

Eirik forced his attention back to Grimar. "If you want your thrall to live long enough to set foot on solid land, you'll need to tend to her. Her gown is still damp, and she needs to eat something."

Before Grimar could accuse Eirik of being far too concerned with his property again, Eirik strode toward the tiller, where Alaric stood.

"So, you're finally willing to confront Grimar," Alaric said casually as Eirik approached. "All it took was a pair of big brown eyes and—"

"Leave it, Alaric," Eirik bit out. By the gods, why was he so angry? And why was he taking it out on his friend?

Alaric only raised a sandy brown eyebrow at him. He stepped aside so that Eirik could reclaim the tiller and stayed next to him. They both watched silently as Madrena warily approached Laurel and handed her a waterskin so that she could rinse her mouth from her sickness.

Laurel nodded her thanks after she'd taken a few gulps and handed back the waterskin to Madrena. Then she returned her gaze to the horizon, her face a detached mask.

Grimar stomped to her side a moment later and without word or pause threw a cloak at her. She caught it, and Eirik could see confusion on her face as she looked up, but Grimar had already turned his back and walked away. The smear of Grimar's blood, a vaguely hand-shaped mark, remained on Laurel's cheek.

Eirik cursed under his breath, which drew another quizzical look from Alaric. Thankfully, his friend didn't say aught else.

"That girl has calluses on her hands, but I doubt she could wield a weapon to save her life," Madrena said with disdain as she approached them at the stern.

"You'd best drop that subject, sister," Alaric said wryly.

Madrena swung her pale gray gaze between the two of them, finally shrugging and rolling her eyes.

"Very well. Let's talk about something more pleasing —like the lands we just raided," she said, leaning back against the tall, carved serpent tail rising from the stern of the Drakkar.

Alaric's green eyes danced. "Never have I seen a land so ripe and plentiful!"

"It was dark, and we only saw the monastery," Eirik said dryly.

Alaric wasn't dampened. "Ja, but the monastery alone was so abundant in riches that the rest of the country must be similarly endowed."

"I saw trees in the distance," Madrena added, "and open fields for grazing."

"There is much more to learn," Eirik replied quietly, "but indeed, it is a land of much promise."

"I can see why the Jutland King hungers for as much of these western lands as he can swallow," Alaric said.

"Jarl Gunvald will be pleased that we are doing our own exploring."

"Then why must we dash home after only one raid, and no real chance to see the country?" Madrena asked with her usual bluntness.

"You wish to be captain now?" Eirik said with more sharpness than he'd intended. What had gotten into him?

Madrena shrugged off his harshness, though. "Nei, I just wish we had more time to explore."

"Ya, so do I," he replied more evenly. "I'd rather not do so with Grimar in tow, though."

"'Twould be nice to leave him in Dalgaard for the next voyage," Alaric said with a half-suppressed smile. "Who knows, perhaps his little thrall will manage to throw him overboard and we will be rid of him at last!"

Madrena cackled at her brother's words, but Eirik only managed a weak smile. He couldn't allow harm to come to his kinsmen—especially not the son of the Jarl. But nor could he continue to allow Grimar to challenge his authority so publicly. The girl, Laurel, was only a minor distraction, he told himself firmly. It was simply his dislike of the practice of slavery that made his blood boil to think of her in Grimar's hands.

Madrena stilled, seeming to sense the line of Eirik's thoughts. "Be careful when it comes to the girl, Eirik," she said soberly. "It is clear to all that you've taken an interest in her, but Grimar will like as not use that against both her and you."

Eirik rubbed the scruff on his jaw, considering Madrena's words as she and Alaric sauntered off.

Unbidden, his eyes drifted to Laurel once again. Her head was barely visible within Grimar's overlarge cloak. What was it about her that drew his eye?

She didn't look like most of the women Eirik had encountered. He'd seen thralls from other lands who had dark hair like hers, but they usually had darker skin to match it. Of course, the women he'd normally taken to his bed had been from the Northlands since he refused to use a thrall for such purposes. Perhaps Laurel was of Saxon blood, or even a descendant of the Romans whose empire had spread wide long ago.

Whatever her bloodline, something about her stirred him. Was he only drawn to her because he loathed Grimar for enthralling her? Was it the contrast she provided compared to the women of Dalgaard?

Madrena was right, though. He couldn't stand between Grimar and his thrall, no matter how much he longed to free her from his cruel cousin and the bonds of enslavement. And yet, Eirik sensed that the tension between them would snap soon. He could only hope that Laurel wouldn't be caught in the middle.

6

Laurel bolted upright with a start. She must have drifted off to sleep while still clinging to the mast, for she had been slumped over it a moment ago. Blessedly, the seas felt calmer now, and the boat only rocked a little. She glanced up at the sky to find that it was late evening. She'd been with her Viking captors for nigh a day.

She tried to swallow, but her mouth was dry and her lips were cracked. Besides the few bites of bread the one called Eirik had given her, she'd had naught to eat for a day and a half. Nor had she had more than the swill or two of water the female Viking had offered. Laurel had been surprised at first to see the warrior woman among the others, but everyone seemed to treat her like she belonged there. What outlandish customs these pagans had.

Her head still spun from seasickness, but she found her way to her feet to search for something to drink.

Presumably they hadn't taken her this far just to let her die of thirst.

As she stood on unsteady legs, she looked around the ship to get her bearings. Some men moved about, pulling on various ropes to adjust the sail, but most sat atop wooden sea chests or on the deck itself. They talked and laughed quietly among themselves, seemingly uninterested or unsurprised by her presence.

Lining the exterior of the ship were wooden shields, the same ones the Vikings had been carrying when they'd stormed the Abbey. They were painted a variety of colors, but the most popular seemed to be blood-red, like the stripes in the sail.

She turned toward the ship's stern and started again when she realized that Eirik was watching her intently from the tiller. The sleeves of his tunic were turned back, revealing tanned forearms corded with muscle. His hand clenched on the tiller, causing the muscles to jump under her gaze.

She looked away quickly, disconcerted by the intensity of his stare. Yet it wasn't the lecherous look Brother Egbert used to give her, nor was it the malevolent sneer so often plastered on Grimar the Raven's face.

Her *master*.

Her throat tightened even to think the word. Nay, she was no man's slave. She'd been little more than a slave at the Abbey all her life. She would not be degraded further as some Viking animal's property.

But of course, what her Viking master could do to her was likely far worse than anything she'd experienced at the monastery. She shivered when she remembered the look in Grimar's eyes when he'd first burst into the chapel. His bloodlust had been replaced with simply lust at seeing her, a young woman among aging nuns and monks. He'd handled her coarsely, with no care for her at all. Would he…would he…?

As if the Devil had risen at her thoughts, Grimar stepped before her.

"I need water," she croaked, placing a hand on her throat to show her meaning.

He frowned and said something in the strange, guttural language these Northmen spoke.

She shook her head. "Water," she said again, hoping he'd understand eventually. For good measure, she made a drinking motion and then pointed to the sea surrounding them. "Water."

A slow grin spread across his face. "Wa-ter," he said haltingly.

"Aye, I need water," she replied, relief flooding her.

Suddenly Grimar snatched her up and carried her to the gunwale. She shrieked in terror as she looked down to find her feet dangling above air—air and the ocean.

She clawed at him, trying to latch onto him so that he couldn't throw her overboard. He leaned farther out, his arms lowering her closer to the sea.

"Water!" he shouted. Despite her desperate attempts to fight her way back onto the safety of the ship, she was nothing compared to his strength and size. He laughed as she screamed again.

All at once, she was jerked backward and the ship's deck reappeared beneath her feet. Before she could say a prayer of thanks, however, she was torn from Grimar's grasp and tossed to the deck.

Shouts erupted all around her. She scrambled back from the cacophony, only to bump into someone's legs. A circle had formed, and she was in the middle of it.

She looked up and realized that actually two men were the center of attention within the circle—Grimar and Eirik. Eirik shoved Grimar hard, his eyes blazing and a string of shouts coming from his mouth. Grimar stumbled backward from the force of the push, but as he came forward again, a blade flashed in his hands.

Everyone around her fell instantly silent at the sight of the dagger flashing in the light of the setting sun. She saw Eirik's face harden and his fists clench, yet he didn't draw a weapon, despite having a dagger at his belt. The two exchanged words once more, but this time they both spoke levelly. Slowly, Grimar lowered the dagger and re-sheathed it. The crowd began to disperse, the men returning to their tasks, yet the air was taut with unspent energy.

The female Viking materialized at Laurel's side, inconspicuously handing her the waterskin she'd offered before. But this time, after Laurel had taken a long, greedy pull, the woman refused to take the skin back.

"Keep," she said in heavily accented version of Laurel's language, pushing the skin back into her hands. Laurel nodded her thanks, unsure of what to make of the kindness of some of these barbarians.

"Be-ware," the woman whispered as she moved to stand. But instead of pointing to Grimar, she leveled her finger at Eirik, who was approaching them.

Before Laurel could ask the woman what she meant by warning her against Eirik, she dissolved back with the rest of the crew.

Eirik crouched before her, his face hard. "Are you all right?" he asked tightly.

"Aye," she said shakily, taking another swig of water to soothe her throat and settle her stomach.

"Why are you so afraid of water?" Eirik's look seared into her, searching, possessive.

"I-I cannot swim," she breathed. "And the nuns used to hold me underwater as punishment."

A look of anger, followed by sadness, flitted across his features. Before he could say more, however, a shadow fell across where they crouched on the deck.

Laurel looked up to find Grimar looming over them. He said something in his language to Eirik, and Eirik's brow lowered. He stood and stepped back from where she sat.

Grimar wrapped a hand around her arm and yanked her to her feet. When she struggled to get out of his grasp, he twisted her arm behind her back painfully, forcing her to follow him. He stepped toward the ship's bow, the farthest point from where Eirik stood as he resumed his grip on the tiller.

She watched the golden-haired warrior over her shoulder as Grimar dragged her after him. Eirik's hand clenched and unclenched on the wooden tiller until his knuckles were white. She could still see his bright blue eyes, blazing with unspent rage, until Grimar tossed her down on the deck.

Grimar lay down in front of her and acted like he

was going to sleep. His large body cornered her into a narrow triangle of deck at the bow, giving her barely enough room to curl up on her side without brushing against him. She pulled his giant cloak over herself to cut the cold wind coming off the water.

Her stomach was empty, her throat dry, her head spinning from the rolling ocean that enveloped them. And yet she could still feel Eirik's gaze trained on her. The heat of it kindled something strange deep in her belly.

EIRIK WAS A FOOL—A fool and a madman to openly confront Grimar about the girl. Yet when he'd heard her screams of terror and saw her wild fight against his cousin, he'd flown to her side without thinking. To hear his cousin laugh at her torment had been the breaking point.

He couldn't simply order Grimar to treat her as a freewoman—she was his thrall, and there was naught he could do about it. Yet at least he could maintain order as the ship's captain. That was the only argument that had cooled Grimar's blood enough to avoid an all-out battle right there on the deck.

But even as Grimar had re-sheathed his seax, Eirik had seen a light of recognition in his cousin's eyes. Eirik cared for the girl's wellbeing too much—and now she could be used against him.

Eirik wasn't sure when the animosity between his cousin and him had begun, for they'd played together as children often enough. Yet even as a boy, Grimar had enjoyed being cruel, taking an extra swing at Eirik's ribs after their play-fights were over, or using farm animals as practice for his sword work instead of a wooden post.

But it hadn't been until Eirik's father, then the Jarl, had died that Grimar seemed to turn truly spiteful toward Eirik.

When Eirik had been a boy, all in the village remarked on how much he looked like his father. Both were golden-haired and strongly built, but it was more than that. Even from a young age, Eirik had demonstrated the level-headedness and strong sense of honor that had earned his father the title of Steady. The Jarlship wouldn't automatically be passed on to Eirik when the time came, but it was widely believed that he would be just as good a leader as his father.

But when Arud had died unexpectedly while on a raid in a neighboring village, Eirik had still been too young to take his father's place. Instead, his uncle Gunvald, Arud's brother and Grimar's father, had stepped into the position, assuring all in Dalgaard that it would make for a smoother transition that way.

Of course, it had remained the assumption around the village that when Eirik was of age, he would take his uncle's place as Jarl. Yet the timing was never right, or at least so said Gunvald. Eirik hadn't minded, for he was more interested in the summer raids and planning this voyage to the west. But Grimar seemed to have grown increasingly sour at the idea that Eirik would take his father's place. And worse, while Eirik was praised as the likely next Jarl, the village remained silent when it came to Grimar's worthiness.

Eirik didn't see himself as Grimar's competition, but he also didn't lust for the Jarlship the way Grimar seemed to. It had been a blow to Grimar's pride to be sent by his father on a mission led by Eirik. Though Grimar couldn't challenge Eirik as the captain, he'd found a way to hold something else over Eirik—Laurel.

Eirik cursed himself all over again for involving himself. Nei, that wasn't exactly it. If he had to do it over again, he would still protect Laurel from Grimar's cruelty. He only wished that he hadn't revealed how much the girl affected him, how much power she had over him—and now how much power Grimar had as a result.

He motioned for one of his men to take the tiller for the night so that he could get some rest. Normally the rocking of a ship at sea could put him to sleep in a matter of moments. Not so tonight. Every time he closed his eyes, Laurel's pale, delicately sculpted face swam before him. He'd stared at her enough to be able to perfectly picture her wide, unguarded eyes, the soft curve of her cheeks, and her full, rosy lips. His chest pinched, and he felt a stirring between his legs.

It was going to be a long sennight's voyage back to Dalgaard.

7

Laurel scrubbed the back of her forearm over her brow, trying to keep the sweat out of her eyes. She rolled her neck from side to side to ease the ache, but moving her head like that only brought on the seasickness again.

She'd slept uneasily last night, though she was grateful to get to rest unmolested. Grimar hadn't made a move toward her during the night, which was a small blessing in these otherwise nightmarish conditions.

When he'd risen and kicked her legs to wake her, however, the blessing seemed small indeed. He'd put her to work all morning and throughout the hot afternoon.

First he had her drag his sea chest to the bow, which was now their apparent residence on the ship—as far away from the stern as possible, where she spied Eirik standing so frequently at the tiller. The sea chest was so heavy and large that she'd had to get on her hands and knees and push it with her shoulder one painful inch at a time. Of course, this had drawn chuckles of derision from her master.

Then he'd forced her to polish each and every last piece of loot he'd stashed in the chest. With trembling fingers, she'd scrubbed the golden candlestick holders and bejeweled crosses that had once adorned Whitby's chapel. When a particular spot wouldn't come out of a silver platter, Grimar had snatched it from her and spit on it. She'd had to hold back tears of rage and frustration at the sacrilege of his actions. Her tears would do her no good, however, so she bowed her head and forced them back.

Now she was on her knees yet again, but this time to scrub the deck at the bow. Grimar had guided her roughly to the middle of the ship and indicated that she get to work cleaning the deck, but then he and Eirik had exchanged words that crackled with animosity. Apparently Grimar couldn't order her to clean the entire ship, just the corner he'd been banished to at the bow. So he'd had her scrub the small triangle of decking over and over for what must have been hours by now.

The hot sun beat down on her unprotected head, and she swiped her arm over her face again. She'd long ago finished the water skin that the female Viking had given her, and besides the heel of flatbread Grimar had tossed her that morning, she'd had naught else to eat. Despite being on this accursed ship for nigh two days, her body still rebelled at the motion of the rolling sea. She'd already dry-heaved once today, and she could feel the bile rising in the back of her throat once again.

Suddenly a shadow blocked out the sun overhead.

Laurel's relief was short-lived, for when she glanced up, she saw Grimar looming over her.

He said something to her in his language. She shook her head, uncomprehending. He pointed to his sea chest, which sat a few feet away, then pointed to the middle of the ship where she'd pushed it from that morning.

"Nay," she said, her heart sinking. "Not again."

Grimar's frown deepened and he pointed once more to his sea chest, barking out what sounded like a command.

Laurel dropped the rag she'd been using to scrub the deck and crawled to the chest, too exhausted to resist him. She was used to hard work, and to taking orders from those above her, yet never in her life had she been treated like this—like less than the lowliest of farm animals. But when she tried to fight him, he was quick to knock her to the deck, kick her, or twist her arm until she yelped in submission. This was as low as a human could stoop—this monster used her weakness, her pain, and her fear to enslave her.

She put her shoulder to the side of the sea chest and pushed it with what little strength she had left. It nudged forward a few inches. She took a deep breath and pushed again, this time gaining only an inch. Bracing herself, she ground her shoulder into the chest.

Her exertions made her light-headed, and she slumped against the wooden sea chest for a moment as she saw spots.

Grimar sent a hail of angry-sounding shouts down on her. He yanked her to her feet and gave her a shake.

It was all too much for her body. The seasickness swirled with her lightheadedness and Grimar's shaking. She leaned over and vomited onto his feet.

Laurel hadn't been aware that any of the other Vikings on board were paying attention to her, but suddenly the ship fell silent. One tittering laugh erupted, then another. *Let them laugh*, she thought with complete desolation. But when she glanced up, she realized that several of the Vikings were pointing and chuckling—not at her, but at Grimar.

She looked up at his face and recoiled. He was turning a deep shade of red, whether from embarrassment or rage she couldn't tell. His pale blue eyes darted around the ship, taking in the other Vikings' derision. But what was so amusing to them, and why would Grimar be shamed?

Before she could consider such questions, Grimar's grip on her arms tightened painfully. He stormed the few steps to the bow, and Laurel braced herself to be thrown to the wooden planks once again. But instead, he lifted her in his arms and swung her past the gunwale —right over the ocean.

It was happening again. He was dangling her over the rushing, swelling waters, just as he'd done yesterday. Despite how much she detested this monster, she clung to him desperately, trying to latch onto him so that he couldn't get her any closer to the water.

But nay, she thought dimly in the back of her mind, *this isn't like last time.* Last time he'd been laughing, tormenting and teasing her for his own amusement. This time his face was twisted into a disgusted snarl.

All her numbness and fatigue burned away in an instant of sheer panic. *He doesn't mean to toy with me*, she realized, *he means to rid himself of me.*

Her nails dug into his back, trying to find purchase against his linen tunic. A scream tore from her throat. She felt her heart freeze in sheer terror.

She was going to die. She was going to drown in the cold, uncaring North Sea.

"GRIMAR, STOP!" Eirik bellowed. He barreled past his crewmen toward the bow. His eyes locked on Laurel, who was overcome with panic.

Eirik skidded to a stop a few feet away from where Grimar stood dangling Laurel over the gunwale. "What are you doing, cousin?" he asked, trying to keep his voice calm.

"What does it look like? I'm ridding myself of this useless thrall," Grimar snapped.

"Just because a few of the men chuckled at you for having vomit on your boots?" he said lightly. "Surely that shouldn't bother you overmuch."

Eirik had observed every horrible moment of the day, from Grimar's lack of concern for Laurel's basic needs for food and water to his grueling physical tasks for her. Thank the gods they were on a ship, for otherwise Eirik was sure that Grimar would have used Laurel's body in other ways as well.

It was a custom as old as the gods that physical intimacies were not to take place on the open ocean—it was considered a disrespect to Aegir and his wife Ran, and their nine daughters, the waves.

Even with Laurel safe in that regard, Grimar had found every other way to be cruel and harsh to her. Eirik had forced himself to watch, promising to intervene if Grimar overstepped the bounds for the treatment of thralls. When he'd seen Laurel empty her stomach onto Grimar's boots, he'd had to grip the tiller to will himself not to intercede. But when some of the crew snickered at Grimar for being so ineffectual at handling his thrall, he knew something terrible was going to happen.

"She's useless!" Grimar shouted. Suddenly he visibly tried to calm himself. "She's a weakling and of no value as a thrall, except perhaps as a warm body to fill my bed."

A voice in the back of Eirik's mind screamed that his cousin was trying to bait him. He forced himself to take a breath before he did something unthinking like lunge for Grimar's throat and strangle the miserable life out of him.

"But if you throw her overboard," Eirik ground out between gritted teeth, "you'll never know if she can be of use to you after all." The words sickened him to say. Taking a thrall to bed was no better than taking a sheep —neither one had any say in the matter.

Grimar eyed him calculatingly. "She's not worth the trouble. She can't carry much, she has no sea legs, and she's far too willful. She's a runt—a runt who should have been drowned a long time ago."

Grimar shifted so that Laurel was completely over the water that flashed alongside the swiftly moving ship.

"Wait!" Eirik exclaimed. He cursed himself a moment later for the urgency in his voice, for Grimar glanced at him with a sideways smile.

"Mayhap…mayhap I can take her off your hands for you, if she is such a burden," Eirik said slowly. "I could buy her from you."

"And what would you pay for such a useless thrall, cousin?" Grimar said, his sly smile widening.

Eirik swallowed, feeling his crew's attention focused on the scene at the bow. "I'll give you my share of the loot from the monastery we just raided."

Several murmurs of surprise rose behind him.

"Eirik!" Laurel cried, her eyes locked on him. "What is happening? Please help!"

Eirik forced himself to ignore Laurel's panicked cries. He couldn't show any more weakness to Grimar, lest his cousin exploit it for his own sick play at power.

Grimar made a show of considering the offer. "Nei, I think not. 'Twould be unfair of me to sell you something so worthless," he said, the smile returning to tease around the corners of his mouth.

Grimar shifted again, and Laurel screamed, clawing frantically at Grimar as she was tilted closer toward the rushing water.

"Double it, then!" Eirik shouted, no longer able to think straight. It was as if he could see naught but Laurel's small frame clinging desperately to Grimar, tears streaming down her dirty cheeks, eyes wide in terror.

A whoosh of air left Grimar's chest. Eirik's eyes flickered to him, and he cursed himself. Grimar's whole body had relaxed. He wore the same smile, and now his eyes blazed again with the light of recognition.

Grimar knew.

He knew as well as Eirik that Eirik had lost and he had won. Eirik had shown his weakness, and Grimar had outmaneuvered him to deliver a blow.

"You truly want her badly, don't you, cousin?" Grimar asked, play-acted sympathy dripping from his voice.

Eirik could only nod. He didn't even have the words to explain to himself why he was so taken with the girl, why he'd acted so foolishly since the moment he'd laid eyes on her. Nor could he explain why Grimar hungered so badly to hurt him. All he could make sense of at the moment was that he had to protect Laurel.

"Very well," Grimar said softly, lifting Laurel slightly in his arms.

Eirik reached out a shaky hand, careful not to spook Grimar. Laurel's dark brown eyes fell on him, widening in desperate hope.

"Go and get her!" With one hard thrust, Grimar tossed Laurel overboard. Her scream cut off sharply as she hit the water.

In one step, Eirik launched himself over the gunwale after her. Grimar's laughter turned to a surprised shout at Eirik's unhesitating move. Alaric bellowed something from the ship's stern, but it sounded distant and small.

As the frigid water enveloped him, all sounds were muffled. He kicked and stroked his arms as hard as he'd ever done before. He had to reach her.

8

Laurel thrashed violently, grasping at the air even as she sank into the water. She flailed her arms and legs, but her woolen gown felt like a stone around her. The ocean pulled her down into itself, its cold fingers embedding into her flesh.

With a gurgled scream, her head slipped below the water. She held her breath as she'd learned to do in the chair, but this time, there would be no one to pull her back up. Still, she fought with all her strength. Her kicking legs tangled in her gown. Her hands uselessly clawed at the sea, finding no purchase. Her lungs burned as she struggled upward.

Her head broke the surface and she inhaled hard, taking some of the sea into her lungs along with the treasured air. She forced her eyes open despite the sting of the saltwater dripping into them. The Viking ship had already glided past her, yet she thought she could hear faint shouts from on board.

A splashing near her drew her attention for a fraction of a moment.

"Eir—"

Sea water flooded her mouth, swallowing her cry for help. The ocean pulled her down once more, but this time, she didn't have a chance to take a deep breath before the cold silence surrounded her.

Her limbs grew feeble as she tried to claw her way toward the blessed air. She felt herself drifting down, too weak to fight against the force of the ocean's pull.

Suddenly a rock-hard arm wrapped around her. There was a rush of water around her body, but she couldn't tell if she was going up or down. Perhaps a sea monster had claimed her, pulling her into its den beneath the waves, she thought dimly. The water felt warm and soft now, like a bed of down feathers.

Her head exploded through the water's surface, waking her from her dream. She tried to inhale, but water clogged her lungs. She was racked by a coughing fit as the salty water expelled itself from her chest and stomach. Finally she could take a gulp of air into her burning, crumpled lungs.

"'Tis all right. I've got you."

Eirik's rough voice filtered through her mind. Was it his hard arm still wrapped around her waist? Was it his strong body holding them both up at the water's surface?

Eirik shouted something behind her, and she blinked her eyes open. The Viking ship, which a moment before had been dwindling in her vision, was now barreling down on them. But it was the carved serpent's tail that rose above the ship's stern drawing nigh, not the serpent's head on the prow. Long wooden oars bristled from each side of the ship. They stroked in unison, tugging against the sea.

Someone shouted something in response from the ship, and a moment later, a rope sailed through the air. She felt Eirik's body jerk as he snatched the rope with one hand, never loosening his grip on her.

Then they were both being lifted out of the water and into the air. Hands reached toward them and pulled them over the ship's gunwale. They both fell into a sodden heap on the deck, Eirik's arm still holding her to his hard chest.

Laurel blinked up into the vivid blue sky, more spent and grateful than she'd ever been. Two heads leaned over her, blocking some of the light. One was the Viking woman, and the other was a man who looked remarkably like her. She'd seen him talking to Eirik before.

They both started talking at once, but she couldn't understand a word they said. Eirik sat up next to her, pulling her upright with him. He responded to them wearily in their language. Laurel paid no heed to what they said. She was content to lean back against Eirik's broad chest, feel his arm wrapped around her middle, and stare up at the cloudless sky. She inhaled air greedily, the salt burning her nostrils, but she didn't care.

All too quickly, her euphoria was shattered.

Grimar stepped before them, his face turned down in ire. He spoke tersely to Eirik, who answered just as sharply. A look of surprise transformed Grimar's face for a moment, but then his features dropped into an even darker rage. A flutter of murmurs rose around her.

"What is happening, Eirik?" she breathed, looking between the two men. "What is he saying?"

Grimar spat on the deck right in front of them and turned, storming toward the bow.

"He demanded that you be returned to him," Eirik said, finally easing his hold around her waist.

She turned to stare at his strained features. "And what did you say?"

"I told him that since he had discarded you, you were no longer his."

Relief flooded her. Grimar was not her master anymore. He could never exert his will over her again. She was free.

Yet Eirik's bronzed face remained taut. Laurel noticed a muscle in his jaw ticking. She recoiled slightly, fearing something that she couldn't put her finger on.

"What else is there?" she breathed.

"To protect you from him, I..." Eirik broke their gaze, his jaw working.

"Tell me."

He finally turned back to her, his bright blue eyes searing through her. "I...claimed you for myself. You are my thrall now."

Laurel's heart froze in her chest. She felt like the world had tipped on its side.

"You...you *claimed* me?" She jerked away from him, scooting back across the deck in her soaking gown. "I am your *slave*?"

"Laurel, let me explain."

"Nay, what is there to explain?" Her voice was high and shrill, but she didn't care. "I went from being Grimar's property to yours. Now I will be forced to serve you just as I served him."

Saying the words aloud made them even more sickening. From the tales she'd been told at Whitby, she knew Vikings were ruthless, merciless heathens who took what they wanted with no thought to anyone else. She'd never imagined that she could be forced into abject slavery by first one man and now another.

She cursed herself, acknowledging for the first time since this ordeal began that she'd looked to Eirik as a protector of sorts. Aye, he was a Viking warrior, and aye, he'd looted the Abbey with the others. But he'd also stopped Grimar from striking her again that first night in the chapel and had intervened when Grimar had dangled her overboard. He'd given her food and spoken to her in her own language. And he'd saved her life from drowning.

But she'd been a blind fool, only seeing what she wanted—nay, needed—to see, to cling to a sliver of hope that she was not completely at the mercy of these savage barbarians.

But he was no different than the others. And now she was his property to do with as he pleased.

"I am not like Grimar," he said through gritted teeth. "He said that you were still his by rights. You are an *utlending*—an outsider—and if I hadn't made a claim to you as my thrall, he would have taken you again for himself."

"You make it sound like you barbarians follow laws and rules," she spat out.

"We do."

She crossed her arms protectively over her chest. The cold from her wet dress was finally starting to seep in.

"Hear me out, Laurel," he said, his voice softer now. He reached tentatively toward her, but she shied away. "I am not like Grimar."

"You said that already, but how can you be believed when you can force me to your will and no one will stand in your way?" Bitter tears rose unbidden to her eyes. It was better to be the thrall of Eirik than Grimar, a small voice said in the back of her mind. She *knew* they were different—Eirik had begun to show her that already. Yet she bucked at the idea of being a slave to any man.

Eirik opened his mouth to respond, but the Viking woman and the other man who was often by Eirik's side reappeared. They spoke to him and he nodded wearily. The man helped Eirik to his feet, and the woman approached Laurel.

"That is Madrena," Eirik said from behind the Viking woman. "And this is her brother Alaric. You can trust them. They will not harm you. No one will harm you now that...now that you are mine."

The woman called Madrena guided Laurel a few feet away and halted her before a sea chest. Madrena opened the lid and produced a large, thick cloak with rabbit fur lining around the hood and collar. The cloak made puddles around her feet, but it helped cut the chill from her damp gown. Laurel realized with a start that the cloak was far too big even for Madrena, who stood more than half a head taller than she did.

It must be Eirik's cloak. That meant that it was Eirik's sea chest that Madrena was now pushing her down to sit on.

Laurel looked around uneasily as Madrena left her side to carry on with her duties. None of the other Vikings were looking at her, yet she felt acutely aware of her presence among them as an outsider—an utlending, as Eirik had called her.

His words floated back to her, ringing in her ears, causing heat to flood her salt-crusted skin.

"*You are mine.*"

9

Only four days remained on their journey back to Dalgaard, five if the winds weren't favorable, and Eirik was determined to prove to Laurel that he wouldn't treat her the way Grimar had.

After the confrontation, Grimar stayed at the bow, glowering and muttering but keeping to himself. Eirik hoped that the distance would make Laurel feel safe, yet she frequently started at unfamiliar noises. Then again, she'd clearly never been on a ship before, so Eirik supposed it was all strange and new to her. Whenever a sea chest would shift or the sail snap in the wind, her eyes would dart to the front of the ship as if to reassure herself that Grimar was still there.

Eirik often found himself clenching his jaw or squeezing his fists at her frightened reactions. It irked him that she did not feel safe under his protection. But judging by her reaction to learning that he'd claimed her as his thrall, she didn't see him as her protector—more like her jailor, or worse, her tyrant overlord.

She had fallen into an exhausted sleep at the foot of his sea chest the evening he'd pulled her from the icy waters of the North Sea. The next morning, however, her guard was back up. She'd stared at him cautiously when he brought her fresh water, flatbread, smoked meat, and a small crabapple. She ate hungrily, yet her wide eyes skittered around the ship as if she expected to be attacked at any moment.

When the midday sun had grown hot, Eirik erected an awning over the stern out of an extra length of sailcloth. Her pale skin was already flushed pink from being exposed to the wind, salty air, and sun for two days, but at least she could find relief from the elements for the remainder of their voyage. She willingly went underneath the woolen sailcloth awning, which made Eirik's chest pinch strangely. She would now be only a few feet away from where he stood at the tiller.

Each night, after she'd eaten and Eirik had passed the tiller to one of his men, she curled up in his cloak under the awning. He slept by his sea chest out in the open among the rest of his crew. But with each passing night, it grew harder for him to sleep. He even began imagining that he could hear her soft, steady breathing as she slept several feet away.

Madrena began rolling her eyes more frequently at him, and Alaric took to watching him with a little smile on his lips.

"Why don't you put yourself out of your misery and

go to the girl?" Madrena blurted out when they were only a day away from Dalgaard.

Eirik's gaze jerked away from the horizon and landed on Madrena, who was standing cross-armed in front of him. He hadn't even noticed her approaching. Yet he was acutely aware that Laurel sat behind him, fiddling with a piece of rope.

Eirik's mood instantly darkened at Madrena's question. "You would have me risk the wrath of the gods to scratch a bodily itch?" he snapped crossly. That was all it was, anyway—a physical desire, a natural if presently inconvenient male urge. They'd been at sea too long. All he needed was a quick tumble—with a willing woman, not a thrall.

"Nei, I'm not telling you to insult the gods. But your eyes give you away, Eirik. They follow the girl everywhere. Why don't you share the awning with her at night if you want to?"

Eirik felt a flood of hot anger surge through him. He couldn't simply crawl under the awning and lie next to Laurel. She was a thrall, which meant she had no choice in the matter. He didn't want her that way. Despite his frustration, he lowered his voice. "You know better than anyone what it means to be forced by a man, Madrena. I would never do that to Laurel—or to any woman."

When Dalgaard had been attacked a handful of summers ago by a neighboring village, many had been killed—and others, like Madrena, had been violated and made half-dead by the damage the event had done. Eirik and Alaric had stayed by her side through the bed rest, the nightmares, and eventually the long hours of training when she'd been well enough to learn how to wield a sword. Eirik's father had always taught him that men's use of force against women was cowardly and dishonorable. After witnessing what Madrena had gone through—what she still lived with—he'd vowed never to do such a vile thing.

Madrena dropped her arms and stepped toward Eirik so that they were practically nose to nose. "Ja, I don't need you to remind me," she bit out quietly. "And I know the code of honor you hold yourself to. But soon enough we will be back in Dalgaard, where she will be expected to behave like a thrall—and you'll be expected to treat her like one. You may not get the chance to treat her as well as you have been these past few days."

If it were possible, Eirik's mood darkened even more. "What do you want me to do, Madrena? Treat her poorly so that she will adjust to what awaits her in Dalgaard? Or treat her as my equal while I can, only to make her place as a thrall that much worse when we arrive?"

"You could at least explain things to her before we reach the village," Madrena replied, though instead of her usually sharp tongue, she softened the words. Her pale eyes searched his face, but he wasn't sure what she saw there. "You clearly care for her."

"What a cursed mess," he muttered. Was his interest in Laurel really so apparent? Grimar had sensed it, but then Eirik had proved him right by rescuing the girl and claiming her for himself. Judging by Madrena's words, he was making a spectacle of himself to his crew as well.

Even now, his eyes tugged to where Laurel sat. He found her watching them closely, her head cocked to one side.

"Grimar has been telling anyone who'll listen that he wants to call a council meeting when we get to Dalgaard," Madrena said lowly.

Eirik's head snapped back to her. "What?"

"He says he wants to put the question of the girl's ownership to the Jarl."

Eirik cursed. Why couldn't Grimar simply let the matter go?

And a council meeting could have more serious consequences than his cousin's vitriol. Eirik feared what a meeting regarding Laurel would mean in terms of his standing with his uncle. If Jarl Gunvald sensed that Eirik's claim on the girl was a roundabout way of challenging his Jarlship, Eirik would have to decide between his desire to protect Laurel and maintaining peace within the village.

"Enjoy her company while you can, or not," Madrena said over her shoulder as she turned away. "But you should warn her about what awaits her in Dalgaard."

Eirik's eyes fell on Laurel once more. Thank the gods she couldn't understand their language, otherwise Madrena's words would have likely confused and frightened her. But that was also another problem to add to the pile. He needed to teach her his language, teach her how to swim, prepare her for life in a Northland village, caution her about how she would be treated as a thrall —and warn her about the council meeting that would decide her fate.

He sighed and stepped toward her. Those dark eyes followed him, unreadable underneath the awning's shadows. He crouched before her, pinning her with his gaze.

"We need to talk."

LAUREL HAD to suppress a gasp of surprise when Eirik's vivid blue eyes took hold of her. When he spoke, she was struck silent for a moment. Even though he checked on her several times each day, he rarely met her eyes or said more than was necessary. Though she was glad that he mostly left her alone, a small part of her felt guilty for telling him he was like Grimar. He'd seen to her needs and hadn't forced her to work—or forced her to do aught else for that matter.

She pushed the thoughts aside, reminding herself that he was a Viking barbarian and she was his slave. Just because he treated her kindly now didn't mean that she should be glad for her situation.

"What is it?" she replied, trying to keep her voice neutral.

"We are only a day away from my village," he said.

Her stomach clenched uncomfortably, though blessedly she didn't fear that she would vomit. Her innards had finally settled to the sea's rhythms in the last day. But the thought of setting foot inside a Viking village had her quaking.

"And…and what awaits me there?"

"That is what we must discuss," he said, his eyes

pinching slightly. "You are my thrall, and you'll be expected to behave accordingly."

She sucked in a hard breath at his words. He didn't need to remind her that she was a slave, yet she realized that she had no idea what to anticipate in his village. "What does that mean?"

"It means that you are to obey my every word, and my every wish."

A spike of outraged heat sliced through her. *His every wish?* He met her gaze, his face hard and...ill at ease? She didn't know how to interpret his apparent discomfort, but suddenly she became acutely aware of how much space his body took up under the low awning.

His broad shoulders, clad only in a thin linen tunic, almost completely blocked her into the point of the stern. His forearms rested easily on his knees, the sleeves of the tunic rolled back to reveal bronzed, corded muscles. This close, she could see just how callused and large his hands were. She'd never seen so much of a man's skin before, especially one so imposing and strong. This was a man who could take whatever he wanted.

She shivered and leaned back, trying to escape not only his dominating presence but also his foreboding words.

A muscle twitched in his jaw as he watched her. "I'd hoped that my actions these last few days would have shown you that I am not the type of man to abuse my power over you."

"Power is always inevitably abused," she whispered, her thoughts flitting back to Abbess Hilda and Brother Egbert.

A taut silence stretched between them until Eirik cleared his throat. "As my thrall, you are also entitled to my protection. I think you should know that...that Grimar wants to call a council meeting to challenge my claim to you."

Confusion swamped her. "He wants to...he can... what is a council meeting?"

"It is a gathering of the village's free men and women to witness the passing of judgements and the handing down of rulings. The village's Jarl, the leader, will preside and have the final say over whom you belong to—me or my cousin."

Laurel swallowed hard. "And who is this Jarl, this leader, who gets to decide my fate?"

"He is my uncle and Grimar's father," Eirik gritted out.

Her heart tumbled to the pit of her stomach. Grimar's father would determine if she would be returned as the monster's slave?

Suddenly she longed with all her being to remain in Eirik's care. The clarity of the thought caught her off-guard. Was being the slave of one Viking savage really better than serving another? Aye, Eirik had shown her consideration and mercy these past several days. Yet being any man's slave made her heart scream in impotent rage.

"Then...then I may be made Grimar's thrall once more?" The words were almost too bitter in her mouth to get out. But she needed to say them, to face the reality that awaited her when they landed.

"Ja, but Laurel—" He cupped her chin in one large,

callused hand. The gentle yet firm touch sent ripples of awareness through her body. "—I promise to do everything in my power to make sure that doesn't happen. As I said, you are under my protection now."

She shook her head, breaking their contact, yet the skin of her face felt unnaturally warm, as if his hands still caressed her.

"Besides Grimar, from what do I need protection?"

He hesitated, as if weighing how much to tell her. She felt her anger rising again. She knew so little and had so little power over her own life. "Tell me. At least I can be prepared, even if I can't have any control over what will happen to me," she choked out.

"There are other thralls in the village. Most work on farms, helping their masters tend animals or bring in crops. Many free men treat their thralls with decency, though there are also those like Grimar who view thralls as lower than sheep or cows."

Laurel fought back the wave of hopelessness that threatened to drown her. This was to be the place she spent the rest of her life? And worse, she might be one of those cows in Grimar's possession soon.

"Most of the thralls in Dalgaard, my village, are from the Northlands," Eirik continued. "They were captured in raids or traded for prisoners of battle. There are only a few utlending thralls."

His voice held a warning that she didn't fully understand. Her confusion must have shown on her face, for Eirik went on. "Utlendings are considered even lower than Northlander thralls. They are outside the bounds of our laws and customs, tossed aside by the gods."

A slave and an outsider. Oddly, the labels felt familiar to her, yet this was far worse than laboring at the Abbey, where she was considered an affront against the holy order. "So I am to be the lowest of the low. What…what will be done to me?"

His eyes pinched again. "Some villagers will likely look upon you with disdain for being an utlending, though most will be more curious than anything. They will expect you to be deferential, even to other thralls. They will expect you to obey me without question." The words seemed to strain against his throat. "But I will not treat you cruelly or…or force myself on you."

She could feel her eyes go wide at his last words. "Why?" she blurted out without thinking. "I mean…I had assumed…" she fumbled, her face growing hot.

She took a breath and started over. "I had assumed that as a thrall I would be subjected to…such abuses. Yet Grimar never touched me, and you say you won't take me against my will." It was humiliating to speak of such horrors so frankly, yet she'd been required to do many things in the last several days that she otherwise never would have.

"No intimacies of any kind can take place on a ship," Eirik replied. "It is considered an insult to the gods of the sea. Only the threat of the gods' wrath stopped Grimar."

"And when we land?" she said shakily.

"I find such acts abhorrent. A man who takes women by force has no self-control and therefore doesn't deserve respect." His blue eyes flamed brightly for a moment, revealing just how strongly he felt about his words.

The smallest tendril of relief soothed her ragged mind for a moment. Eirik wouldn't abuse her, and if his words could be believed, he wouldn't rape her either. But only if she remained his thrall, she reminded herself with a sinking feeling. If Grimar could convince his father, the Jarl, that she should be passed back to him...

Sickness that had naught to do with the gently rolling seas rose in the back of her throat. Her position was so tenuous that she dared not hope to remain under Eirik's protection. Yet she couldn't deny to herself that he was preferable over Grimar.

More than preferable, a voice whispered in the back of her head. Something about his presence both comforted and disquieted her—not because she feared him, as she did Grimar, but because he made her very aware of his largeness and her smallness, of his strength and her weakness. Even the feel of his gaze on her sent little threads of unfamiliar heat through her body.

Something shifted in the air between them as he continued to crouch before her on his heels. His gaze moved over her and his eyes flickered with a fleeting look of...could it be called anything but hunger? She shivered again despite the warmth under the shade of the awning.

He leaned back so that he was clear of the awning and then stood. "We'll make landfall on the morrow if the winds stay behind us," he said, his tone controlled. "Ready yourself."

10

As the fjord sheltering Dalgaard came into view, a shout of joy erupted from the crew.

Eirik wished he could share in their unfettered merriment. He thanked the gods that the Drakkar had returned home safely and that none of his crew had been harmed in their raid. But the dark eyes watching him from under the woolen awning bore into him. She tried to hide her fear of what lay ahead, yet her wide eyes darted anxiously.

He ducked his head under the awning. "We are almost home."

The words were strange to say, considering her home had been the monastery from which his cousin had stolen her. Yet Dalgaard would be her home now, and no matter how much Eirik wanted to make this easy on her, she'd have to face the village sooner or later.

Several men lowered the sail while others began passing around the wooden oars that were stored until needed. The familiar sound of the oars being fitted through the oar holes and making contact with the water calmed Eirik's nerves somewhat. He passed the tiller off to one of the men and sat on his sea chest to take up an oar himself. He wasn't too proud to row alongside his crew. Besides, he needed to burn off some of the tension in his shoulders and back.

He fell into the pulling rhythm of the oars with the others, relieved to occupy himself with something besides thoughts of Laurel. Her pale skin, dark eyes and hair, and small form had increasingly plagued him during the journey home. The only way he could explain her strange power over his body was that he hadn't been with a woman in a while, so preoccupied with preparing for this voyage had he been.

He leaned back with the oar firmly in his grip, digging it deeply into the fjord waters. She was too small, too boyish in the nigh-shapeless brown woolen gown she wore. She was nothing like the tall, buxom, fair-haired women who populated Dalgaard—and who occasionally caught his eye. Yet even the comely village women had never stirred him the way Laurel did. He was beginning to feel a bit sore between the legs from his sleepless nights and wandering thoughts.

Sweat broke out on his brow and between his shoulder blades as he plowed the oar through the water again and again. He gritted his teeth as he admonished himself for his own bodily reaction. If she had been a free woman, he'd approach her and see if she was interested in sharing a bit of pleasure with him.

But she was his thrall, his property. To bed her

would be no better than rape, for no true free will could exist for her. He would not put her in such an impossible position—for even if she acquiesced to his desires, he could never be sure if she hadn't felt obligated or coerced.

He let his gaze travel down the length of the fjord in search of Dalgaard's docks. In the distance, he spotted a smattering of wooden houses fitted snugly in the narrow strip of land between the water and the mountainsides that rose sharply above the fjord's termination. The docks were a speck that grew larger with each pull of the oars. Now Eirik could make out the village long-house, which stood nestled against the steeply sloping mountains above the docks.

As the Drakkar drew nearer, figures began gathering on the docks in anticipation of their arrival. No special woman in the village awaited Eirik's return. He'd occupied himself too much with raids to have time for a wife and family. And his closest friends were on board with him already. Even still, his chest pinched oddly at the thought of having someone to love and care for him—and someone for him to love and care for in return. Perhaps he would need to consider a wife soon after all.

He pushed the thought away with another stroke of the oar. He had more pressing matters to attend to. Unbidden, an image of Laurel's face flitted across his mind.

As the Drakkar drifted into Dalgaard's docks, another cheer from the ship went up, to be echoed by those on land. Ropes were tossed across the gunwale, and Eirik's crew began leaping onto the docks and into the waiting arms of their loved ones.

Madrena and Alaric clasped arms, their faces wide in playful grins, as was their tradition whenever they returned successfully from a voyage. Then they jumped onto the dock, happily making their way through the crowd of villagers. Eirik also caught sight of Grimar slipping from the ship to make his way with purposeful strides toward the village longhouse. He was likely wasting no time in plying the Jarl's ear about the events of the journey.

Eirik ducked his head under the awning in search of Laurel. She was pressed as far back against the stern as possible, her eyes wide with fright.

"I'd have thought you'd be more eager to get your feet on solid ground, girl," he said, trying to ease her fear.

To his pleased surprise, her eyes widened even more, and then one corner of her mouth quirked in what threatened to be a smile.

"Come," he said more seriously. "There is nothing to fear, for I will be at your side."

She nodded, all hints of lightness vanishing. She crawled toward him, her face surprisingly composed. What could have taught this little wisp of a woman such strength in her short years?

He helped her to her feet and guided her to the gunwale. He leapt over, landing with a thud on the wooden dock. The villagers cheered heartily at his victorious show. But then he reached up and wrapped his hands around her waist. He lifted her up and over the gunwale and lowered her to the dock. By the time her feet brushed the wood, the crowd had fallen silent.

"Our voyage to the western lands was successful," he called out in a loud, steady voice. "We have many treasures to show for it, and none of our people were harmed."

The crowd cheered, but it was laced with murmured questions about the girl standing at his side.

"This is Laurel, a girl from the monastery we attacked," Eirik went on. "She is *mine*."

More confused whispers filtered through those gathered on the docks at his brusque words. He didn't want to leave any doubt in their minds that Laurel was not to be trifled with. Yet most of the villagers knew that he didn't keep thralls and didn't approve of the practice. They would never expect him to claim an utlending as his thrall—it went against his very nature. At least that was how Eirik felt now as the owner of a thrall.

A little boy darted through the crowd and skidded to a halt right in front of Eirik. "Jarl Gunvald calls a council meeting," the boy panted. Clearly he had just sprinted from the longhouse at either Gunvald or Grimar's command. "He wishes to discuss your voyage, and the thrall girl."

More surprised murmurs swelled in the crowd, but Eirik paid them no mind. Truly, Grimar had wasted no time, but mayhap it was better this way. The matter needed to be decided once and for all.

He took Laurel by the hand and began weaving his way along the docks toward the longhouse, which stood a long stone's throw away and slightly up on the banks of the fjord. His crew, along with the villagers, followed him.

As he stepped inside the longhouse, he had to blink several times to let his eyes adjust to the dim interior. He could feel Laurel's hand tense within his own at the scene. In the middle of the longhouse stood an enormous stone fire pit, where flames burned year-round. The smoke trailed out a hole in the thatched roofing. Wooden tables and benches lined the longhouse's walls, to be pulled out for the next community meal.

On the back wall stood a raised dais. An ornately carved chair took up most of the dais, though smaller chairs also stood at the ready for honored guests.

Eirik's eyes sought out a flicker of movement at the base of the dais. His cousin and uncle stood talking quietly, Grimar's pale blond head nearly touching Gunvald's gray-white one. Then Gunvald's attention jerked to the villagers filing in all around Eirik and Laurel. He straightened away from his son and mounted the steps leading up to the dais. With all the command of his title, the Jarl seated himself in the large chair and banged a fist against the chair's arm.

Silence fell over the gathered crowd within the longhouse.

"Welcome home, nephew," Gunvald said, his icy blue eyes, so like Grimar's, narrowing on him. "We have much to discuss."

GUNVALD TOOK in the scene before him, forcing himself

to keep his gaze neutral as it swept over the girl at his nephew's side.

This must be the girl over whom his son was nigh incensed. He'd expected some great beauty, but instead the girl looked small and weak cowering next to Eirik. Her dark braid was mussed, her skin pale in the dim light, and her frame thin and hunched in fear.

Gunvald suppressed a snort of derision. This was the girl his son had been babbling furiously about a moment ago when he'd burst into the longhouse and demanded that Gunvald call a council meeting?

Yet Grimar could not be dissuaded when he set his sights on something. It would be useless to try to talk him out of his claim on this utlending girl. Silently cursing the weakness of his son's temper, Gunvald adjusted the thick animal furs he wore over his shoulders.

He would have to make a point of following procedure, of course. He couldn't simply take the girl from Eirik, who stood half in front of her protectively, and give her to Grimar—too many in the village would see that as unfair favoritism. It could raise unfavorable comparison between their current Jarl and Arud the Steady—and Arud's level-headed son.

Instead of starting with the girl, however, Gunvald would test Eirik's amenability with a safer topic.

"You have been successful in your voyage to the west?" Gunvald said loud enough for those in the back of the longhouse to hear.

"Ja, Jarl," Eirik responded just as loudly. "We

reached the western lands and have brought back many treasures to show for it."

Eirik turned and motioned behind him. One of his sailors stepped through the parting crowd with his sea chest hoisted on top of his shoulder. The man set the chest down with a loud thump in front of the dais and opened the lid.

Gold, silver, and jewels glinted in the firelight. The crowd gasped and a ripple of excited whispers spread through the longhouse. Gunvald leaned forward, making a show of inspecting the sparkling loot.

"That is just a small portion of what we recovered," Eirik went on, never taking his eyes from Gunvald. "My crew and I would like to give you a share of the loot, to honor you as our leader, and to give thanks for your foresight in sending us on the voyage."

Gunvald's head snapped up to level Eirik with a narrowed stare. Without doubt, that had been a veiled jab at him.

It had been Eirik who'd insisted that Gunvald send a ship to the west. He'd adamantly claimed that others, especially in Jutland, would soon stake all the land and its wealth for themselves. While Gunvald had thought it safer to keep raiding closer to home, Eirik had convinced most in the village that their future lay to the west. When it had been clear that public opinion had turned against him, Gunvald had ordered Eirik to sail west, as if it had been his decision. Was Eirik attempting to remind the others of this?

Gunvald slowly placed a hand over his heart and bent his head.

"You have made the Jarl of Dalgaard proud," Gunvald said, giving an extra breath of emphasis on his title. The crowd cheered their approval of Eirik's gesture and their Jarl's gracious acceptance.

At least Eirik was still willing to acquiesce to Gunvald in the symbolic gesture of sharing their takings. If he hadn't played his part in this little ceremony, the issue of the girl would have been moot. Yet even now Gunvald had to proceed carefully. If Eirik's firm grip on the girl's hand was any indication, he may not be so willing to part with that particular piece of loot.

"Before we feast in honor of your success—" Gunvald began. The villagers gave a titter of anticipation for the promised festivities. "—there is another matter we must settle."

Eirik's hardening gaze was visible even from the dais, but Gunvald went on. "It has come to my attention that you've also brought home an utlending thrall," he began loudly for the villagers' benefit. "There seems to be some dispute about who is the rightful owner of the girl."

Just then, Grimar stepped out of the crowd so that he faced Eirik at the base of the dais. Though his son's face was smooth, it was obvious to Gunvald that he worked to keep his temper in check.

"I was the first to see the girl when we raided the western monastery," Grimar said to the crowd. "I claimed her as my thrall in front of many witnesses."

Those gathered in the longhouse murmured among themselves for a moment.

"Then why is Eirik, son of Arud, now holding the girl?" someone shouted from the back.

Eirik stepped forward, bringing the cowering girl along with him. "My cousin did indeed claim this woman as his thrall," he said levelly. Several in the crowd muttered their confusion. "But Grimar discarded her. He said she was useless and threw her overboard on the voyage home. I retrieved her and claimed her for myself."

Now the noise from the villagers was overwhelming. "Silence!" Gunvald shouted, pounding his fist on the arm of his chair once more. He cursed internally. His son had left out any mention of discarding the thrall. He'd only said that Eirik had taken the girl despite his previous and rightful claim to her.

"Do you have any witnesses to these events?" Gunvald said, trying to disguise the weariness in his voice. If it was as Eirik said, he could never rule in favor of his son. The groundlessness of such a decision would leave him open to criticisms from his people, and more dangerous, to a challenge for the Jarlship.

"I saw both events, Jarl," the young man called Alaric said, stepping forward.

"So did I," said his twin sister Madrena, coming to his side. If Gunvald remembered correctly, both were close companions of Eirik. Yet they were also well-liked and respected in the village, as Eirik was. Their words would be hard to discount.

"Speak," he said tersely.

"Grimar did indeed claim the girl as his thrall as soon as he laid eyes on her," Alaric said in a clear, loud voice. "But he treated her so poorly on the voyage back that she almost died. He gave her neither food nor water and forced her to work for his amusement."

Those gathered made their opinions heard. Some shook their heads in disapproval at Grimar, while others laughed at his incompetence in tending to his thrall. Grimar's face flushed bright red, his hands clenched at his sides. He clamped his mouth shut in a frown. At least he was keeping a rein on his temper—for now.

Gunvald waved his hand. "Grimar's treatment of the thrall matters not. She was his to do with as he wished. What of this issue of him discarding her?"

"Everyone on the Drakkar saw it, Jarl," Madrena said, though she spoke to the crowd. "Grimar said she should be drowned for being useless. I believe his words to Eirik before he threw her overboard were something to the effect of 'if you want her, go and get her.'"

Gunvald pinched the bridge of his nose. His son's words damned any case he might have had. The crowd knew it too. Their shouts made it clear that they sided with Eirik.

Gunvald glanced at Eirik to gauge his reaction. His nephew's face remained unmoved, yet he drew the girl closer to him, shielding her from the stares and shouts. Gunvald's gaze traveled to his son, whose chest heaved in impotent rage. Grimar's icy gaze shot between Eirik and the girl. Clearly his son longed to slice both of their throats right here and now and was barely stopping himself. Once the longhouse had cleared, Gunvald could count on Grimar plotting revenge.

The girl was going to be a problem. If she remained

in Eirik's possession, Grimar's hot head and black temperament were sure to bring an open conflict. And the last thing Gunvald needed was for more attention to be drawn to the tension between his son and his nephew. It would inevitably lead to questions of the Jarl's succession.

A thought fluttered soft as a feather in the back of his mind. If he could rid both men of the girl and put the matter behind them, mayhap the uneasy balance of his power could be maintained a little longer. The thought tickled again, growing stronger. He would remind both the village and Eirik who had the authority to make decisions while also appearing even-handed.

"I have come to a ruling," he said, still forming the idea as those in the longhouse fell silent and turned their attention toward him.

"Grimar made a claim to the girl first," he began. A few people nodded in agreement, but several faces turned down in frowns. "But Eirik also has a claim," he went on quickly. "They are both rightful and justifiable. Grimar apparently discarded the girl, yet his initial claim could be thought to still hold."

Villagers whispered to each other, some in disagreement, some in confusion. Before they could take his momentum, he spoke again. "It seems that the only *fair* thing to do is disregard both claims."

This time the villagers erupted with their opinions. Grimar's eyes flashed to him, and Eirik's face darkened threateningly. The girl, clearly not understanding what was going on, looked around wide-eyed. Gunvald had to bang on the arm of his chair several times to regain order.

"She is still a thrall, and an utlending," he said, his argument taking shape in his mind as he spoke. "She is not one of us. We all know that having an utlending in our midst is repulsive and upsetting to the gods. Tell me, Eirik, does this girl worship the gods, or does she hold them in contempt?"

Eirik's gaze narrowed. "She knows naught of our gods, so she cannot hold them in contempt," he said slowly.

Before he could go on, Gunvald cut him off. "It will displease the gods to have a nonbeliever in our village. Should we risk their wrath over this outsider?" he said. Some of the villagers began to nod slowly.

"She can be someone else's problem," he added, drawing more nods and murmurs of agreement from the crowd.

"But father," Grimar said, his eyes flaming with outrage. "I claimed her as part of my share of the loot from the raid. You can't simply take her from me!"

"You and Eirik will each get your share of her worth," Gunvald replied. Then he turned to the crowd. "The girl will be sold at the slave market in Jutland. The profits will be split between Grimar the Raven and Eirik, son of Arud. That is a fair outcome. This dispute is resolved."

A flurry of surprise and shock filled the longhouse. It was an unusual plan, yet Gunvald had successfully come up with a way to get rid of the girl and appear unbiased and even-handed in a ruling involving his son.

More important, his decision should serve as a reminder that he was still Jarl. Eirik wanted something, and Gunvald was the one with the power to take it away.

Eirik was visibly fighting for control of his temper, yet for once Grimar seemed to have a handle on his. Grimar shot a displeased look at Eirik and the girl yet he kept his mouth shut. Eirik, on the other hand, growled loud enough to be heard over the noise of the crowd.

"When will she be taken to Jutland?" he bit out.

Gunvald stroked his bearded chin in thought. "We were planning to embark on a trading voyage there at the end of the summer raiding season," he said casually. "She can be sold then."

Several of the people surrounding Eirik, including the twins who'd spoken on his behalf earlier, began to protest. To Gunvald's surprise, it was Eirik who held up a hand to silence them.

"She will remain with me until then, unless anyone has objections to that," Eirik said flatly. He pinned Grimar with his hard gaze, then shifted it to Gunvald.

Though Eirik's commanding tone and bold gaze sent a slice of apprehension through him, Gunvald forced himself to take a deep breath. He could not act rashly now. He'd tested Eirik's willingness to defy him, yet his nephew hadn't taken the opportunity to openly challenge his Jarlship. But he'd come close. He would have to acquiesce to Eirik's wishes in this comparably small matter. It may even make him appear to be benevolent to those watching.

Yet Gunvald still made a show of deciding, just to be

sure that all those gathered knew who had the power to have the final say.

He inclined his head slightly in agreement. "Let us put this matter behind us and prepare a feast," he said, closing further argument. The villagers began dispersing, eager to gossip about the unusual council meeting and the evening's festivities.

Eirik held Gunvald's gaze for a long moment before turning, the girl in tow, to exit the longhouse. Gunvald slowly let out a breath he hadn't realized he was holding. A small smile of victory spread across his face.

"What in the name of Thor was that?" Grimar hissed once everyone had filed out of the longhouse. He stepped unthinkingly onto the dais and stood towering over Gunvald's chair.

"Shut your mouth, boy," Gunvald shot back. "Instead of firing off your temper, you should try to learn something."

Grimar slouched in one of the smaller chairs on the dais. "Why don't you just explain to me why you are going to sell the girl," he muttered.

"Because we have bigger things to worry about without the distraction of a tug-of-war between you and your cousin over some thrall. Would you rather have a limp, shrunken girl or a secured Jarlship?"

Grimar sat up a little, his eyes lighting. "You think I'm still in position to take your place?"

Gunvald snorted. "Not yet, not by far. But think beyond your pricked pride, boy, and consider the long game. You act rashly when what is needed is planning— and finesse. Eirik is unhappy about my decision, but once the girl is gone and things return to normal, we can once again continue building your claim to the Jarlship."

"Why must I wait?" Grimar said testily. Then a gleam came into his pale eyes. "Why can't he just meet with an accident, as his father did?"

Gunvald bolted to his feet and slapped his son across the face. "Never speak so carelessly about such things!" he hissed. He glanced around the longhouse, but thankfully it remained empty and quiet. "The death of a kinsmen is always a tragedy. Eirik is our blood. You risk the gods' anger even thinking of killing him for your own gain."

Once he calmed himself with a deep breath, Gunvald straightened his fur mantle and resumed his seat. "Arud's death, though *accidental*, still hangs over this village. The last thing we need is for Eirik to follow his father to Valhalla and leave any doubt that the memory of his leadership is better than your actual power as Jarl."

The words came out through clenched teeth. Gunvald knew all too well that ruling in the shadow of his dead brother left him vulnerable to critique. He wanted his son to rule—when the time came—without any pall of doubt hanging over him. They had to do this the right—and slow—way, building up Grimar in the villagers' eyes and guiding Eirik away from thoughts of power. As long as Eirik remained interested in the lands to the west, he took himself out of the running. Besides, all manner of tragic accidents happened on raids. They simply needed to play the long game.

"Leave me," Gunvald said with a dismissive wave to Grimar. "And don't do aught about Eirik or the girl!" he hissed to Grimar's back. Grimar didn't bother turning to acknowledge his father's command. He stormed out of the longhouse, the door banging after him.

If only his son understood the subtle maneuverings required of a Jarl. Grimar would never be the beloved leader that Arud had been, or that Eirik could be. Nor would he be as shrewd and calculating as Gunvald. Yet the time would come soon enough when Gunvald could no longer defend his hold on the Jarlship. Whether the challenge would come from Eirik or someone else, he would be displaced. His best hope was to put his son, whom he could control, in his place.

Gunvald stood to retire to his private chamber off the longhouse for some much-needed sleep before the evening's festivities began. He would need to be at his best to be ready for the trials that lay ahead.

11

"What is happening?" Laurel had to take two steps for every one of Eirik's long strides. He pulled her behind him by the wrist as he weaved through the crowds.

Though she couldn't understand anything that had been said during what must have been the council meeting Eirik had warned her about, she knew from the weight of so many sets of eyes that she had been the topic. While Eirik's grip on her hand had loosened somewhat partway through the meeting, by the end he was nearly crushing her fingers. He was clearly unconscious of what he was doing, but she'd watched his face closely and saw that his eyes were filled with hate for Grimar and the man on the dais.

She yanked her arm back, and though her wrist still remained firmly in Eirik's grasp, she caught his attention.

"Answer me—what was the decision?"

"I'll explain when we get to my cottage," he snapped over his shoulder. He pulled her forward once more, ignoring the curious stares of the surrounding villagers.

Alaric and Madrena fell in beside him, ignoring her. They talked quickly and quietly to each other, yet Eirik never slowed their pace.

She tried to take in her surroundings as they plowed through the village. The water and docks were to her left. Steep mountains rose sharply not far behind the wooden building they'd just come from. In the small space between the water and the mountains, there were several wooden and stone huts, all with thatched rooves. Some villagers entered the huts while others lingered in the open square, either watching them or talking among themselves.

Eirik didn't hesitate as they passed the last of the structures. He picked up a trail through the green underbrush on the fringe of the village, skirting the narrow strip of flat land between the water and the steep, rocky mountains. Madrena and Alaric fell in behind her.

When they were nearly out of sight of the village, he halted suddenly. It was so abrupt that Laurel ran into his broad back, bouncing off with a whoosh as the air left her lungs. Eirik hardly noticed. Instead, he was focused on Madrena and Alaric as he spoke rapidly to them.

When she'd recovered her air and her footing, she peered around his wide shoulders to find a sturdy looking if solitary cottage clinging to the mountainside. The first three or four feet of the cottage's base was made out of large stones mortared together. Then tight wood paneling rose to the thatched roof, with a few fur-covered openings for windows.

The three Vikings seemed to be having some sort of dispute. Both Madrena and Alaric started talking in tight voices over Eirik. But Eirik barked what sounded like a command to them. They looked cross, with Alaric scowling and Madrena folding her arms over her chest, but then they turned and walked back down the path toward the village.

The apparent dispute settled, Eirik turned to open the cottage's wooden door and led her in.

She reluctantly followed him into the cottage. It was dim inside. Like the larger building they'd just come from, there was a fire pit in the middle of the room with a gap in the thatching overhead to let the smoke out. A simple cooking station took up one corner of the cottage. There was a table with two benches between the fire and the rudimentary kitchen, a few wooden chests, and little else in the single-roomed cottage.

Her eye snagged on one other item pushed back into the far corner. She hadn't noticed it at first, for linen cloth was draped around it to create privacy. As her eyes adjusted to the dimness, she realized it was a large bed. A wooden frame held a mattress piled with furs off the ground. Her eyes widened. She'd never seen such a luxurious bed before.

As she continued to look around in silence, she began to notice other things about Eirik's cottage. The still air held a lingering smell of wood smoke, salty sea air, and something else—something she'd detected whenever he was near. Was it his own clean, masculine scent?

A flutter of nervousness settled in her belly. She was suddenly aware of how intimate this was—she was alone with him for the first time, in his home, staring at his bed, close enough to smell his skin.

She forced her mind from such thoughts and turned to him, reminding herself firmly of the task at hand. She needed to know what had transpired at the council meeting, for though she was presently in Eirik's keeping, she sensed that something hadn't gone as he'd wished.

Just as she opened her mouth to demand that he explain what had transpired, he turned to her and pinned her with his gaze.

"I'm sure you want answers, Laurel." His eyes, normally so vivid, were dark with unspoken rage. "Jarl Gunvald has decided…he decided that…" That muscle in his jaw was ticking again. Eirik swallowed, his eyes hard as he continued to look down at her. "He has decided that you will remain my thrall. Indefinitely."

"W-what?" Her voice sounded distant to her own ears.

So that was it. Her fate had been decided. She would remain a thrall to a Viking barbarian forever.

She tried to remind herself that between Eirik and Grimar, she should be grateful that she'd been given to Eirik. Yet to hear his words—that she was his slave, for the rest of her life—cut deep. Aye, Eirik was better than Grimar, but why must she only have those two options? Why did she get no say in her fate? What of her freedom?

The thought sent her head spinning. Suddenly her legs, which already felt unsteady on solid ground, gave out beneath her. Eirik caught her under her arms and eased her to the floor, crouching in front of her.

"I've told you before that I will never mistreat you," he said, his voice unusually gruff.

A low moan ripped from her throat. Had God abandoned her? She was to be a slave to a heathen Viking, to be done with as he saw fit—forever. It was apparently her fate to suffer. Even still, she whispered a prayer for her safekeeping.

Yet through the haze descending on her at the news that she was to remain Eirik's thrall, a whisper of apprehension breathed in the back of her mind. This outcome didn't seem to match with Eirik's reaction in the large wooden building earlier. Unless he didn't want her as his thrall. Could that be possible? Nothing seemed to fit together. Was there more that he wasn't telling her?

Something cracked inside her. She was completely at Eirik's mercy. She didn't know his language, didn't have a soul to rely on, and had naught but a life of enslavement ahead of her. A flood of hopelessness drowned out any thought of escaping this nightmare. A sob of utter devastation shook her, followed quickly by another. Her eyes brimmed over with tears she'd held at bay for what felt like years.

She wept for her life at Whitby, for all the pain and fear and cruelty she'd lived with there. And she wept for the loss of that life, for even it seemed better than to live in this strange land, surrounded by strange people and customs, as little more than a soulless, will-less animal.

Through the aching sobs racking her body, she was distantly aware of Eirik lifting her in his arms and walking toward the back of the cottage. She didn't care what he did now. He'd said he wouldn't rape her, but he was also a raiding, pillaging Viking, and the world was a cruel place. She was too deep in her own grief to fight him.

He spread her out gently on his bed, but instead of lying on top of her, he stretched out next to her. He pulled her against his chest and held her tight, absorbing her shaking cries.

He began whispering words in his own language to her, running a hand up her back and to the nape of her neck. His hand was warm and large. He could have snapped her neck if he'd wanted to, but instead he gently massaged the tension from her nape and scalp. His fingers tangled in her braid. He found the tie at its tail and pulled it free so that his fingers could weave through her hair.

Though she didn't understand his words, she sensed that they were meant to soothe her. His voice was low, and it rumbled through his chest and into hers. His lips brushed her ear and she shivered. They were so soft, a feather touch on her skin. They trailed down to her tear-damp cheeks. Ever so gently, he kissed first one tear and then another, barely brushing her face.

Slowly, the racking sobs began to ebb and a numbness settled over her. She was in shock, a voice said in the back of her mind. That explained why she couldn't form a coherent thought, couldn't do aught except lie frozen in Eirik's arms, the willing recipient of each deliberate, soft kiss.

His lips drifted from her cheek to hover over her mouth, a hair's breadth away. She realized dimly that she longed for their touch, longed for the relief they promised from the pain and misery. She lifted her head slightly to close the distance between them.

He inhaled in surprise, yet she barely noticed. She was completely focused on his soft yet firm lips. They weren't demanding and forceful the way Brother Egbert's had been. Eirik recovered from his surprise and took control of the kiss, but with tenderness. He tilted his head so that their lips met more fully. She yielded her lips to him as he pressed more firmly against her.

She suddenly became aware that their lips weren't their only points of contact. She still lay in his arms, pulled against his chest. One of his hands held her close by her back while the other was twined in her loose hair. She realized that her breasts were molded against his hard chest. When she inhaled, their stomachs brushed together. And lower, she felt something long and hard pressing into her pelvis.

Her eyes popped open, and she gasped in shock at the intimacy of what they were doing. But he took the opportunity to flick his tongue against hers. A strange liquid heat shot through her at the foreign contact. Brother Egbert had tried to shove his tongue in her mouth before, which had repulsed her, but she had no idea it could feel like this. The heat of his tongue as it caressed hers seeped through her limbs, pooling in her breasts and between her legs.

The door to the cottage banged open and she nearly screamed in surprise. Both she and Eirik bolted upright on the bed.

"Alaric!" Eirik snapped. The sandy-haired man stood in the doorway with a large wooden tub on its side. He deliberately looked over the two of them on Eirik's bed and raised one eyebrow.

Eirik barked something else to Alaric, who casually rolled the wooden tub into the center of the cottage, then strolled out the door, a small smile playing on his face.

"I thought you might enjoy a bath after the…trying journey," Eirik said once Alaric was gone. "Unless…you aren't as afraid of bathwater as you are of the sea, are you?" His eyes clouded with concern.

A burst of laughter erupted from her. Laurel quickly clamped a hand over her mouth, embarrassed at her wild behavior, first in kissing Eirik then in laughing like a madwoman. The ridiculousness of the question paired with Eirik's thoughtful gesture and the lingering feel of his lips on hers was simply too much to make sense of at the moment.

"Nay, I'm not afraid of bathwater," she finally replied.

"I also asked Madrena to bring one of her old dresses."

She blinked at him, even more overwhelmed than before. She didn't have a chance to put words to her swirling thoughts, however, for the next moment

Madrena barged in just as abruptly as her brother had. She, too, eyed them sitting on Eirik's bed. Without comment, she tossed a pile of clothes on top of a nearby chest and left.

"There's a stream behind the cottage. I'll need to haul the water, and there won't be time to heat it," Eirik said, standing.

"I'm used to cold baths," she replied, finding her feet. She tried to smooth her wrinkled and dirty woolen dress, but the poor garment had been through too much. She could relate. What had just happened between them? Was she losing her mind in the presence of the tall, golden-haired Viking before her?

Eirik went about filling the tub using a wooden bucket. She stood awkwardly as he moved in and out of the cottage, unsure of what to do with herself. Finally, when the tub was full enough, Eirik cleared his throat.

"I suppose I'll bathe in the stream," he said. His gaze moved slowly from her eyes to her lips and lower across her body. Then suddenly, his brow lowered in frustration and he spun on his heels. He snatched a random garment from one of the wooden chests and exited the cottage without another word.

She wished she had more time to puzzle over the events that had just transpired, but she was acutely aware that Eirik would return shortly. Her face heated at the thought of him walking in on her while she bathed —but it wasn't just shame that made her blush.

Laurel shoved the emotion aside brutally. What a sinful idea to blush over—a Viking barbarian searing her with his gaze, and naught between them but air.

She scurried to the pile of clothes Madrena had deposited and found that the Viking woman had not only left her a shift and overdress, but also a strip of linen to dry herself with. Most prized of all, she'd placed a lump of fragrant soap on top of the pile. She raised the soap to her nose and inhaled. It was piney, fresh, and crisp.

She quickly pulled her rough wool dress over her head and tossed it aside. Bringing the soap with her, she gingerly stepped into the tub. The water was frigid, but she'd never had aught but cold baths all her life, so she didn't waste time shivering. She quickly slipped in and dunked her head. She worked the soap in her hands and then scrubbed her skin and hair thoroughly. The crisp scent of the soap combined with the cold water made her feel cleaner than she'd ever felt before.

Once the soap was rinsed away and she couldn't take the cold water anymore, she stood and dried herself with the linen cloth. Then she slipped the shift over her head and sighed. She had never been given a shift at the Abbey. Abbess Hilda believed that having scratchy wool against her skin would remind her of the bodily sins of her parents.

If her wandering thoughts of Eirik bathing in the stream nearby were any indication, Abbess Hilda had been right about her. Mayhap she did deserve naught but scratchy wool after all.

But nay, she was no wanton. Eirik was different. He was kind to her when he could easily be cruel. But would he truly treat her better than her status as a thrall warranted? The tenuousness of her situation chilled her more that the icy stream water ever could.

Suddenly the cottage door opened and there stood Eirik.

Bare-chested and dripping water.

She shrieked in surprise and snatched up the over-dress, trying to cover herself from his gaze. She'd dallied with her thoughts for too long, and now here they stood, both in varying states of undress, alone in his cottage.

"I forgot to bring a clean tunic," he said by way of explanation. Yet instead of moving to one of the chests for the garment, he stood rooted in the doorway, his eyes piercing her. He wore a pair of fitted leather pants she hadn't seen before, but it was his naked skin on which her eyes were riveted.

Like the parts of him she'd seen already, his torso was bronzed from the sun. His shoulders seemed even more broad and imposing without a layer of loose linen over them. She could see every contour and corded muscle in the light streaming in from the open door behind him. His wide chest narrowed into the hard planes of his stomach. With each of his inhalations and exhalations, the ridged muscles on his torso popped. Her mind skittered back to the feel of his stone-hard body pressed against her on his bed. What would it feel like to touch his bare skin?

His damp hair was finger-combed away from his face. She noticed the muscle in his jaw was ticking again, as it often did when he was frustrated. She sought his eyes, unsure what she'd find there. Instead of annoyance or even anger, she saw a raw heat blazing in their bright blue depths.

She broke their gaze quickly. "I…I need to finish getting dressed."

He finally stepped forward to one of the nearby chests and opened the lid to remove a linen tunic. He tugged the garment over his head, then closed the chest and stood still once more.

When she only gaped at him, he lowered his eyebrows. "What are you waiting for?"

She felt her eyes go even wider than they already were. "You expect me to simply…dress in front of you?" The overdress blocked her front from his gaze. Without it, the thin linen shift would do little to protect her modesty. This level of intimacy was surely wrong.

Slowly, he pivoted on his heels to give her his back. Not waiting for any more privacy, she yanked the over-dress on and tugged it down over her body. But once the finely woven wool covered her, she twisted and turned, unable to make sense of the strange cut. There were no sleeves, only two strips of material draping down her back. Two fine brooches with beads strung between them sat on the front of the gown, but they appeared only ornamental.

After struggling for several long moments, she sighed and gave up.

"Eirik?" she said softly.

"May I turn around?" His voice was unusually rough, though he didn't sound angry.

"Aye. I can't seem to…where are the sleeves?"

Eirik faced her and pinned her once again with that heated stare. As he approached, her stomach clenched.

"It is the style here for women to wear these sleeveless overdresses in the summer," he explained. One of his large hands reached out and nearly brushed her damp hair. She inhaled, expecting his touch, but instead, he grasped one of the strips of wool dangling down her back. He pulled it over her shoulder and fastened in at her chest with one of the silver brooches.

She held her breath as his fingers worked the pin, which sat just above her breast. He did the same on the other side, so that the strips sat on her shoulders and were each fastened by one of the brooches.

He stepped back and let his gaze trail over her. He muttered something in his own language, and that blue fire flickered in his eyes.

She glanced down at herself, feeling awkward in the strange garments. Her arms were bare except for the thin linen shift, which went to her wrists but clearly showed her skin underneath. The two brooches were intricately wrought silver, far finer than anything she'd ever worn before. Several strings of beads were looped between the brooches. The beads draped over her breasts, drawing attention to them. Both the shift and the overdress fit her fairly well through the waist and hips but were far too long on her and puddled around her feet.

"Come," he said, extending a hand toward her. "We'll be late to the celebration."

"What celebration?"

"The one honoring our successful voyage. 'Twould

be an insult to the Jarl if I didn't attend," he said flatly, though his mouth turned down slightly.

"And why must I attend?" she asked, feeling her stomach twist in foreboding. "Am I to serve those at the feast, as my status as a slave warrants?"

The strange spell that had been hanging in the air between them shattered. Her throat was thick with the bitterness of her own words, yet she couldn't simply escape to the safety of Eirik's arms or let herself be swept away by his kisses. She was his thrall—the reality of her situation was still horrifyingly raw.

His face hardened. "You must attend because I will not leave you here alone."

"Do you expect me to attempt escape?" she blurted.

Strangely, the thought hadn't crossed her mind since she'd been taken from Whitby Abbey. Of course, she wouldn't have been able to simply jump overboard and swim to safety while they were on Eirik's ship. But even now that she was on solid ground, she was in a foreign land where she didn't speak the language or know a single soul who might aid her. Eirik had spoken of the enslaved monks from Lindisfarne from whom he'd learned her language. Mayhap she could find them and…

"Nei, for if you tried to escape, you'd be either dead or captured in a matter of hours," he ground out.

Her spine stiffened. "Then why? Do you wish to parade me about for all to see your helpless, utlending thrall?"

He closed the distance between them so fast that she gasped and took an involuntary step back.

"Nei, you are coming with me because I fear for your safety if I leave you alone, Laurel," he said, his voice cold but his eyes flickering with emotion. "Grimar was not satisfied with the Jarl's ruling. He or his supporters may try something."

"You said you'd protect me," she whispered.

"That is what I am doing. Now come. They will be waiting on us."

How could she have been so foolish to let herself kiss this man, let her thoughts run wild about how he was different from the others? He was still a heathen, a barbarian. And she was still his property. She hardened herself to the events that awaited her. She was among his people now, people who had no care for her and who saw her as lower than an animal.

Laurel followed him out the door into the slanting sunlight of the midsummer evening. She had to be stronger than she'd ever been before—strong enough to resist her own desire to trust Eirik.

12
_____

E irik slowed his pace along the path toward the village. Laurel struggled to keep up with him in Madrena's too-long clothes. He'd told his friend to bring something she'd worn as a younger, smaller girl. He'd forgotten that even as a youth, Madrena had been tall.

He tried to cool the heated frenzy of thoughts that swirled through him, threatening to make him—what? Lose his temper at the innocent young woman trailing after him?

This situation wasn't her doing, he reminded himself. Grimar had captured her, Gunvald had made the decision to sell her at Jutland's slave market—and he had claimed her as his thrall. He was as guilty as his uncle and cousin in this cursed tangle.

Nei, he was more guilty, for he was the one who'd kissed her even after vowing to himself that he wouldn't touch her, thrall that she was. But seeing her devasta-tion at the news that she would remain his thrall, and feeling her small, slight, yet womanly body pressed against him in his bed—it had been too much. The cold dunk in the stream had done little to cool his blood.

And he'd nearly lost all hold on his control at seeing her in Viking women's garb. Her slim figure was finally visible in the more fitted clothes. Her breasts were fit to her frame, yet they were more womanly and shapely than they'd appeared in her old formless brown dress. The traditional double brooches and strings of beads only added to the effect. Her narrow waist flared delicately into gently curving hips. And her pale, thin arms and shoulders were visible through the shift Madrena had provided.

He was weaker than he'd thought. First he was lusting after his thrall, and next he was lying to her about his uncle's ruling. He simply wouldn't accept Gunvald's decision that she be sold at Jutland's slave market at the end of the summer raiding season—a little less than two months from now. He would just have to find a way to convince his uncle that Laurel should be allowed to stay—but not as his thrall, as a free woman. The task was almost too much to contemplate, yet he wouldn't give up until he found a way to protect and free Laurel.

He ripped his mind from the impossibility of the situation he'd gotten them into. It didn't matter that he found her so completely entrancing. He would keep trying to think of a way to avoid the fate Gunvald had decided for her, but it didn't change the fact that for now, she was his thrall. It was easier to be angry about the situation, angry at her for her sharp remarks, than to dwell on their reality.

He halted outside the longhouse, where merriment from within could be heard. "Stay close to me," he said over his shoulder to her. "Keep your eyes lowered and do as you're asked by others, but don't leave my side."

She looked up at him, her eyes wide and dark in the surrounding twilight. He couldn't tell which emotion ruled her—fear or frustration. It didn't matter, he reminded himself icily.

He opened the door to the longhouse and was met with a blast of noise and the smells of cooking food and ale. All the villagers were gathered for the celebratory feast, some shouting merrily to each other, others singing over raised horns of ale. A few near the door cheered as they spotted him.

"Remember what I said," he whispered once again before stepping fully into the midst of the celebration.

He received several pounds on the back as he made his way through the now-full wooden benches and tables. He caught sight of Alaric's sandy head and Madrena's pale blond one pressed together near the dais and weaved his way toward them.

"The clothes are too fine for a thrall," Madrena muttered when they reached her.

"You were the one who selected them," Eirik snapped back.

"I don't *have* any clothes fit for a thrall!" Madrena hissed, eyeing Laurel. "You still haven't told her?"

"Nei, and I'm not going to," Eirik said flatly to Madrena. "She doesn't need to know yet. There may still be a way for me to convince my uncle to change his mind."

"Take care, Eirik," Alaric said, his brow lowered. "You say you don't want her treated as a thrall, yet you are controlling what she knows of her own fate. This may come back to bite you in the ass."

"Eirik!"

Before he could respond to Alaric, Eirik's head snapped to the dais, where Gunvald, Grimar, and a few others sat at the table of honor. Gunvald motioned for Eirik to join them. Eirik cursed under his breath but gave his uncle an acquiescing nod. He took Laurel by the wrist and mounted the stairs to the dais.

Just as Grimar took a swig from his drinking horn, he noticed Eirik's approach with Laurel in tow. Grimar sputtered, sending ale spewing from his lips.

"A thrall cannot sit at the high table with us!" he said loudly. The noise in the longhouse died as all eyes shifted to the dais.

Gunvald's attention was pulled by his son's sharp words. "What is the girl doing up here, nephew?" he asked, frowning.

"And why is she dressed like a free woman?" Grimar demanded as he stood, pointing a finger at Laurel.

"She is mine to dress and take where I want," Eirik said just as loudly. He forced himself to relax the tension in his shoulders. He couldn't let Grimar dictate his actions or rile his anger.

"She is an utlending! She deserves neither a free-woman's clothes nor a place at the high table." Grimar's ice blue eyes flashed in outrage. "In fact, she doesn't even deserve the hair on her head."

Without thinking, Eirik shoved Laurel behind him as Grimar drew the seax at his waist. A ripple of surprise went through those gathered at yet another spectacle involving Grimar, Eirik, and the utlending girl.

"You'll not cut her hair, Grimar, unless you wish to go through me first," Eirik said, his voice deadly calm even as his heart pounded faster.

"What is he doing?" Laurel breathed behind him.

"He wants to cut your hair," Eirik replied over his shoulder. "Thralls normally have their hair cropped short to distinguish them from free men and women."

"Enough!" Gunvald shouted. "Grimar, put down your arms." In a lower voice likely only meant for his son, he hissed, "I told you to leave it be!"

With a grumbled curse, Grimar re-sheathed his seax and slowly took his seat.

"You tread a dangerous line, nephew," Gunvald said, turning to Eirik. "She is a thrall, not a freewoman to be dressed like that, her hair still long. Do with her as you will, but she is not fit to sit at the high table."

That seemed to placate Grimar somewhat, but Eirik felt his lips curl in a snarl. "Very well, Jarl," he managed. His uncle watched him closely. Ever since Eirik and his crew had returned from their voyage, Gunvald seemed bolder in testing both his own power and Eirik's submission.

He motioned for Alaric and Madrena to fetch Laurel. "'Tis all right," he said quietly to her. "You'll sit with Alaric and Madrena. They'll look after you."

"But you said not to leave your side!" she said frantically as his friends guided her down off the dais. The noise swelled once more as the villagers returned to their merriment, cutting off his attempt to reassure her.

He took a seat next to the Jarl, but his eyes trailed after her as Madrena and Alaric sat her between them at the nearest bench.

"Forget the thrall," Gunvald said crossly to him.

With effort, Eirik tore his gaze from Laurel and accepted a drinking horn from his uncle, if only to give Gunvald the satisfaction of thinking he was obeying him.

"This night is a celebration of your victorious voyage. To many more ahead!" Gunvald raised his horn and Eirik tapped its rim with his own. He drank deeply of the ale, trying to soothe his frayed nerves.

Steaming meats, fresh bread, and a cabbage and carrot stew were soon passed around, along with many more pitchers of ale. Eirik tersely responded to all of Gunvald's slathered-on praise for the voyage's success and his outpouring of enthusiasm for future raids on the lands to the west. Yet as the meal progressed, Gunvald's droning voice grew faint as his attention narrowed on Laurel's slim back.

Her dark head remained bowed throughout the meal. She ate and drank little, though Madrena kept nudging food toward her. Madrena seemed at a loss when it came to interacting with Laurel. Though he appreciated his friends' kindness toward her, neither Madrena nor Alaric seemed to know what to make of her—or of his strange behavior regarding her.

The longhouse grew so loud with gaiety that soon Gunvald was having to shout to be heard. Eirik was finally feeling the effects of the plentiful ale, but instead of soothing his nerves, it seemed to make him more agitated at what was going on around Laurel.

Those at her table were already drunk. Even Madrena and Alaric were leaning across her so that they could talk to each other. A flicker of movement behind her drew Eirik's eyes. Haakon, the large, aging warrior with a bushy red beard, stumbled past where Laurel sat stiffly. The giant stopped right behind her, swaying slightly from too much drink.

"A thrall with long hair," Haakon slurred. He reached out and pinched some of Laurel's dark hair between his fingers, giving it a tug.

Eirik bolted to his feet so fast that he knocked over the chair he'd been sitting in. Gunvald clamped a hand over his wrist before he could move to Laurel's side.

"I thought I told you to forget her for the evening," Gunvald said lowly. Clearly his uncle was willing to exert his authority to keep Eirik away from Laurel. The thought made Eirik's blood boil.

At the tug on her hair, Laurel jerked to her feet and faced Haakon. Her eyes were wide with outrage at his boldness, but he only laughed and then belched in her face.

"Fetch me more ale, thrall!" Haakon said, shoving his drinking horn at her. Madrena and Alaric had risen at her sides, unsure if they should intercede or not. Alaric made eye contact with Eirik, but Eirik forced himself to give a little shake of his head. They couldn't afford another scene, especially since it was apparently Gunvald's goal to make Laurel's presence a non-issue.

Laurel looked between the red-bearded giant before her and the horn he'd thrust under her nose, clearly not understanding his command.

"Utlendings…" Haakon muttered, then snatched a pitcher of ale from a nearby table and pushed it at Laurel, forcing her to take hold of it. "Now…refill… my…horn…thrall." Haakon annunciated each word as if speaking slowly would make her understand their language.

After a moment, Laurel tilted the pitcher and poured more ale into Haakon's horn. He took a swig and turned to where Eirik stood on the dais.

"You have much work ahead of you in training your thrall, Eirik!" Haakon called out, drawing laughter from those around him. Eirik remained silent but tried to kill the man with his gaze. Normally Haakon's blunt manners didn't bother him, but something about the sight of the man's hand on Laurel's hair made him see red.

Gunvald gave Eirik's sleeve a little yank, drawing his attention back to him. Slowly, Eirik righted his chair and resumed his seat at the Jarl's side. But his eyes remained locked on Laurel. Several more villagers around her held up empty drinking horns for her to refill. Her back stiff, she moved from one to another, emptying her pitcher.

The villagers didn't mean any harm by it, Eirik tried to tell himself to cool his temper. She was a thrall. Besides, they were likely more curious than aught else to get an up-close look at the utlending who'd already caused so much trouble.

Yet as he watched her rigid back, he hated each and every one of them for treating her like that. Nei, he hated himself, for he was the one who'd made her his thrall and stood against Grimar and Gunvald publicly over her.

He clenched his fists as several more villagers fingered Laurel's long, dark hair when she turned her back on them to serve others. Some were even bold enough to feel the material of her dress and shake their heads, either in disapproval or confusion at its fineness.

He'd had enough. And she certainly had as well.

"I am wearied from our journey," Eirik said brusquely to Gunvald as he stood. "Please excuse me for the rest of the evening."

Gunvald eyed him for a moment, but then gave a little nod of permission. Not bothering to take the stairs down from the dais, Eirik simply leapt the several feet to the floor and made his way toward Laurel, who had resumed her seat between Alaric and Madrena.

"…can't fight, can't swim, can't speak our language, and doesn't even—" Madrena jerked away from Alaric and clamped her mouth shut when she realized Eirik was practically on top of them.

The combination of the unspent anger at Laurel's treatment and the ale made Eirik feel ready to throttle Madrena. "If you have something to say, Madrena, say it to my face," he bit out.

Her pale eyes flared at him. "Very well, I will. Why do you insist on making things difficult when it comes to the girl? She's an utlending." She lowered her voice and leaned in, though everyone around them was too drunk to pay them any mind. "You know I would support you if you ever get your head out of your ass and challenge the Jarl, but the girl is distracting—"

"Enough!" Eirik roared.

Alaric took a step between Eirik and his twin sister. "Easy, both of you," he said quietly.

"I am going home," Eirik said, willing himself to speak levelly. "And I am taking Laurel with me. She needs protection—perhaps more than I realized." He let his words sink in as he gazed coldly at Madrena.

He took Laurel by the arm and stomped out of the longhouse, the sounds of merriment fading behind him.

"I thought Madrena was your friend," Laurel huffed as she hurried behind him. "What was that all about?"

Eirik sighed and slowed his pace somewhat. In truth, Madrena was right. Laurel was an outsider, ignorant of his people's ways. He didn't have to defend his protection of Laurel to Madrena or anyone else. But he couldn't simply expect Laurel to live with him in Dalgaard as an utlending thrall. Even if he was successful in convincing his uncle to reconsider his ruling, she couldn't remain an utlending forever.

"She...she is worried about you."

"I doubt that," Laurel said. "I seem to bother her."

He almost smiled at her perceptiveness. "She doesn't like that you know so little of life here."

Laurel stiffened under his hand, which was still wrapped around her elbow. "I didn't ask to come here," she said coldly.

"Nei, but you are here now, and it is time you learned something of our ways," Eirik said, an idea forming in his mind.

"And what if I don't want to learn? What if I don't want to have any part in your heathen ways?"

He was beginning to learn that underneath her meek, small exterior, Laurel was actually quite stubborn, even hot-headed at times. Eirik halted suddenly and turned to her. He couldn't simply command her to learn more about life in the Northlands. "It…it might make things easier for your time here," he said softly. She didn't need to know that her time in the village might end with the coming of fall.

"My time here?" Though her voice was hard, her eyes shimmered in the blue light of midsummer's false night. "You mean as your slave?"

A flicker of doubt had him looking closer at her in the twilight. Did she sense that he wasn't telling her everything? Nei, she couldn't know that Eirik hoped that in teaching her some of their customs and language, he might be able to convince his uncle that she should stay on with them.

She held his gaze for a moment before her shoulders slumped slightly. "I know how to work hard. I know how to serve. But I do not know how to be a slave, and I doubt I will ever understand your ways," she whispered.

Gently, he lifted her chin so that his eyes met hers. "At least try. You may even find that your spirit will serve you well here."

As he watched her, he saw a glimmer of something he'd never seen in her eyes before. It was hope.

13

Eirik pointed to the stack of wood next to the fire pit.

"*Brandr,*" she said.

"Good." He brought his fingers to his sleeve and gave it a tug.

"*Ermr.*"

He pointed to the small wooden table in the corner of his cottage.

She froze, fumbling for the word. "*Baru?*"

"Nei, *borð,*" he replied.

He stood and stretched his back, clearly restless in the dim, confined space of his cottage. They'd spent most of the last sennight inside the little hut. He'd apparently made it his mission to teach her his entire language as quickly as possible. If only her brain would cooperate. There were many different words and unfamiliar combinations of sounds.

She imagined based on his tanned skin and honed

physique that he normally spent most of his time working outdoors. She, too, was used to putting her body to work, but that didn't fully explain her restlessness in the small space.

The night of the celebration, they'd arrived back at his cottage and she realized that there was nowhere to sleep—nowhere, that was, except his large bed. He must have read the panic on her face, for he took a few of the furs from on top of the bed and threw them on the floor in the far corner. She had the enormous, down-filled bed to herself, yet she'd been restless that night and every night since.

The bed smelled of him—of wood smoke, pine, fresh air, and his warm skin. Then of course she had remembered what they'd done earlier on the bed—that slow, simmering kiss, their bodies pressed together, his hot tongue entering her…

Each night, she listened to him breathing and grew itchy and embarrassed at the intimacy of sharing such a small space with a man. If Abbess Hilda could see her now, she'd have a fit.

"I've been pushing you too hard," Eirik muttered, interrupting her thoughts.

"Nay, keep going," she said. "I just need to concentrate."

"I think I've been asking you to concentrate a little too much," he said, pacing the short distance from the door to the makeshift kitchen.

"At least it is something to focus on," she replied quietly, folding her hands. She hadn't allowed herself to dwell on her fate as Eirik's thrall. Learning his language so quickly had been a welcome distraction. Besides, she could either accept her new life or resist it, but either way she was stuck in this Northland village. Learning all she could might benefit her in the future—whatever it held.

Eirik paused in his pacing, his large body poised for action. "I know what we need. We need to get outdoors. We need a *svima*." He eyed her, waiting.

She sifted through the hundreds of words she'd learned in the last sennight. "*Svima*..." A sense of dread crept through her as the memory flitted back. "*Svima*... swim? You want to go swimming? Nay, Eirik, I can't!"

"Easy, Laurel. I want to teach you. You need to learn sometime, and I'm an excellent—"

"Nay!" Her voice rose frantically, but she didn't care. "I can't!"

He knelt before her so that their eyes were level. "Yes, you can."

"Is this an order, then? Do I have no choice in the matter as your thrall?" She was desperately grasping at straws now, she knew. He'd never treated her like a slave or forced her to do aught in the fortnight since she'd been taken from the Abbey. Yet she felt cornered and terrified. She would never willingly enter water other than to bathe.

He leaned back on his heels, watching her closely. "You mentioned on the Drakkar that the nuns at the Abbey punished you with water. What did you mean?"

She took a deep breath, trying to slow her pounding heart. She didn't speak for a long moment, but he simply waited, his bright eyes pinning her.

"They used to—to tie me to a chair and lower me under water," she finally replied, her voice quavering. "I never knew how long they'd keep me under, or how many times they'd dunk me."

His brows lowered. "Why would they do such a thing to you?"

"For little things, like being late to prayer or not cleaning the refectory or outhouses well enough." She felt her lip beginning to tremble and she lowered her eyes. "But sometimes it was simply to remind me of my parents' sin."

"What sin could your parents have committed that would warrant such treatment?"

"As I told you before, I was born out of wedlock," she replied simply. At his confused look, she went on. "My parents weren't married when I was born. The Abbess and the nuns told me *I* was their punishment."

He shook his head slowly. "The monks from Lindisfarne I spoke with tried to explain your Christian concept of sin, but it makes little sense. Children are a blessing, and their parents' dishonor does not determine their fate. A man or woman's own actions are what determine if a place in Valhalla awaits."

She raised her head, tentatively eyeing him. "Is Valhalla your version of heaven?"

He rubbed the golden stubble along his jawline. "It is similar, based on what the monks told me. Valhalla is a great hall in the kingdom of Asgard. It is where Odin, the Allfather God, resides, along with some of the other gods. When a warrior dies an honorable death, the warrior maidens called the Valkyries swoop down and transport him to Valhalla, where warriors feast and drink and fight happily for all eternity."

"That sounds terribly sinful," she said, though she had to acknowledge a flicker of curiosity within herself.

"Sin is a strange weapon you Christians use against yourselves," he replied. "For Vikings, there is no such thing as sin. There is either honor, or dishonor."

She lowered her head again, unsure of what to make of his words. He was a heathen, and his people's ways were strange, yet she couldn't deny that he was an honorable man.

She sighed and let her gaze fall to her lap. "'Tis a very nice idea that one's actions alone can determine one's place in the afterlife," she said. "But even then I may be beyond saving. The nuns always said I was too proud, too willful. Even when I'd do as I was told, they said my eyes gave me away."

He chuckled, which brought her head snapping up.

"They were right," he said, his eyes soft. "Not that you deserved their ill treatment. But the more I come to know your eyes, the more they reveal your spirit to me. You don't look it, but I think you have a warrior's heart, Laurel."

Her skin flushed under his words and his gaze.

"Now I understand why you are afraid of water," he said, breaking the spell. "But I don't know why you refuse to learn to swim."

She opened her mouth to protest, suddenly feeling a surge of anger. But before she could respond, he went on.

"You have two choices, of course. You can either

continue to be afraid as you always have, or you can face your fear and overcome it. It sounds like the perfect opportunity to prove your honor to the gods. Who knows, perhaps your god will be watching too."

Her eyes widened at his audacious words, but then the most unexpected thing happened. He winked at her, the normally hard lines of his face transforming into a lively grin. She couldn't help but feel the corners of her own mouth tug up. How could this man have so much power over her and yet exert it only to draw a smile from her?

He stood, taking her hands in his and drawing her up. "I have just the place in mind for our first lesson."

"Just a little farther," Eirik urged as he guided Laurel by the hand along the overgrown path. Though a quick dunk in the fjord or the stream behind his cottage normally sufficed, he sometimes took the long walk to this secluded lake tucked between the steeply sloped mountains rising all around.

They crossed out of the tree line and into the small open meadow that bordered the south side of the lake. They were close now.

He quickened his pace. The balmy summer air and high sun weren't the reason he was so eager to reach the lake, though. Nei, the weather had little to do with it.

She'd taken so quickly to his language. Every day she picked up new words. She was even able to piece together some of what he and Alaric had discussed when his friend paid a visit to retrieve his bathing tub. Though he didn't want to shove his people's customs down her throat, over the past sennight she had also asked him more questions about their views and habits. To now have the chance to teach her something as important as swimming—Eirik felt a surge of pride at the thought.

But he had to admit that it was more than admiration of her sharpness and willingness to learn that had him dragging her to this secluded lake. She was more terrified of water than aught else, yet she trusted him to try to teach her how to swim. She was brave in facing her fears. And she was coming to know that he would never harm her. For some reason, the realization of her growing trust in him over the last sennight made his chest pinch strangely.

He caught sight of the glimmering lake across the grass- and flower-filled meadow, and something else, something far lower than his chest, pinched as well.

He hadn't kissed Laurel again since the night after the council meeting. He'd tried to rein in his unruly lust for her, tried to control his body despite being in such close proximity to her day and night. All he'd gotten for his efforts were sleepless nights on some furs in the corner of his cottage, an aching cock, and of course his own cursed sense of honor left intact.

Mayhap it was a mistake to take her out here alone, where they would be undressing and swimming together. Then again, his body was wound tight enough that the ever-quieter voice in his head about the wrongness of his attraction to Laurel seemed far less urgent.

He halted at the water's edge and immediately unbuckled his belt from around his tunic.

"What are you doing?" Laurel gaped.

"Getting ready for a swim. What does it look like?"

Her wide-eyed stare in response doused the heated, fervent need to undress and enter the water with her. Of course, while he was growing more and more eager to reach the lake, she'd likely been sinking deeper into her fears. He silently cursed himself and his lust-filled body. Why did he feel like such a fumbling, untried boy when it came to her?

"We can take this slow," he said, stilling himself. Her dark eyes darted first to the smooth, clear lake, then over his body. By Thor, if he was reading her right, she was nearly as hesitant at the idea of seeing his body as she was at getting into the lake.

It didn't take the gift of Sight to know that Laurel was innocent. Her reaction to their kiss had told him that. Yet could she truly be so completely ignorant about the ways of the world to be uncomfortable just at the sight of his body? She had been raised with both nuns and monks, yet if the monks from Lindisfarne were to be believed, these Christians intentionally denied themselves any knowledge—or pleasures—of the body.

He casually pulled his leather boots off, followed by his tunic. Ignoring her, he went to the water's edge and crouched, running his fingers through the cool water. He'd let her get used to seeing him like this.

"Fear is your worst enemy when it comes to swimming," he said, still facing the lake. "If the water feels you struggling against it, it will fight you in return."

Everyone in Dalgaard, and likely everyone in all the Northlands, knew how to swim. Water was simply too central to their way of life to avoid it. Whether it was fishing, sailing to other lands, or just bathing in a lake or fjord, all people had need of the ability to swim. He'd never had to teach anyone before, yet he'd learned as a very young boy from his father.

She tentatively stepped next to him at the waterline. "If I didn't struggle, I'd simply drown. That doesn't seem like a good alternative."

He glanced up at her. Her face was tight with anxiety as she stared at the water in front of them. At least she was distracted from his semi-nakedness. Even still, he'd better keep his pants on while they were in the water.

He stood and began wading into the lake.

"You're going in...like that?" She was eyeing his pants with a look of worry. "Won't they pull you under?"

He looked down. Thankfully, he was wearing his double-lined linen pants and not his heavier wool or leather ones for cooler weather. "I'll be fine. Unless you'd rather I remove them?"

Her face flushed bright red. *Good*, he thought. *I'm distracting her.* Then an idea so audacious, so brazen, popped into his mind that he almost discarded it out of hand. Whether it was more for her benefit or his, though, he began forming a plan.

"You can leave your shift on if you prefer," he said, facing her and stepping backward still deeper into the lake. "But your dress will be too heavy and cumbersome.

You'd best remove it." He halted, his eyes locked on her. Even from a dozen paces away, he could see the redness in her cheeks and her gaze flickering in uncertainty.

Her hands began fumbling with first one brooch and then the other as she unfastened her dress's shoulder straps. Every few seconds, her eyes flew up to his and fluttered away just as quickly. She pulled the overlong dress up and over her body. The muddy hem passed her hips, then her waist, then her breasts, and finally over her head.

She carefully set the garment on a nearby rock. Then she bent and removed her leather boots. Her blush had moved over her neck, her pink skin contrasting against the off-white of her linen shift along her collarbones.

"Mayhap your shift will tangle in your legs once you enter the water," he said casually, never taking his eyes from her. "You could leave it on the shoreline as well, I suppose."

She glanced down, unsure. Then she got a glimpse of the view he was being treated to and gasped in shock. The bright sunlight made the shift all but useless in hiding her form. He could clearly see the outline of each of her slim yet shapely legs, along with the darker patch of hair between them. The enticing inward curve of her waist was also visible. Her high, round breasts brushed against her shift, each with a rosy tip that was barely obscured by the thin linen.

She threw her hands across her body, but they did little to hide her beauty. Even waist-deep in the cold northern lake waters, Eirik's cock jumped and began throbbing. Mayhap this plan was ill-conceived. Or was this exactly what he wanted all along?

Laurel rushed toward the water, seeking its refuge to hide her exposed body. She was knee-deep before she hesitated. At least his little trick of pitting her modesty against her fear of the water had gotten her that far.

"Come, Laurel," he said, reaching a hand toward her. "You are brave enough to face this." Though he formed the words to lure her deeper, he surprised himself by believing them. In the little time he'd known her, he'd learned that she wasn't one to cower or run from her fears—except when it came to water.

Slowly, she inched closer to him. The cold water was making her nipples pebble under the shift. He forced himself to focus on her face. Her lower lip was captured between her teeth, the anxiety evident on her delicate features.

"What if…what if I go too deep and drown? What if I take you down with me?"

Even as she spoke the shaky words, she continued toward his outstretched hand.

"You've already tried that once," he said, quirking one eyebrow at her.

She let out something between an exhalation and a laugh just as she reached his hand and placed hers within it. He drew her to him so that the water lapped just under her breasts.

Eirik cursed the lake water for its fortune in being able to envelop her, caress her skin, and wrap around her curves. Then he cursed himself for such thoughts. He needed to get his lust under control and focus on the task at hand. He was teaching his thrall how to swim, not seducing this captivatingly beautiful woman before him.

"First of all," he began, but had to pause to clear his throat. "You've learned that when you claw at the water, it will slip right through your fingers. But it will actually hold you up if you let it. Watch."

Eirik leaned back so that he floated face-up on the lake's surface. He kept his hold on her hand to show her how relaxed he was. The cool water enveloped his nape and his free-flowing hair, tickling his ears. He gazed up at the cloudless blue sky for a moment, savoring the sensations.

He popped upright. "Now you try."

She seemed to shrink in on herself and shook her head. "Nay."

"I'll hold your hand the entire time, and I'll be right here to keep you safe," he said.

She locked her dark, frightened eyes on him for a long moment. Without breaking their gaze, she slowly started to lean back. Her loose chestnut locks fell into the water inch by inch until the back of her head was submerged.

Her fingers dug painfully into his hand. She finally broke their gaze to squeeze her eyes shut, her breath coming short and shallow.

"'Tis all right, Laurel," he said as if she were a spooked animal. "I'm right here."

He wasn't sure if she registered his voice or not, but after a moment first one foot and then the other appeared at the water's surface.

"That's it. You're floating."

Her eyes popped open in surprise. "How am I…" Her body tensed in uncertainty, and almost instantly she sank, her head dipping under the water.

Reacting on instinct, Eirik jerked her up hard by the hand. Her head emerged immediately from underwater, but he misjudged his own strength and her lightness. Her whole body rose from the water and slammed into him.

He held her to him, trying to steady her as she sputtered and panted. His skin felt unnaturally hot at all the points of contact they shared. Her breasts pressed against his chest with naught more than the wet linen shift separating them. One of her hands, the one he didn't still have captured in his own, had come up to take hold of his neck. Their torsos were plastered together, and he was certain she could feel his cock throbbing against her belly.

He coughed and set her down. "You tensed up. But when you were relaxed, the water was holding you."

She nodded and averted her eyes. "Is that all for today?"

"Nei, Laurel, it is not." For some reason, his words sounded laden with meaning that he didn't intend to give voice to. "That is, you should at least try a few strokes on your stomach."

Her eyes flitted to him, wide and questioning. By the gods, he couldn't seem to find words that didn't seem suggestive. "Like this," he said quickly. He let go of her hand and took several strokes farther out into the lake, his hands slicing through the water and legs kicking.

He swam back to her side, trying to look anywhere but at the wet shift plastered to her breasts. Thank the gods she still stood in waist-deep water, or else he might forget himself completely.

"That looks a lot more complicated than floating," she said dubiously as he stood at her side.

"I'll help keep you up," he replied. "Sink down so that only your head is above water."

Surprisingly, she did as he said with only a moment's hesitation. She truly was coming to trust him. She lowered herself until just her head and neck were on the water's surface.

"Now lift your feet behind you. I'll have you, don't worry."

She slowly raised one foot so that her heel was above the water. He reached for her stomach as her body tilted forward. Her weight shifted onto his two hands, one of which spanned from just below her breasts to her navel, the other of which was planted on her low belly.

Her other heel appeared at the surface and her weight was fully suspended by the water and his hands. She exhaled in shock at what must have been a terrifying position for her, and he could feel her stomach contract. Unbidden, his cock stirred once more below the water.

"Now use your arms as I did," he instructed, forcing his mind from the ache between his legs. "Place your hands together and slice them forward, then separate them and make an arc back to your sides."

She did as he said, and to give her the feel of moving through the water, he stepped sideways as if she'd pulled herself forward. A surprised noise came from her lips, but she repeated the motion.

"Now kick your legs."

With her heels above water, her kicking sent a shower of spray into the air. He laughed as the cascade of droplets fell all around them.

"That's it! Now combine the kicking with the strokes."

This time he didn't have to move—she propelled herself forward. He sidestepped to keep his hands on her stomach as she continued to kick and stroke.

"Am I swimming?" she breathed, glancing over her shoulder at him.

"Almost," he said. "Keep going." As she returned her attention to her arms and legs, he eased his hands slightly lower to let her take more of her own weight. Her head dipped into the water up to her chin, but she kept her limbs working. "This is what it will feel like as you get better. Soon enough, you won't need me to support you."

Suddenly she stopped her limbs and tilted herself upright, breaking his contact with her stomach. She looked up at him, her eyes unreadable. She was close enough that he could see the little flecks of gold in their depths. "I like your support."

Her words caught him completely off-guard. He sputtered to come up with a response, but before he could scrape together the words, she went on.

"Eirik...why do you not treat me as a thrall? You warned me that thralls are the lowest members of society, especially utlending thralls. Yet you treat me as an equal. Why?"

He combed his damp hair back with one hand, searching for a way to explain things to her.

"As I've told you, enslaving our enemies and even trading for slaves is part of our way of life," he began. "We believe that our own free people should have more rights that the enemy thralls we have in our midst. So thralls don't get a say at council meetings, nor do they get to enjoy as much leisure as free men and women. They are put to work, often doing the most menial or grueling tasks."

She nodded, so he went on. "But my father taught me that keeping thralls to do your work should be considered shameful. What kind of man would make another do the hardest work for him? What kind of leader could claim to hold others' respect, yet be unwilling or unable to work alongside the strongest and hardest-working men?"

"You believe that having thralls tarnishes your honor in the eyes of your gods?" she asked softly.

"Ja, that's exactly it," he replied, stirred that she seemed to understand. But then he realized that her voice held a note of sadness in it. She broke their gaze to cast her eyes at the water between them.

"So I am a stain on your honor," she said flatly. "I understand now why you were acting so strangely the night the Jarl decided that I would remain your thrall."

Eirik cursed himself silently. It hadn't been his imagination—she'd sensed that something was wrong regarding the council meeting. Thank the gods she didn't suspect that he'd actually lied to her and that his uncle still planned on selling her at the slave market come summer's end.

"Nei, that is not it, Laurel," he said quietly, taking her hands in his. "Your presence in my life is far from a stain. 'Tis more complicated than that."

She blinked up at him, absorbing his words. "What do you mean, more complicated?"

He frowned, struggling for words. How could he explain things without revealing Gunvald's true ruling about her fate? Alaric and Madrena continued to pester and question him about his decision not to tell Laurel yet, but he didn't want to worry her unnecessarily. He *would* find a way to change his uncle's mind, he vowed.

And how could he explain to her that though he was drawn to her like no other, he felt honor-bound not to act on those feelings because she was his thrall? Would an innocent, an utlending, understand his sense of honor, yet also the ever-deepening pull he felt toward her?

He sighed. "Even though you are my thrall, I will not force you to...serve me in any way," he said, his voice gruff. "It is true that I don't keep thralls because I consider it dishonorable. But now that you have fallen to my keeping, I won't treat you as other thralls are treated."

"Why did you kiss me?"

By Odin, Laurel's blunt questions would send even a mountain goat scrambling for solid ground. "I didn't force you to kiss me as my thrall," he said quickly.

She waved away his objection. "Nay, of course not.

But you said that because you didn't think having thralls was honorable, you wouldn't treat me like one, including…intimacies…"

Finally, she faltered, which gave Eirik a moment to collect his thoughts. "I shouldn't have kissed you," he said levelly. He needed to say the words out loud to remind himself. Even now, gazing down at her delicate features, he longed to take her mouth with his, to pull her against his body, to bury himself—

He cursed, this time out loud. Thankfully, he hadn't taught her the words he spouted, and she blinked in confusion.

"Thralls are regularly used for such…intimacies, as you call them, and more."

Her eyes widened and her lips parted. By the gods, he was going to need to back up farther than this.

"Where you grew up, men and women aren't supposed to touch, let alone have sex. Is that correct?"

A blush was creeping from her neck to her face despite the cool water all around them. She only nodded.

"Here in the Northlands, we don't believe our gods want us to ignore our bodies and the pleasures they can bring us." Her eyes looked everywhere but at him as he spoke. He was reminded yet again that even just his bare torso was probably a foreign and shocking sight to her.

"You said that sometimes even nuns would become pregnant, though, so you must be at least somewhat aware of what goes on between men and women."

She nodded again, yet she pulled her hands from his

and began fidgeting with her fingers. "But such things are sinful," she said quietly.

"Ja, and according to those people, your parents, who weren't devoted to holy life, were also sinful. But as I told you before, we don't view things that way here. Of course, we are still governed by the rules and customs of our community. We are not the savages some of your monks make us out to be. Yet we believe that bodily pleasures, and the union between two people who care for one another, are natural and good."

"Why are you telling me this? What does this have to do with me being a thrall?" she blurted out. Clearly she'd never had a frank conversation about such matters before.

He paused and chose his words carefully. "Because while free men and women of the Northlands get to choose how and with whom they share their bodily pleasures, thralls cannot. Thralls must do as they are ordered. Some people treat thralls with dignity and respect. Others do not."

He watched as understanding seeped through her embarrassment.

"Thralls have no ability to choose. And you find the use of thralls, either for labor or for…intimacy…to be dishonorable," she said slowly

"That is why I shouldn't have kissed you," he replied, his voice low.

"But why *did* you?"

He felt like he could drown in her depthless, dark eyes. If he did, he would die a happy man.

"Because I wanted to…and because I wanted *you*."

His voice sounded gravelly to his own ears, but he couldn't muster aught other than the truth at the moment. Not with her standing before him, all but naked to his gaze in her wet, transparent shift, her eyes wide and searching him.

She visibly swallowed, her slim throat bobbing. He cursed himself silently yet again. Had he frightened her away? Had he shredded the delicate web of intimacy and trust that had been building between them?

"And…and what if I said I wanted you to kiss me again?" she breathed.

Before his mind could reiterate all the reasons why he shouldn't, his body acted. He closed the distance between them in one step and his mouth descended on hers.

14

W here she found such bold words, Laurel would never know. Abbess Hilda would have strapped her to the chair and dunked her until she was blue for words like that—and to a Viking heathen, no less.

But Abbess Hilda and all her strictness about sin and denial held no weight in this foreign land. Though Laurel still didn't understand the strange ways of Eirik and his people, the more distance she gained from Whitby Abbey, the less she felt bound to the old rules that had restricted her life.

The memory of her first kiss with Eirik had crept into her mind as she lay restless in his bed each night. His scent, of pine and salt and skin, hovered in the air around her as he drilled her on his language. And the feel of his warm, rough, large hands on her belly, brushing the undersides of her breasts and coming dangerously close to her most private spot—

How could she want the touch of a Viking barbarian? How could a savage man stir such base, sinful desires deep within her? Yet here she was, asking him to kiss her again.

Before she had time to regret her words, he moved so quickly that she inhaled in surprise. His hard body collided with her. The skin of his bare chest was warm compared to the lake water in which they stood.

He lowered his head and captured the gasp on her lips. His hands wound around her back, pulling her firmly against him. His body was rigid, hard, yet his lips were soft on hers.

There was too much to take in all at once. Her head swirled as her body yielded to the flood of sensation. One of his hands rose to the back of her head, tangling in her damp hair. The other dropped to her lower back, molding to the inward curve and pulling her snugly against him.

Her breasts tingled where they came in contact with the taut skin of his chest. Below the waterline, she could feel his hard manhood pressing against her. She knew it meant that he was aroused, yet that didn't frighten her for some reason. Instead of wanting to pull back, to fend him off, she longed to be even closer to him. She wanted to feel his desire, for her own was coursing hotly through her limbs, delicious yet uncomfortably urgent.

Her hands found his shoulders. The muscles beneath her fingers were corded and tense, yet his mouth was still soft, gentle. She let her fingertips trail from his shoulders to his neck. His thick golden hair was damp and clung to his skin. As she entwined her fingers in it, a noise that sounded almost like a growl came from deep in his throat.

He tilted his head, melding their mouths together more firmly. She leaned into him, greedy for more contact. He made another noise that sounded half-hungry, half-pained. His tongue brushed her lips, asking for entrance, yet his body under her hands was pulled tighter than a bowstring. She realized vaguely that he was fighting for control, forcing himself to go slow for her benefit.

She parted her lips, remembering their first kiss and the liquid heat his tongue had brought. This time was no different. Nay, it was different, for the heat was already lapping at her. As his tongue entered her mouth and swirled with hers, instead of the lazy, slow-spreading warmth, she was hit with a jolt of white-hot lightening that singed her everywhere.

His tongue was so wet and hot. It caressed her, teased her, slowly explored her. It was only her mouth, but his motions implied something else far more intimate, something she didn't fully understand. Yet her body responded on its own, seeming to instinctively know the same carnal language he spoke.

Without realizing what she was doing, she moved her hips against his underneath the waterline. She pressed herself into that hard column of his manhood, which strained against his linen pants. She could feel it pulse. Needing relief and needing more of the torturous sensation at the same time, she rubbed the part of her that throbbed and ached against that ridge of rock-hard flesh.

He said something that sounded like a curse against her mouth. His hands turned into talons, his fingers sinking into her hair and the skin of her lower back. He met her pressing hips with his own, grinding his manhood along the mound just above the crux of her legs. She heard a whimpering moan and realized the sound had come from her own lips. Even as the ache grew between her legs, so too did the desire to make it more intense.

He ripped away the hand on her lower back, and she would have lost her balance had he not kept his grip on her nape, steadying her and keeping their mouths fused together. Before she could mourn the loss of the hand on her back, however, he found her waist. His thumb strummed along her ribs, inching upward. She wasn't sure where he was going until his thumb traced the underside of her breast and she inhaled sharply.

His thumb played there for a long moment. She leaned into him, hoping he understood her bodily reaction to his touch better than she did. She didn't know what she wanted, but she knew she needed more.

Finally, his hand rose to cup her breast. Through the thin, wet material of her shift, she could feel each exquisite callus on his warm palm. One in particular rested right over her already-hard nipple. She arched into his hand with a moan. Even the slight movement of her nipple against his hand sent more bolts of heat through her. It was as if a fiery trail led from her breasts to the crux of her legs, for hot sensation seemed to shoot between them.

He broke their kiss, leaving her panting and dazed.

But she couldn't form the words to ask for his lips never to leave hers again. Her lips were swollen from his kisses and the soft scratch of his golden stubble. His taste lingered on her tongue.

His mouth fell on her neck, and she arched her head backward to give him more access. He nibbled and sucked his way lower to brush kisses and flicks of his tongue along her collarbone. His nose trailed lower still to meet with the line of her shift as it cut across her chest. But he didn't stop there. She felt a hot breath against her breast, and then before she could comprehend what he was doing, his tongue flicked across her nipple.

The wet linen may as well have not been there. She gasped and jerked involuntarily as his tongue circled slowly, torturously, around her nipple. Her head fell back on another gasp and moan as his hand and tongue completely overpowered her. She was lost in a sea of sensation, drowning in fiery sin.

That thought brought another gasp to her lips, but it wasn't wrought of pleasure.

Something in the air shifted between them. Eirik's head snapped up and he dropped his hand from her breast as if he'd been burned.

He took a step back from her, raking his hands through his disheveled hair. "I shouldn't have...I shouldn't have done that."

"Nor should I have," Laurel breathed, feeling as if she'd been doused in icy water.

"You are my thrall," Eirik said, but he sounded like he was trying to remind himself of what that meant.

"Do not blame yourself," she replied, feeling her cheeks heat with embarrassment. "I asked you to kiss me." It was hard to say the words out loud—far harder than it had been for her to make such a bold, wanton request of him in the first place.

She lowered her eyes away from his rapidly rising and falling chest. How could she give herself over so completely to such base desires? Was Abbess Hilda right about her? Was her very existence a sin, the result of her parents' lasciviousness? Perhaps she had inherited their sin after all—for hadn't she wanted more of the deliciously wrong sensations that Eirik induced in her? Wouldn't she have kept going down that path? Might she end up just like her parents?

"Nei, it matters not that you asked. I should not have allowed myself to…to be overcome by my desire for you." His eyes looked everywhere but at her.

Confusion mixed with embarrassment, swamping her. He clearly desired her, and he admitted as much. Even though it shouldn't, the declaration made her stomach flutter. Yet he said it didn't matter that she'd let her own desire be known?

"You think that because I am a thrall, my wants and requests don't matter?"

"Laurel, you can't consent to such things by your very existence," he said, his voice tight with what must be his own shame.

"My *existence*? I was not born a thrall. I was made one by Grimar—and by *you*." It was as if all the passion between them from a moment ago was turning into hot anger.

She might as well have slapped him, for he recoiled, his eyes wide and vivid blue. "You need not remind me," he bit out.

"Just because I have been made a thrall doesn't erase my free will. Not all of my desires and actions are coerced simply because I am your *slave!*"

Anger she hadn't known still simmered in her heart bubbled over now. She had plowed forward, doing little more than shed a few tears at the news that she had been made a slave by these barbarians. Yet she wasn't just scared or sad to learn that her fate was to serve a Viking—she boiled with unspoken, unspent rage that her life was being taken away from her. Freedom, something she'd barely even tasted in all her nineteen years, was snatched from her—forever. She couldn't even *feel* something for Eirik, couldn't even desire him, without that freedom being taken away.

She stood there panting before him. His eyes sliced through her, unrelenting.

"I will not touch you like that again while you are my thrall," he said in a low voice.

Though she knew his reasons, knew he valued his honor above all else, his vow still felt like a blow. She took a staggering step back but managed to right herself.

She should be happy. They had treaded into dangerous waters with their first kiss. Yet she'd convinced herself a moment ago that she could give in to her desire, that no harm could come from another kiss.

They'd gone too far. Nay, she admitted deep within herself, the truth was that *she'd* gone too far in letting herself believe that she could want this Viking warrior, that she could protect herself from her own sinful desires, and that their attraction could be shared without her position as his thrall interfering.

She waded out of the water and onto the shoreline, her eyes downcast. She snatched her dress off the rock she'd left it on and hastily donned it over her wet shift. She heard splashing behind her as Eirik emerged from the lake, but she didn't look up as she fastened the shoulder straps to the brooches on her chest.

He dressed faster than she, but he waited at the faint trail that led back toward the village through the meadow and the woods. Once she'd shoved her feet into her leather boots, she went to his side. Though he'd held her hand the entire trip to the lake, he simply turned and began walking along the path.

She followed without a word. Her chest pinched, and she told herself that she was hardening her heart to her own desire for the kind, honorable Viking before her, yet somewhere inside she knew the truth.

She wanted him. And she couldn't have him.

GRIMAR LET the pine branches fall back into place before Eirik and the thrall girl turned toward him. It had been surprisingly easy to follow them from Eirik's hut to this secluded mountain lake. He'd kept an eye on Eirik's hut for several days, yet both his cousin and the thrall rarely left except for their basic necessities.

Rumors were already swirling that Eirik was treating

the girl like a freewoman—letting her keep that long, dark veil of hair, dressing her in the garb of those who were far above her in station. Grimar spat on the forest floor.

Some even said that mayhap his cousin was bedding the girl. Knowing Eirik's ridiculous code of honor, Grimar very much doubted that he'd lain with her yet, but it was obvious that he was captivated by the utlending girl. And that long, passionate kiss they'd just shared in the water revealed Eirik's weakness—he wanted her, even if he tried to deny himself the benefits of having her as his thrall.

Grimar frowned. Eirik was growing careless when it came to the girl. Normally, Eirik, like all good warriors, would have brought more than the seax at his belt and certainly would have swept the area before taking a swim exposed and unguarded. Grimar probably could have stabbed him in the back a few moments ago, so lost were they in their embrace.

Of course, Grimar reminded himself bitterly, he couldn't simply bury his seax in his cousin's back and be done with the competition for the Jarlship. Nei, his father insisted that he had to wait. He had to be patient.

His father's voice rang in his head and he longed to spit again. The path to the Jarlship had been far easier for Gunvald. Grimar's uncle Arud had simply met with Gunvald's blade while raiding in a neighboring village. Gunvald had been the obvious choice for the next Jarl, especially because no one knew he'd slain his own brother.

All these years later, Grimar couldn't just take up his

father's mantle. He had to compete with his honor-bound cousin. Grimar didn't understand why so many in the village spoke so highly of Eirik. It was a Viking's way to take what he wanted, when he wanted it, by any means necessary. Eirik's sense of honor and duty made him weak. But Grimar wasn't afraid to fulfill the North-men's destiny.

Yet everyone wanted Grimar to be different, to be softer. Eirik thought him lawless, while his father was always insisting that he plan and plot instead of act. Well, perhaps he would show his father that he was just as capable of political maneuverings as he was at wielding his sword.

Gunvald was always so cautious, always thinking ten steps ahead. According to his calculations, Eirik's distraction from the Jarlship was supposed to be a good thing for Grimar. Yet Grimar doubted how much Gunvald understood the bond that was forming between Eirik and the thrall girl. When the time came to sell her, Eirik wouldn't take it well, if his current behavior was any indication.

But apparently the Jarl hadn't considered what it would mean for their plans if Eirik longed to keep the girl enough to oppose Gunvald's ruling. Mayhap Grimar would have to take matters into his own hands, to *act* rather than plot.

The two in the water were beginning to emerge, and Grimar stilled behind the tree line where he watched them. Even from this distance, he could see the contours of the thrall girl's body, the dark patch between her legs, and her two rosy, hard nipples through her wet shift. His cock stirred. She was supposed to be his. Yet his rage flared hotter than his desire.

He wanted something far more important than a warm place to bury his cock—he wanted the Jarlship and all the power that came with it. If it meant getting rid of the girl sooner rather than later, so be it. And if it meant going farther against his own kin—well, his father had proven that such a path was viable.

He had power over both the girl and his cousin's fates. Grimar smiled. Eirik and the girl moved away, completely unaware that he lurked so close.

15

"Good. Now how would you say, 'I would like to buy three goats'?"

"I want to work."

"What?" Eirik's head snapped up from the block of wood he'd been about to chop. Laurel sat on a nearby rock with her hands in her lap.

"I want to work," she repeated, her eyes on her hands.

"You are working," he replied, raising his ax once more and taking a swing at the wood. Even though they didn't need a fire burning continuously in the cottage at this time of year, there was always much to be done during the summer in preparation for the coming winter. "You are learning my language. 'Tis enough for now."

It was strange to exchange so many words with her that didn't involve the instruction of his language. Nigh a sennight had passed since their day at the lake, and an uncomfortable tension had settled between them. They still lived in close quarters within his cottage, but beyond necessary communication and her lessons in language, they rarely spoke. And now she was asking to get away from the cottage—to get away from him.

She traced one booted foot along the moss in front of her. "I do not enjoy sitting idly by while everyone else in the village is occupied," she said quietly.

He tossed the pieces of firewood he'd just cut in a pile near the rear of the cottage. "I don't think you understand how important you are to the village, Laurel."

"Why? Because I am an utlending?" Her eyes flickered up to his, but they were unreadable.

"Ja, because you are an utlending. You'll learn our language first, but eventually I want you to teach us your tongue as well."

"So that you can conquer more of my lands and enslave more of my countrymen?"

This time he had no difficulty interpreting the barely contained hostility and frustration in her voice. He sank the ax into the block on which he'd been chopping and turned fully toward her.

"Mayhap. And mayhap also to trade with your people, or to settle—peacefully—in the west."

She let that subject drop but tried a different tack.

"I know that you do not wish to treat me like a thrall, but I am not afraid of hard work. In fact, I'm used to it. I find it shameful to sit with idle hands all day."

He sighed. She was too astute by far. Although

everything he'd told her about the importance of their language exchange had been true, he'd also hoped that keeping her thus occupied would shield her from the need to stoop to thralls' work.

He didn't doubt her capability—he'd seen the small calluses on her palms and heard her explanations of the work the nuns and monks at the monastery had put her to. Rather, he hated the thought of how the villagers would view her—and treat her. To them, she was just an utlending thrall who'd been put above her place through Eirik's attentions. He didn't need them abusing their power over her. Though she couldn't know all the subtleties of the village's social order, she'd clearly picked up on the fact that he was shielding her from thralls' work.

Before he could form a suitable response, she interjected.

"Would you deny me this?"

She didn't say the words, but a silent *as well* hung at the end of her question. His mind leapt back to that afternoon at the lake. He'd been sure he was doing the right thing by rejecting his desires for Laurel. After all, she was his thrall. Even if she had been the one to ask him for a kiss, she was in no position to choose in such matters. What if he'd gone farther than she'd wanted? What if she feared saying no to him?

Of course, he'd come to know Laurel well enough to trust that she would voice her wishes. She wasn't one to cower or remain silent. And he knew himself well enough to be certain that if she had indicated she'd wanted him to stop, he would have—he'd never forced himself on a woman, nor would he ever.

Yet he still clung to the principle of the matter. As a thrall, her desires meant naught and she had no choices. He'd never push himself sexually on a creature with no power.

But he'd never considered her role in this mess. She'd kissed him back willingly that first time on his bed. And she'd asked him to kiss her again in the lake. Luckily, he'd gotten a rein on his lust and stopped things before they went too far. But he'd never considered what she said—that she should at least be granted the freedom to make her own choices in such matters.

He never wanted to treat her as his thrall, an object to do with as he wished. Yet by protecting her from his lust, was he also taking away her ability to choose desire for herself? He had been tugging on this tangled knot for the last sennight with little to show for it—except that the code of honor he prized so highly in himself had fallen into doubt.

Her question still hung in the air: would he deny her this, as he denied her the ability to choose for herself what she wanted from him?

He opened his mouth, still unsure of how to explain his thoughts.

"Eirik!"

Madrena's voice floated from the front of the cottage, cutting him off before he could speak.

"Around back!" he shouted in response, his face falling into a frown. He couldn't decide if Madrena had terrible or perfect timing.

"At least you're not cooped up inside again," Madrena muttered as she rounded the corner of the cottage. She wore her practice garb, with her skirts cinched up to expose the boots that encased her calves and her bare knees above them. A padded vest covered her torso, and her pale hair was braided back from her face. She had her bow and quiver slung over one shoulder, and a short sword fitted to her frame over the other.

"You haven't trained with us since we returned home," she said, her eyes drifting to where Laurel sat.

"I've been busy," he said flatly.

"So everyone says."

Eirik yanked his ax from the chopping block. "What does that mean?"

Madrena shrugged casually, though she gave Laurel another sidelong glance. "It means that people are talking about you and the utlending thrall spending all your time inside your little hut."

"You think I care about some flapping jaws?" Eirik bit out. In truth, he should pay the gossip more heed, he knew. Sooner or later there would be trouble.

"I can't seem to tell *what* you care about these days," Madrena retorted, finally letting her underlying frustration show clearly. "I thought after our successful voyage you'd be eager to make plans for the next raid, or at least keep up with your training. But all you do is stay in your cottage with the girl."

"Are you jealous, Madrena?" He knew the question was a low blow, but he was sick of her questioning and finding fault with him when it came to Laurel.

"Jealous? Of being forced to share this hovel with your stinking hide?" Her pale eyes flared.

He kept his ax in his hand just in case she decided to draw a weapon on him. It wouldn't be the first time they'd had to settle their differences with force. Of course, they usually called it off when they'd both gotten out their pent-up energy. But something had been building between him and Madrena ever since Laurel appeared.

"Nei, I don't envy her your attention," Madrena went on, eying his ax. "I only wonder what's happening to you. Where has your wanderlust gone? What of your drive to make Dalgaard and its people better?"

"What do you think I'm doing with her?" he nigh shouted, gesturing with the ax at Laurel, who sat wide-eyed watching them. "We can't simply raid our way to a secure, prosperous future. We need to learn, to adapt. She can teach us!"

Madrena opened her mouth to shout something back, but before she could form the words, Laurel stood abruptly.

"I...want...work?" she said brokenly in their language.

Madrena rounded on her, mouth agape.

"Work," Laurel repeated, mimicking the motions of sweeping and scrubbing.

Madrena turned back to him. "She's a thrall after all. Why not put her to work?"

"Madrena, nei," Eirik said darkly. "I'll not allow her to be mistreated—"

She sighed with exasperation. "I don't want her to

be harmed either. Alaric and I might as well be your kin, remember? If she is so important to you, then she's important to us too." The last was said grudgingly, but Eirik nodded slightly to acknowledge her effort.

"Can you help me with her?" he said quietly. He doubted Laurel would be able to piece much together from their conversation, but even still, she was learning his language faster than he'd expected. "We've both been cooped up too long, and there is some…tension between us."

"Tension?" Madrena actually shot a cocky smile at him. "So why don't you just…relieve it?"

"Madrena, you know—"

"I know, I know!" She rolled her eyes at him. "But it is plain to see that you are *both* drawn to each other. Doesn't that circumvent your code?"

He hefted the ax in his hand as a warning. She was far closer to knowing his thoughts and desires that she realized, but he didn't want to get into it with her.

"She wants to work, but I don't want any of the villagers mistreating her."

Madrena snorted in frustration. "You put her above all other thralls. You're asking for trouble." But before Eirik could respond, she turned to Laurel.

"Can you weave?" Madrena asked loudly, motioning with her hands.

Laurel looked puzzled for a moment, then seemed to comprehend Madrena's question. "Nei," she replied.

"Can you cook?" She mimicked eating and stirring a pot.

Laurel shook her head, her brows coming together in despondency.

"Can she do anything?" Madrena said to Eirik in exasperation. She exhaled. "Just go get into your practice gear and meet me in the training fields," she said under her breath. "I'll come up with something."

~

THOUGH LAUREL only understood bits and pieces of Eirik's conversation with Madrena, she was sure she'd won a minor victory when Madrena took her roughly by the elbow and started pulling her toward the village. Eirik remained behind, watching them with a creased brow as they went.

"Work?" Laurel huffed, resorting to the word that seemed to have come through the clearest earlier.

"Ja, work," Madrena said sourly, never slowing her long strides.

They traversed the distance between Eirik's cottage and the more densely packed village quickly. Madrena made a straight line for the long wooden building where the council meeting and the feast had taken place.

"Longhouse kitchens," Madrena said by way of explanation as they entered the dim interior. The tall Viking woman made her way to the back of the structure where a narrow door led to a separate cooking area. Unlike the longhouse, the kitchen walls were made of stone, likely to protect against the dangers of fire.

The kitchen was mostly quiet, and only a few women moved about, some chopping vegetables, others preparing flatbreads to be cooked on an iron griddle on the far wall. She noticed that half of the women had their hair cropped almost to their skulls. Thralls.

Laurel hesitated for a moment. She thought she'd made it clear that she had no skill when it came to cooking, but perhaps she'd gotten her words confused.

Madrena spoke rapidly to one of the women with longer hair. The older woman motioned toward a bucket in the corner and then to Laurel. The woman's pale blue eyes flickered over her in disdain before dismissing her altogether.

"Clean," Madrena said bluntly, picking up the bucket and thrusting it into Laurel's chest.

Laurel's heart sank. So, it was to be like the Abbey all over again. But she had been the one to ask for work. Even scrubbing floors was preferable to living in such close quarters with Eirik.

Madrena muttered something under her breath, and Laurel caught the words "too busy," "warrior," and "nursemaid" before the Viking spun on her heels and exited the kitchen.

The older woman, who apparently hadn't completely forgotten her after all, pointed toward the door at the back of the kitchen. Laurel went outside and quickly spotted a stream where she could fill her bucket. When she returned, the older woman, who was apparently in charge of the kitchen, handed her a lump of lye soap and a coarse bristled brush. The familiar scent of lye filled Laurel's nostrils. At least she knew how to clean.

The woman nodded with her square jaw toward an

enormous iron cauldron near the cooking fire. Laurel needed no more instruction. She emptied half the bucket of water into the cauldron and set about scrubbing it.

The mindless labor was surprisingly soothing. It gave her a chance to chew on the uneasy routine she'd settled into with Eirik ever since that day at the lake. As he'd vowed, he hadn't touched her since then, but the memory of what he'd stirred in her still rose fresh to the surface several times each day. She'd catch herself watching his hands as they ate in his cottage, or see the bunching and shifting of his muscles beneath his linen tunic, and an unbidden flush would come over her skin.

She never knew that she was capable of so much sensation, so much pleasure. Abbess Hilda had warned of such things, yet Laurel had hardly thought it was possible to feel so much lightning heat between her own body and Eirik's.

Sinful lust was one thing. But even worse, she feared that her hatred and disgust of all things related to these Northern barbarians was slipping. Eirik was nothing like what she thought a Viking savage would be. He was honorable and kind and loyal, as were his friends. Even gruff, hot-headed Madrena was never cruel or violent toward her.

Of course, there was Grimar, who was just as bad as all the nightmarish stories about Northmen had warned. And his father the Jarl seemed more cold and calculating than kind. But Brother Egbert and Abbess Hilda had been no better.

Mayhap if she acknowledged that there were good

and bad people everywhere, she could come to terms with her new life among the Vikings. She saw no way to escape it even if she wanted to. But far more frightening, she wasn't sure she was even trying to find a way to free herself.

Free herself from what? From Eirik's kindness? From his protectiveness and sense of honor? Nay, she repeated to herself firmly, she was still a slave. Even if it was only in name, she could not accept such a thing. Especially if it meant that Eirik would deny her the ever-growing feelings deep in the pit of her stomach that she couldn't refute anymore.

She wanted him.

Abbess Hilda would turn purple if she knew. But Abbess Hilda wasn't here, she reminded herself. Why should she continue to live her life by a code imposed upon her from afar by a cruel, harsh woman? She would never abandon God, no matter that she now lived among pagan people. But God had seen fit to throw her into Eirik's care. Could she remain true to herself and still desire such a man? Could she finally have a say in the direction of her own life?

Time slipped away as she scrubbed, ensnared by such thoughts. The increasing noises around her finally drew her out of her own musings. She glanced up from the thoroughly clean cauldron to find that the kitchen now buzzed with activity. It must already be time to prepare the evening meal for the Jarl.

Laurel stood and arched her back to ease the aches. She half-dragged, half-carried the heavy cauldron out the back kitchen door and dumped the cleaning water.

Then she used the rest of the fresh water from her bucket to rinse the cauldron and hauled it back indoors.

The older woman turned from giving directions to the bustling workers to inspect the cauldron. She looked closely, even running her fingers along the inside. Finally, she gave a satisfied nod and seemed to look Laurel full-on for the first time.

"*Góðr*," she said. *Good.*

Laurel's chest swelled with pride. The older woman waved her away and returned her attention to the other tasks around her. Laurel returned the bucket to its place in the corner and quietly exited the kitchen.

After quickly rinsing the residual lye soap from her hands in the stream, she made her way toward the path that led to Eirik's hut on the far side of the village.

Before she reached the trail, however, the sounds of clanging metal and shouts filled her ears. A brief moment of panic seized her before she realized that none of the other villagers milling around her paid the noises any heed.

Curiosity drew her in the direction of the sound. She found a path that led between two thatched build-ings and toward the steep mountainsides rising all around. But instead of finding a sheer wall of rock, there was an opening that wound through the steep, moss-covered rocks that rose on either side.

The shouts and clanging grew louder as she made her way deeper into the mountain. Then suddenly the rock walls opened into a little grass-filled clearing. She had no idea what force could create such an opening in the rocks, but she marveled at the beautiful, hidden meadow.

The clearing was filled with battling Vikings. They roared and bellowed as they leveled their weapons at each other. This must be their idea of practice, Laurel thought, her eyes struggling to take in all the activity.

Some of the fighters used wooden swords and spears against each other. They looked to be younger than the others. But the bulk of the warriors squared off with each other using sharp weapons that glinted in the slanting sun.

As her eyes flickered over the surging mass of bodies, she caught sight of Madrena's pale blond hair, braided and pulled into a topknot. She had a short sword in hand and was lunging at a helmeted, bare-chested warrior. The warrior blocked Madrena's initial thrust and tried to pin her blade beneath his, but she spun and plowed her shoulder into his to free herself. The man toppled backward, and before he could right himself, Madrena's blade was leveled at his throat.

The woman warrior held the blade there just long enough to prove she'd won, then quickly sheathed it on her back and extended a hand to the man she'd just bested. The warrior popped up at her side and removed his helm, a wide grin on his face. It was none other than Alaric, Madrena's brother. Laurel shook her head in disbelief. This was the way of life here in the Northlands.

As she turned to leave the training meadow the way she'd come, her eye snagged on a broad, bare back. She recognized it immediately as Eirik's. He was fully concentrated on a giant, red-headed warrior before him. The warrior carried a round shield and sword, yet Eirik held naught but his long blade.

The red-haired warrior blocked a powerful blow from Eirik and thrust his own sword toward him underneath his shield. Eirik spun out of the way just in time. He attacked the warrior's other side so that he had to pull the shield awkwardly across his body. As a counterattack, the giant warrior plowed into Eirik's body with the shield, throwing him backward. Yet Eirik turned the tumble into a roll and popped up on his feet in the blink of an eye, his sword still in hand.

Laurel clamped a hand over her mouth to cover the unbidden gasp that rose to her lips. He moved so fluidly, so assuredly, even without the protection of a padded vest, chainmail, or a shield.

Suddenly the memory of gliding through the cool water of the mountain lake—his hands splayed across her stomach, the water kissing her skin—came back to her in a rush of heat. She turned to retreat back through the rocks and to the village, ashamed of her own lust-filled thoughts.

"Laurel!"

Eirik's voice was unmistakable, even over the clangs of wood and metal. She turned back to the practice field slowly, willing her blush down, but to no effect.

Eirik had apparently called a halt with the red-headed giant, for both had lowered their weapons. Even from across the meadow, Eirik's vivid blue eyes pierced her. He crossed the field swiftly, never taking his eyes from her even as he weaved through swinging swords, thrusting spears, and arcing axes.

"What are you doing here?" he said, his breath coming fast from his battle.

"I…I finished working and heard the noise…"

She felt completely ridiculous standing before him, his golden head towering over her, his bare chest heaving and slick with sweat. His scent, of pine and warm skin, drifted around her. Suddenly there was nowhere to look except at his bronzed torso, the muscles bunching and chording under her gaze.

"I'll take you back to the cottage," he said. "Did Madrena…help you?"

"Yes," she replied quickly, not wanting to cause any more tension between the friends. "I cleaned in the longhouse kitchens."

He eyed her with a frown for a moment but didn't comment. She suppressed the surge of victory—she'd done as she wished, and she felt useful for the first time since being taken from the Abbey.

"Tomorrow I'd like to return to the village to help out wherever there is need," she said, forcing her eyes from his torso to his face. His bright eyes held her in place, stilling the breath in her lungs.

"Very well," he said after a long moment. "But either Madrena, Alaric, or I will escort you to and from your work. And you'll not escape your language lessons either," he said firmly. "We will have to continue them in the evenings."

She nodded as if she were acquiescing to his demands, when in truth he'd just acquiesced to hers. A flutter of excitement tickled her chest. Mayhap she could find a place here after all. Mayhap she could be of use and even gain the respect of the rest of the village.

Eirik placed his hand on the small of her back to guide her out of the clearing and back toward the village. Another flutter brushed her insides, but it was unlike the one of excitement and pride she'd just experienced. This one was lower and deeper in her belly.

His merest touch lit the still-new flames of desire within her. What could ever come of such an impossible longing?

16

"Old Asta claims she's never seen an utlending learn the Viking way of weaving so quickly."

Alaric moved aside so that Laurel could pass into Eirik's cottage. She smiled at him as she glided by, as if she understood the praise Alaric was passing on. By the gods, she just might understand, for she was learning their language so quickly that even Eirik was caught off-guard at times.

Laurel had smiled more in the last sennight than Eirik had seen in the previous fortnight. They had fallen into a comfortable routine, with her spending her days on various tasks around the village and him training with the other warriors. In the mornings and evenings they would talk in his language, haltingly at first but with increasingly more fluidity.

"I'm surprised the old woman still knows any words of praise," Eirik said, drawing a chuckle from Alaric. In truth, Asta was one of the most respected elderly women in the village. It was a high mark of honor to Laurel to receive such words.

Though she'd said she didn't know how to weave or cook or do aught besides the most menial tasks, each day in the last sennight she returned to his cottage, either at his side or guided by Madrena or Alaric, with tales of all she'd learned that day.

Indeed, in a sennight's time, Laurel had apparently learned how weave, dress and smoke a slain deer, and even fish—from the safety of the docks, of course. As Eirik walked to and from the training grounds tucked in the mountains behind the village, he often heard snippets of gossip about the utlending thrall who was a quick learner and a hard worker.

Though he refused to accept the idea that he owned her, he felt a swell of pride in his chest for her success. Of course, some of the villagers grumbled that she was only finally seeing to the duties she should have been doing all along as a thrall. Yet most took their cue from Eirik and accepted the leniency with which he treated her.

"Besides gossip from Asta," Alaric said, stepping into the cottage, "I've brought you another treat." He removed the hand he held behind his back to reveal an ornately carved box.

Eirik grinned widely at his friend. "Are you sure you want to be embarrassed again?"

Alaric scoffed. "If you're lucky, I'll allow you to look good in front of Laurel before I take you."

Eirik dragged out his wooden table and each of the benches on either side.

"What is that?" Laurel said, eyeing the box as Alaric set it down on the table. She had been about to sit down to hem another borrowed dress from Madrena but was clearly curious.

Alaric lifted a tiny peg on the outside of the box, and it opened to reveal several carved pieces of wood, each the size of a thumb. He then flipped the opened box over to form a board.

"Hnefatafl," Eirik said to her. "King's Table. 'Tis a game."

"How do you play?" She'd all but forgotten her stitch work now and approached the table.

Alaric began setting up the board as Eirik spoke. "These white pieces are the attackers. And the red ones are the King's protectors. This," he hefted the one larger, more ornately carved red piece, "is the King."

Laurel watched, her eyes following Alaric's arrangement.

"Why are there so many more attacking pieces? And why is the King in the middle, surrounded on all sides?"

"The King is the most powerful piece. He can move in several ways, while the attackers and defenders, the pawns, can only move in one direction. Yet as is so often the case in real battle, even a powerful King can be surrounded and outnumbered. He has to use skill, cunning, and force to stay alive."

"Which side will you play for?" she asked, gliding one finger along the red-painted King.

"He'll play the part of the King, of course," Alaric said with a roll of his eyes. Laurel smiled faintly, clearly understanding Alaric's words, if not his rib directed at Eirik about taking the role of a leader.

As the attacker, Alaric made the first move. Eirik studied the board for a long moment before making his own countermove. Laurel watched the next several exchanges before stepping away to retrieve her borrowed dress and the needle with which to hem the garment.

"I saw Grimar lurking around the weaving house today," Alaric said, his eyes flicking up from the board.

"Be careful what you say in front of Laurel," Eirik replied quietly. "She understands far more than you would imagine already."

Alaric nodded and lowered his voice. "He pretended to be occupied at the smith's, but he was clearly watching the weaving house. Of course, once he saw me at Laurel's side, he returned to the longhouse, likely to report to the Jarl."

Eirik cursed softly. Neither Gunvald nor Grimar had caused trouble over Laurel moving so freely about Dalgaard. In fact, both had been unusually reclusive of late. Eirik had barely exchanged pleasantries with Gunvald since the night of the feast. But he had seen Grimar slinking around in the shadows frequently, always watchful and silent. He was glad he'd asked Alaric to see Laurel back to his cottage when he'd left the training field early to bathe in the little stream nearby.

"What do you suppose they are up to?"

Alaric shrugged. "You know better than anyone that Gunvald has an unquenchable thirst for power. They could be scheming something, but I don't know why, since she'll be gone in a month anyway."

Eirik gritted his teeth until his jaw ached.

"You continue to withhold the information from her?" Alaric asked.

"I still believe there's a way for me to persuade my uncle to change his ruling. Clearly Laurel is worth more to the village than her thrall price would fetch at the market."

Laurel's increasing happiness and comfort in the village were good in and of themselves. But even better, Eirik hoped that her willingness to learn, to work hard, and to find her place within the village would help his cause to convince his uncle that she should not be sold in Jutland a month from now.

Alaric eyed him, a glint of something unreadable in his green eyes.

"Don't look at me like I'm a fool, Alaric," Eirik bit out. "Madrena has already told me that my behavior is the focus of much gossip and that my…attentions toward Laurel are obvious. But things are not as they seem. I have not dishonored myself or her."

He had come cursedly close that day at the lake, though.

"You mean to tell me that you've been playing house with the girl for more than a fortnight and you still haven't—"

A low growl from Eirik's throat cut Alaric off, but his

friend only chuckled. "Are you blind, man? Have you seen the way she looks at you? She clearly wants you just as badly as you want her."

Eirik's head snapped around just in time to catch Laurel's dark eyes fixed on him. She started at his sudden motion and quickly averted her gaze, a slow blush creeping up her cheeks.

Alaric barely covered another chuckle with a cough. "You are still trying to come up with a way to overturn your uncle's ruling, ja?"

Eirik returned his attention to the board, but he was having a hard time concentrating on the game. "Ja."

"There's always the obvious way." Alaric's voice was filled with a barely restrained merriment.

"Nei," he said firmly, though his chest pinched strangely.

Eirik had discarded the thought of marrying Laurel almost immediately when it had occurred to him days ago. It would be wrong to ask Laurel if she would marry him as a way of securing her freedom. He would shame himself to coerce her in such a way. Wouldn't she feel that she was being forced from her position as his thrall into the role of wife?

Besides, he didn't want a wife. Or at least he'd always thought that having a wife and family would get in the way of his voyages. Madrena's words kept floating back to him, however. She'd said that something had changed in him in the last few sennights. He no longer spent so much time dwelling on the next voyage. His mind seemed to be occupied with matters here at home.

"But you have to admit that it would solve the

immediate problem," Alaric went on, clearly testing Eirik's mood. "Marriage to a free man would raise Laurel from thralldom. And Gunvald can't sell a free woman—especially not his nephew's wife."

"I said *nei*, Alaric," he breathed.

"There's another way, I suppose," Alaric said, the mirth leaving his eyes as he leaned forward on his elbows. "Challenge Gunvald's Jarlship."

Eirik pounded his fist against the table, causing the carved pieces of wood to jump on the board. "If you want the Jarlship so badly, why don't *you* challenge Gunvald?" he grated through clenched teeth.

This conversation was nothing new. He'd had it a dozen times with both Madrena and Alaric over the last few years. Yet for some reason, the fact that Laurel's fate hung in the balance sent an unexpected rage surging through him.

He could feel Laurel's eyes on his back and imagined that she was straining to pick out the words of their conversation.

"But I don't want the Jarlship for myself, brother," Alaric said quietly. The last word was meant as a reminder that though they were not blood kin, they had chosen to consider themselves family. Alaric was only saying what he thought Eirik needed to hear. The thought cooled Eirik's blood somewhat.

"Besides, I would make a piss-poor Jarl. I don't have your level-headedness, your foresight and vision for our people, or your sense of honor and responsibility," Alaric went on, looking Eirik directly in the eyes.

Eirik sighed and rubbed a hand along his jawline.

Both Madrena and Alaric thought it was past time for Eirik to make a move toward the Jarlship. He'd told them the reasons why it wasn't for the best many times before. Just because his father Arud had been a great Jarl didn't mean that Eirik could or should lead the village. His uncle was doing a good enough job at it. And besides, Eirik was more interested in raiding and voyaging to new lands than staying home.

But as he ran through his objections in his head, they sounded hollow even to him. Everyone agreed that Eirik was much like his father in temperament and character. Though Gunvald was clever and calculating, it had become apparent in the last few years that he longed for power more than a secure and prosperous village. And in the last few sennights, Eirik's lust for new adventures had strangely faded within him—he much preferred spending his evenings conversing with Laurel.

"I wouldn't go so far as to say that you'd be a piss-poor leader," Eirik said wearily. "Then again, if this is the best you can do…"

Eirik moved the King piece into action, evading Alaric's attack even while forcing him to go on the defensive. Alaric swore as his attack fell apart.

Unbeknownst to Alaric, his strategy hadn't been a complete loss. His words swirled within Eirik's head, threatening all his defenses.

As their game progressed, Eirik only gave the red and white pieces half his mind. The other half churned with thoughts of Laurel—of a life with her as his wife, not as his thrall. He could hear her breathing steadily behind him as she worked her needle. Was he honor-bound to marry her to secure her freedom?

Nei, it wasn't his honor whispering in the back of his head that he would never be happier than by her side. It was his heart.

.

17

"Laurel, are you awake?"

Laurel's already-open eyes widened. "Yes," she whispered back into the darkness inside the hut. Unlike when she'd first arrived in the Viking village, the sun now sank past the horizon for a brief time each night. Thankfully, the tightly thatched roof and the furs hung over the window openings blocked most of the light. Even still, she hadn't been able to sleep.

"I think we should talk." Eirik's voice came from the far corner where he always slept atop a thick fur.

"Very well."

He'd been unusually quiet in the few days since his game with Alaric. Laurel's stomach squeezed at the memory of that evening, when she hadn't understood everything they'd spoken of, yet she could make out enough to know that they'd discussed her—that some danger loomed ahead of her. Even more shocking, she thought she'd heard her name combined with the word for—a union of some sort? It couldn't mean…

She didn't hear him move through the cottage, but suddenly his weight bore down on the bed near her hip, making the wooden frame creak slightly.

A long silence stretched and she could faintly make out his blue eyes, which were darker than usual, pinning her to the bed.

"I cannot stop thinking about that day at the lake," he said, his voice low.

She inhaled in surprise. She'd hoped he would explain what he and Alaric had been discussing that involved her. She hadn't expected such a bold declaration.

"N-neither can I," she breathed. Even at the mere mention of the lake, her skin flushed and her lips tingled at the memory of his kisses. Of course, he had kissed her elsewhere as well. Her nipples drew taut underneath the shift she wore—the only thing between her skin and the air.

"I would like to know what you'd think about …"

His voice was thick as he struggled to form the words.

"What is it?" She held her breath.

"I wondered if perhaps you would consider…if you would consider marrying me."

She sat bolt upright so quickly that she almost knocked foreheads with him. "What?"

First he was reticent and taciturn for several days. Then he was whispering to her in the middle of the night, but instead of explaining things, he reminded her of the heated kiss—and more—they'd shared nigh a fortnight ago, and now he was asking her about marriage?

"What do you...where is this...what?"

He lifted a shadowy hand and brushed his fingers along her cheekbone. "This is obviously sudden and unexpected," he said. Even as he spoke, her eyes drifted closed for a moment at the feel of his callused yet gentle fingers playing along her skin.

"I do not know how these things are done in Northumbria," he said. In the dim light, she could see that his brow was furrowed.

She opened her mouth to respond, but then a realization struck her. "Nor do I."

She'd never given much thought to marriage. Since Whitby Abbey was all she'd ever known, marriage wasn't part of daily life. Even though marriage was proper for people outside the Abbey, the nuns and monks within its walls looked down on such earthly unions as somehow less pure that their own relationship with God.

Of course, she wasn't a nun, so she wasn't bound to their way of life. Yet she had never considered a life outside of her servitude to the Abbey before.

"Why would you want to marry me?" Asking such a question made her blush, but she was so caught off-guard that she didn't bother worrying about the boldness of her words.

Eirik cleared his throat. "There are several reasons,"

he began, his voice low and earnest. "I admire your bravery given this…difficult situation. You are a hard worker, and you awe me with how quickly you learn new things. And we seem to be…compatible…in other ways."

His fingers trailed down her cheek to her neck, the touch feather-soft.

"I know I said I wouldn't touch you like this again," he breathed. "By the gods, I've tried to stop myself, yet your skin, your lips, your eyes—they haunt me. I am drawn to you, Laurel. I long for your company when you are not with me, and I feel calm and excited all at once when I am in your presence."

She shivered at both his touch and his words. Something deep within her wound tight, ready to break. "I…I feel the same way. I've fought against myself all this time, telling myself that it is wrong to care for a Viking heathen, wrong to have such sinful thoughts and desires, wrong to give up my old life, my old self."

Tears brimmed in her eyes as she spoke, blurring the shadowy outline of his ruggedly hansom face. "And I have fought myself as well," he whispered, letting his fingers play along the top of her shift. "I've held myself to my code of honor, yet it leaves me cold when all I want is you."

She exhaled, and it felt like all her fears, all her worries, left with the air from her lungs. She could no longer pretend that she didn't want him too, or settle for the idea that she couldn't have him. She could no longer cling to the edicts of Abbess Hilda about her sinfulness, how wrong it was that she was willful, how her life was a punishment from God.

For in Eirik's deep blue eyes she saw herself anew. She saw that her willfulness and quick mind were gifts, not burdens. She saw that the heat now coursing through her body meant that she was alive, a small vessel for pleasures as old as time itself. She saw that the world was far wider, far richer, far more vivid that she'd ever imagined.

She leaned forward and brushed her mouth against his, trying to communicate the swirling emotions overflowing within her. She didn't know what marriage to this man would mean. She wasn't sure if she was ready to decide, but her body needed to touch his. She needed to feel the heat she had tried to deny herself for so long.

He responded to her kiss immediately, pulling her into his chest. He tilted his head and deepened the kiss, stealing her breath with his soft yet firm caresses. His hands dug into her back possessively.

She inhaled through her nose and swam in his clean, masculine scent. Her fingers couldn't find a resting place, so eager were they to skim over his arms, his back, his neck, and to twine in the golden waves of hair hanging around his shoulders.

"I've thought about having you in this bed every cursed night," he breathed against her lips. He leaned forward so that she eased back onto the down-filled mattress.

Even as she sank back into the bed, a flicker of doubt threaded through her. "I'm not ready to…"

He propped himself on his elbow above her, his eyes glimmering hungrily. "Nei, you are an innocent. Not yet. But let me give you a taste of the pleasures we can share."

His words held a dark promise that sent a shiver through her. Her body seemed to be acting separately from her mind, for though she still felt the weight of guilt for her wanton ways, she craved to delve deeper into the pleasures they had waded into that day at the lake.

Before Abbess Hilda's voice could castigate her, Eirik's hand skimmed down from her collar bones to her breast. A jolt of sensation had her bucking at the light touch. His thumb brushed over her already-hard nipple, which strained against the linen of her shift.

"I have dreamt of tasting you again," he whispered. "But I long to taste you more fully."

His tongue twined with hers for another moment, but then he tore his mouth away and lowered his head to her breast. As he had done before, he flicked his tongue across the peak of her breast. Even through her shift, the sensation was almost too much. She writhed and moaned as heat pooled between her legs.

She clung desperately to his shoulders, her fingers sinking like talons into his muscular flesh. After several torturous moments of his attention on one breast, he shifted to the other, and she was treated to another fresh bolt of pure heat.

One of her knees rose of its own accord so that it cradled the outside of his hip. He made a satisfied noise in the back of his throat at her unconscious motion. He reached down and wrapped one large hand around the back of her other leg, pulling it up so that his torso rested between her two bent knees. She felt exposed like this, but instead of being frightened, it only heightened the swirling heat in her limbs.

His hand remained wrapped around her leg, and he began slowly pulling her shift higher. When the material was to her mid-thigh, he shifted slightly to let his fingertips trail down the inside of her leg. Closer and closer his fingers drew to the apex of her legs while his tongue swirled and teased her breasts.

She gasped as his fingers brushed against the damp curls protecting her most private place. No one had ever touched her there before. Once, when she was younger, she had been caught by one of the nuns touching herself there. She had only been exploring with childlike curiosity, but Abbess Hilda had beaten both of her hands with a switch, then strapped her to the cursed chair and dunked her.

She tensed as one of his fingers slid down the damp seam, remembering the Abbess's harsh words and punishment.

"Does this feel good?" he whispered against her breast.

She had never considered such a question before, yet the answer was so clear. It felt *incredible*. Her insides were knotted in exquisite anguish, longing for more. Her skin felt flushed and tight, her breasts heavy and needy. And between her legs, she was wet and hot and hungry.

Something was building within her, and it made her feel empty and greedy.

And it was Eirik—strong, honorable, kind Eirik—sharing this moment with her. How could this be the terrible sin Abbess Hilda had claimed it was?

"Aye," she breathed. "I want more." It was an affirmation of her choice, a rejection of her past, a glorying in this perfect moment.

His finger resumed its trail down her damp, aching flesh. He parted the folds of skin and brushed against that spot of pure pleasure. She arched her back instinctively, her body seeming to know what to do.

He caressed her, teased her, brushed and rubbed and circled until her breathing was shallow and she thought she'd go senseless from the pleasure. Then he slipped one large finger inside her and a whole new, deeper sensation filled her. He lifted his mouth from one of her breasts, and the cool air hitting the damp linen shift over her nipple sent fresh ripples of hot and cold sensation through her.

She was too deep in her own pleasure to comprehend what he was doing at first. Then she felt his hot breath right against the dampness between her legs and she jerked up onto her elbows.

"What are you doing?" she panted, eyes wide on him.

"Giving you pleasure," he breathed. Before she could ask what he meant, his tongue flicked out and over that most sensitive spot.

She gasped and moaned, her knees shuddering

around his shoulders. As his tongue stroked her, he slowly began moving his finger in and out.

"You taste even better than you did in my dreams," he said, his hot breath teasing her flesh.

Though the words were bold, for some reason they made her head spin even faster. There was something so raw, so carnal about this act. She had no idea what to expect when it came to the ways of bodily pleasure, yet this was far more animalistic than she'd imagined. Her body responded of its own accord, greedy, hungry, open. She cared not whether she should be embarrassed by the rawness of this moment. All she knew was that she wanted more.

She felt herself climbing toward something just out of reach, some promised relief from the nigh-overpowering sensations coursing through her. His tongue flicked and swirled while his finger moved faster, pumping in and out. She spiraled higher still, her breath hitching as she reached.

Then something broke within her and a flood of pleasure washed over her, drowning her. She cried out wordlessly as her body shook and clenched and twisted, drenched in ecstasy. Slowly, the waves of pleasure ebbed, but she felt washed clean by their power.

His touches slowed and finally ceased as he pulled away and brought himself up alongside her.

"That was..." She couldn't find the words for what she'd just experienced.

"That was just the beginning," he finished for her.

She became aware of the rock-hard shaft jutting into her hip. He was still wound tight as a bowstring, his pleasure unspent. Could they share the kind of intense sensations that had just claimed her? She reached out to let her fingers brush his rigid manhood. He sucked a hard breath through his teeth at even that light touch.

He let her explore him through his linen pants, occasionally groaning or inhaling as she discovered what he liked.

But then he stilled her hand with his.

"You haven't answered me," he said. "About marriage." His eyes glinted softly in the dim light, penetrating her deeply.

She froze, considering. It was all so much to take in —the question of marriage, the shift taking place within her heart, the pleasure he'd just given her.

She opened her mouth to answer when a dull snapping sound filtered into the cottage.

Eirik tensed, listening. The snap sounded again, though it wasn't the sharp, higher noise of a branch breaking in the wind. It was lower, duller, and more distant than the trees clinging to the mountainsides around them.

Eirik bolted from the bed and had a hand around his sword, which stood in the corner, faster than she could blink.

"Stay here," he whispered. Sword in hand, he eased the wooden door open and peered out into the bluish light of the midsummer night. A long, strained silence hung in the air for what felt like ages.

"What is it?" she finally whispered, unable to stand the tension.

"Something is out on the water, but I can't tell—"

He cursed violently. "Stay inside the cottage no matter what, Laurel. Do you understand?" he barked.

"What's happening?" she hissed, her voice rising in panic.

"There are at least three ships sailing straight for the village. We are under attack!"

18

"Stay here," he repeated. "If it comes to it, make a bolt up the mountainside. Climb as high and as fast as you can and don't look back."

If it comes to it? What did that mean? If the attackers cut Eirik down and breached the cottage? Terror squeezed her throat until she felt like she couldn't breathe.

"I need to warn the village before the ships are upon us." He tugged on his leather boots but didn't bother taking the time to don a padded vest or his chainmail and helmet. With one last look at her, he slipped out the front door and closed it silently behind him, his sword dull in the blue light of half-night.

Laurel jerked to her feet, frantic to do something, yet she didn't know what. She pushed the heavy wooden table and two benches across the cottage floor so that they blocked the front door. But then she realized that the windows were completely unprotected. They were only covered with furs so that the mild air on these long summer days could be enjoyed.

She glanced around for some sort of weapon and had to settle for a dull knife from the kitchen and an iron poker for the fire. She stood for a moment, facing the door, weapons shaking in her quavering hands.

Longing to reassure herself that Eirik was all right, she moved to one of the front windows and eased the fur covering back a few inches. The air outside was cool and twilight blue, though she guessed it was after midnight. Her eye was immediately pulled to the fjord waters in front of Eirik's hut.

Panic twisted her stomach at the sight that met her eyes. Three ships were indeed moving up the fjord, nearly to the village already. Their sails were white and red, just as Eirik's had been on that terrifying night they'd attacked the Abbey, but instead of stripes, there were red diamonds on a white background. The white glowed almost blue, whereas the red diamonds were darker than blood, nigh black. The high, curving prows of the ships rose like ghosts over the calm waters.

She heard the same dull snapping sound that had alerted Eirik and realized that it was their sails flapping in the weak breeze. She prayed that somehow the other villagers would hear the noise and rouse themselves.

Her eyes moved down the trail that connected Eirik's hut to the village. Even from the distance he had already covered, she could make him out clearly, for his off-white tunic glowed vividly in the bluish light. A terrible realization struck her as she watched him move swiftly toward the village. His tunic made him a beacon, an obvious target for the ships that drew nearer by the second.

As if her thoughts brought the nightmare to fruition, Laurel heard several muffled shouts coming from the direction of the ship. Her eyes locked on Eirik as a scream of warning rose in her chest.

But the scream never made it past her throat, for in the next instant a sickening thunk of an arrow sinking into flesh met her ears, and then it sounded again. Eirik's body jerked unnaturally, first in one direction, then another.

She didn't comprehend the noise of the kitchen knife and fire poker falling to the ground, but in the next moment, her free hands were flying to a dark woolen cloak that hung on a peg near the door. She flung the cloak around her shoulders to obscure her pale colored shift. She didn't bother trying to move the table and benches from the front door. Instead, she ripped back the fur window covering and leapt out the window.

Laurel landed painfully on the side of one foot but threw herself forward, forcing her legs to sprint toward where Eirik had fallen on the path. She didn't dare glance toward the fjord and could only pray that the dark cloak obscured her from their attackers' sight in the low light.

She fell to her knees when she reached Eirik. He lay motionless on his back, two arrows bristling from his body. One was buried in his left shoulder, while the other protruded from his right thigh.

"Oh God, nay! Eirik!" she whispered, trying to keep

her voice low even as panic threatened to steal her senses completely.

He groaned and moved a fraction of an inch. She breathed every prayer of thanks she could think of as the air whooshed from her lungs.

"I told you...to stay inside," he ground out. She almost laughed, so great was the surge of hysteria in her veins. But then reality crashed back down around her.

"What do I do?" she whispered through trembling lips.

"Get back to the cottage." His voice was strained, and he still hadn't moved more than a twitch.

"But I must get you to safety. Oh God, the villagers!"

Without Eirik to warn them of the impending attack, they were defenseless. Her eyes shot up to the ships. They were gliding slowly past them and farther into the fjord. In a matter of minutes, they would be level with the rest of the village and in a perfect position to attack.

"Leave me," Eirik whispered. "Get yourself away."

"Nay," she said firmly. "I'll not abandon you, nor will I let everyone in the village fall under attack while they sleep." Her mind raced. She had to choose. She couldn't stay with Eirik and tend to his wounds and also warn the villagers. She glanced down at Eirik. His face was twisted in agony, and dark blood was seeping over both his tunic and his pants.

She sent up another prayer for strength and grabbed Eirik underneath his arms. He tried to muffle a moan of pain at having his wounded shoulder moved, but Laurel winced at the noise. She couldn't stop, though. She leaned back with all her weight, dragging him backward off the path. He groaned again and she had to stop, panting at the exertion of moving his limp weight.

She pulled again with all her might, managing to drag him another foot into the underbrush along the trail. Again and again she threw her weight back, gripping under his arms even as one hand grew slick with his blood. Finally, he was fully off the path and into the tall grasses and shrubs that lined it.

She stood back on the path and looked down on him. His pale clothes were now obscured by the underbrush, hiding him from view. If their attackers made their way toward Eirik's hut, he would be concealed—and safe, she prayed.

"I'm going to warn the village," she said quietly. He tried to protest, but it came out garbled and turned into a moan of pain. He was growing worse. She steeled her heart against the desire to huddle next to him and hide. She had to be brave. She had to live up to his words that she had a warrior's heart.

With one final look, she threw herself down the path toward the village. She held the cloak closed at the front, concealing her white shift from the eerie blue light. She could only pray that she looked like a shadow flitting along the shoreline to those on the approaching ships.

The dark outlines of buildings began to emerge before her. She dared a glance toward the fjord. The ships were almost right on top of them. Then she heard a splash and realized that their attackers were already leaping from their ships and into the water.

There was no time left. Even though the village was

still several dozen strides away, she inhaled and screamed as loud as she could.

"We are under attack! To arms!"

More splashes rose from the fjord, as well as muffled voices.

"Wake up! We are under attack!" she screamed again. As she sprinted forward, the whiz of an arrow sounded behind her. Another arrow darted directly in front of her. If she'd been one step farther down the path, the arrow would have found her chest.

She dove behind the closest building, only to hear the sound of an arrow sinking into the building's outer wood planking. Blessedly, the village had begun to stir at her first scream. Now activity erupted from the small clump of huts around the village square. Men and a few women poured from the huts, their weapons dull in the low light. Other shouts rose all around her as the warriors scrambled to meet their attackers.

At the first sounds of clanging metal, she scrambled to her feet. She was about to be in the middle of a Viking battle, and she had no weapons, no armor, and no idea how to defend herself. Yet there was nowhere to go for safety.

A bright flare of light caught her eye. An attacker had set a torch to one of the thatched rooves several houses over from where Laurel stood. The dry thatch went up in flames quickly. Screams of pain and battle cries filled the air along with quickly thickening smoke as several more buildings caught fire.

Laurel edged around the side of the house behind which she hid. Along the shoreline, Viking warriors poured from their ships, splashing in the water and making their way toward the village. The armed villagers met the surging attackers. Yet the attackers were managing to press up the rocky beach and into the outskirts of the village.

While most of the shadowy forms of the villagers rushed toward their assailants, Laurel's eye caught on a few smaller figures moving back into the mountainsides. She squinted through the smoke. They must be the village's children and the women who didn't fight, along with the aged and sick. A clump of them were stumbling toward the narrow path through the steep, rocky mountain walls that led to the hidden practice fields.

It was Laurel's only chance to survive this battle. She took a deep breath and forced her feet to move. She shot from behind the building and into the village square.

The attackers had already pushed into the square and were hacking their way deeper into the village. Laurel tried to skirt around the pairs of warriors locked in deadly combat, yet there were already too many fighting in the open square. She veered out of the way as a villager toppled backward, slain. Yet she stumbled over another body and fell to her knees.

The cloak and her shift tangled in her legs as she struggled to find her feet once more. A deep bellow sounded over her, and she looked up to find a warrior standing above her. He held a huge ax in both hands, which he raised, taking aim at her head. In the blue light, she saw that his eyes were filled with pure bloodlust.

It was as if time slowed in that moment. The ax's

curved blade glinted in the light of the fires all around. It arced through the air in a half circle. Soon it would bury itself in her skull. Everything went quiet, her ears muffling the screams and clashing metal around her. A strange calm stole over her. There was nowhere to run, no time to scream.

The blade's slicing motion suddenly halted. A sword appeared right over her head, catching the ax's handle. Breaking her terrified paralysis, she scrambled back.

The bearer of the sword absorbed the force and weight of the ax's swing. Her savior was brought to one knee but managed to deflect the ax to one side. The warrior popped back on both feet and spun the sword to swipe it across the back of the attacker's legs. The ax-wielding attacker screamed in agony and fell. With one more flick of the sword, Laurel's defender ended the attacker's life.

The sword-bearer turned, and Laurel realized it was Madrena. Her pale hair trailed out from under her helm, her face partially obscured by the nasal guard.

Even still, Laurel saw that Madrena's eyes widened on her.

"Where is Eirik?" Madrena barked, bending to pull Laurel up by the elbow.

Laurel couldn't find the words to explain all that had happened, so she simply shook her head. Madrena visibly swallowed. "You need to get to the practice fields with the others."

She yanked Laurel back by the arm, all the while scanning the square. Both the villagers and their attackers were locked in deadly combat. Neither side seemed to have the upper hand yet.

"Alaric!" Madrena shouted. Laurel's eyes caught sight of Madrena's twin brother. He was engaged with an attacker who was swinging two short blades at him. It seemed like all Alaric could do to block first one blade and then the other as the attacker slashed and thrust.

Madrena released Laurel's elbow and flew to Alaric's side. She swung her blade at their attacker, forcing him to use one of his short swords to block it. That was enough of an opening for Alaric to deal a death blow with his own sword to the intruder's neck.

Just as Madrena and Alaric turned to her, several of the attackers broke through the line of villagers to spill deeper into the square. Some went straight for the buildings and huts surrounding the square, either to loot them or set them on fire. Others were simply looking for their next kill.

Laurel bolted toward Madrena and Alaric, closing the distance between them. The twins put their backs to her, their weapons pointed outward to fend off this new wave of attackers. As they each dispatched more of the Viking attackers, they backed up toward the path leading to the training fields.

At the mouth of the path, Alaric and Madrena paused.

"If any of these whoresons makes it into the fields—"

Madrena didn't need to finish. They all knew it would be a mass slaughter of the women, children, elderly, and sickly who were hiding behind the towering mountain walls.

"I'll stay," Alaric panted. Like Madrena, his face was partially obscured by his helm, yet Laurel could see the weighty look that passed between the siblings.

"We both will," she replied.

"Nei, sister. More warriors are needed in the village. Go!" With that, Alaric shoved Madrena hard in the direction of the village square. She didn't look back, but a battle cry ripped from her throat as she dove into the fray once more.

Alaric grabbed Laurel's elbow and pulled her down the narrow path toward the hidden meadow.

"Where is Eirik?" he snapped, just as Madrena had done.

"He...he was shot. He was trying to warn the village, but the attackers spotted him."

"Does he live?" Alaric's voice was suddenly calm and low.

"I..." Laurel thought back to how quickly he had begun to fade once she'd gotten him into the underbrush. "I do not know," she choked out, her voice thick and raw.

Alaric remained silent, though his hand clenched reflexively around her arm.

As they emerged from the trail into the field, dozens upon dozens of figures came into view. Families huddled together in clumps around the meadow. A few children cried softly as their mothers tried to shush them. The noises from the battle underway in the village echoed eerily around the stone mountainsides surrounding the clearing. Shrieks of the wounded and dying, clashing metal, and battle cries filled the night air.

Alaric released her arm and turned to face the entrance to the practice field, weapon poised. He would be their last line of defense should any of the attackers find the path. He was only one man, yet at least the narrow opening to the meadow worked in his favor, providing a funnel only wide enough for one person at a time to pass through.

Time stretched as the battle raged on. Laurel fell to her knees and whispered prayers for the fallen men and women who had begun to accept her as one of their own, for the safety of those gathered in the field, and for Eirik. She may have rejected the cruel ways of the nuns and monks at Whitby Abbey, but she would never abandon her faith.

She shifted on her aching knees and looked up to stretch her neck. The sky had lightened considerably from pale blue to the thin yellow of early dawn. It would still be only a couple of hours past midnight, yet the northern summer sun was already spreading its light.

Laurel realized that most of the battle noises had faded. She had no idea what the fate of the village would be, but beyond the mountain walls, the battle had been determined.

Just then she made out the crunching sound of loose rocks underfoot along the hidden path. Alaric visibly tensed in front of the opening, his knuckles white on his sword hilt.

Laurel caught a glimpse of a pale blond head before

Madrena fully emerged into the clearing. Alaric lowered his sword with an exhale of relief.

"The battle is over," Madrena said loud enough for everyone in the meadow to hear. "We are victorious!"

Those huddled in the clearing sent up a brief and relieved cheer, yet the sobering reality was that many of them had likely lost a loved one in the attack. And Laurel had seen enough before retreating to the field to know that many homes had been destroyed.

"See to your kin," Madrena said to the crowd. "And look to your homes for what can be saved."

The villagers began filing out of the field wearily. Laurel hung back with Madrena and Alaric as they waited to ensure every last villager returned safely.

"What of Eirik?" Madrena asked lowly. She was blood-stained and smoke-smudged but appeared uninjured.

"He heard the ships approaching," Laurel replied. "He went to warn the village, but he was shot twice. I… I tried to pull him to safety, but when I left, he was falling into unconsciousness."

"And how did you end up in the village?" Alaric said as he re-sheathed his sword.

"I ran here to send up the alarm that we were under attack," she said.

Madrena and Alaric looked at her for a long moment, and then exchanged a glance that seemed to pass some unspoken communication between them.

"That was you?" Madrena finally said. "You were the one who sent up the alarm?"

Laurel could only bob her head. Madrena's eyes glinted with respect and Alaric gave her a little nod.

"Without that warning, we would have been slaughtered in our beds," Alaric said. "The village owes you its existence this morning, Laurel."

Laurel's vision blurred with a combination of exhaustion and pride. Before she could speak, though, Madrena motioned toward her hands.

"Are you hurt?"

Laurel looked down to find that her hands and the left sleeve of her shift were covered in dried blood. She lifted her shaking fingers to her face. "Nay. This is Eirik's blood."

"We have to retrieve him," Madrena said to Alaric, who only nodded. "Take us to him, Laurel."

Laurel fell in between Madrena and Alaric as they wound their way back through the rock walls and into the village. As she emerged from the trail, she froze in horror.

Bodies and blood filled the village square. Most were their unidentified attackers, but many were the villagers she was coming to know. Smoke still filled the air, stinging her eyes, but the fires had been almost completely extinguished. The living moved among the dead, looking for family members and trying to salvage what was left of their homes.

"Who was it?" Alaric asked as they strode through the square.

"They were from the east, likely Jarl Thorsten's men," Madrena replied. "The survivors fled on one of their ships, but the other two remain here."

"Good," Alaric said darkly. Laurel could only imagine how much time and effort went into building each one of the long, high-prowed ships like Eirik's Drakkar. Capturing two from their enemies must be an incredible prize. Compared to the lives lost, however, it was little consolation.

As they hurried through the square, Laurel's foot snagged on something. She looked down to find that she'd tripped on the arm of a dead warrior. Through the blood spatters, she recognized the man called Haakon, the enormous red-bearded warrior who'd pulled her hair and ordered her to pour him ale her first night in the village.

Laurel clapped a hand over her mouth to stifle the cry that rose to her lips. The warrior's eyes were open, frozen in death. She had been terrified of him that first night, yet he had proved harmless to her. He didn't deserve to die.

"Leave him," Alaric said, taking her by the arm. "He died a warrior's death. He's probably already riding with the Valkyries to Valhalla."

She squeezed her eyes shut, trying to get the sight of Haakon's dead eyes out of her mind. Abbess Hilda would say that the warrior was going to eternal damnation for being a heathen. Yet in that moment, Laurel understood the comfort that the Vikings' pagan religion could give in times like these. She let Alaric guide her away from Haakon's body and toward the trail that led to Eirik's cottage.

"Take us to him," Madrena said as she stepped aside to let Laurel lead.

Laurel hurried down the trail until she neared where she thought she'd left him. She slowed, scanning the underbrush. When she spotted him, she fell to his side.

He was pale in the warming sunlight. Blood had soaked most of his tunic and the right leg of his pants.

"Eirik," she breathed, desperately pressing a hand to his chest in the hope of feeling his heart beat.

She felt the thump of his heart, though it was weak and slow. A new wave of fear tightened her throat. If he didn't make it through…

She couldn't let herself think of such things when he clearly still needed help. She and Madrena each lifted one of his arms while Alaric picked up his legs. The three of them slowly shuffled back to the hut. Once they pushed their way through the blockaded door, they set his limp body on the wooden table, which now sat askew in the middle of the room.

Madrena immediately moved to grab the small cauldron hanging over the kitchen fire. She disappeared out the cottage's back door, presumably to get water.

"Hold him," Alaric said grimly to Laurel. She didn't understand what he meant until he wrapped his hand around the arrow shaft protruding from Eirik's leg.

She swallowed and leaned her weight into his good shoulder, hoping she could contain his thrashing if it came to that.

With one swift jerk, Alaric removed the arrow from Eirik's right thigh. He moved to Eirik's left shoulder, but frowned and muttered something Laurel didn't understand as he examined it.

Madrena returned with the cauldron full of water. She stoked the fire and set the cauldron over it.

"What's wrong?" she said at Alaric's muttering.

"This arrow is too deep. We'll have to push it through."

"Won't that hurt him?" Laurel said, frantically looking between Madrena and Alaric.

"It must be done. He's likely too far gone into the pain to notice," Madrena said flatly.

The siblings rolled Eirik onto his right shoulder. "Steady him," Alaric said. He quickly snapped off the majority of the arrow shaft protruding from Eirik's shoulder. Even that small amount of motion drew a muted groan from Eirik.

Alaric and Madrena braced themselves on either side of Eirik's body. Laurel felt useless and helpless, yet she took hold of Eirik's head between her hands.

With a quick nod, Alaric jammed the remainder of the arrow shaft deeper into Eirik's shoulder. Even in unconsciousness, Eirik thrashed and bellowed in pain. Laurel watched in horror as the tip of the arrow emerged through Eirik's skin on the other side of his shoulder. Madrena took hold of the blood-slick arrow tip and drew it all the way out.

All the while, Laurel gripped his head, keeping him from thrashing and hurting himself more. "'Tis all right, Eirik," she whispered. "I'm here. You'll be fine." The words felt hollow and meaningless, so great was her fear for him, yet she hoped that somewhere in his agony-addled brain he took comfort from them.

"We'll need to wash the wounds and keep them

clean," Madrena said in a strained voice. "Let us hope that a fever isn't already setting in."

Alaric and Madrena went about boiling water, soaking strips of linen in it, and cutting away the linen tunic and pants around each of Eirik's wounds. They seemed to know what to do, so Laurel stayed out of their way and remained by Eirik's side. The two must have seen their fair share of battle wounds and knew how to treat them, whereas Laurel had done little more than treat splinters.

The hours slipped by as they tended to Eirik, for the sun was high and hot by the time Laurel emerged from the hut to see to her needs and rinse her hands in the stream. It wasn't until then that she realized she'd been comprehending and communicating with Alaric and Madrena in their language. Eirik's lessons had come to fruition.

A lump caught in her throat. She wanted naught more at that moment than to be able to talk with him once more, see his tanned face transform in a smile, feel his warm, lively hands on her.

As she turned to re-enter the cottage, she froze.

Grimar was coming up the path toward her, his ice blue eyes locked on her.

"You survived the attack," he said, his cool eyes unreadable. "How fares Eirik?"

"He'll be fine," Madrena said, stepping from the cottage to stand between her and Grimar. "Just a few scratches."

Laurel's mind worked slowly to untangle why Madrena would lie so baldly to Grimar. Of course,

Grimar was a cruel, callous man. But why would Madrena need to maintain the appearance of Eirik's wellbeing? Was Eirik in some sort of danger? Was she?

Grimar eyed Madrena calmly for a long moment. "My father has called a council meeting to assess the damages of the attack on the village," he said finally. "Everyone who is able must attend."

"Eirik is resting now, but my brother and I will be there," Madrena replied smoothly. "I assume you don't want this thrall to attend?" She casually gestured toward Laurel.

"Nei, of course not," Grimar responded dismissively. "The meeting is already getting underway. You and your brother had better hurry."

With that, Grimar turned and strode back toward the village.

"What was that?" Laurel said once he was out of earshot.

"It would suit Grimar's plans to have Eirik out of the way," Madrena replied as she ducked back into the hut.

"He would harm his own cousin?" The thought was horrifying, yet Laurel should know by now not to put anything past Grimar.

"Nei, I don't think he would go that far," Madrena said. "To harm one's kin is a grave violation of the laws of both mortals and gods. Yet he is clearly more interested in Eirik's health than he should be. We have to go in for a council meeting." The last was said to Alaric, who nodded.

"I heard," he said.

"You'll have to stay here with Eirik and tend to him." Madrena turned to Laurel.

"But I…I don't know how…"

Madrena took her by the shoulders and pinned her with her pale gray eyes. "You dragged him to safety earlier, and you ran into the village to warn us all of an attack. You can do this also."

Though the thought of having Eirik's life in her hands terrified her, Madrena's new confidence in her buoyed her somewhat.

"Just keep the wounds clean and dry. Try to get him to drink some water. I'll see if I can get some herbs from the village healer, though she'll likely be stretched far too thin as it is."

Laurel nodded numbly. Once Alaric and Madrena filed out of the cottage, however, her ears rang with the silence and her heart hitched.

She turned her attention to Eirik, who still lay limply on the large wooden table they had so often eaten on. His normally bronzed skin looked sickly and pale in the cottage's dim interior. She dipped a wooden cup into the cauldron of hot water and brought it to his side. Raising his head with one hand, she tried to pour some of the liquid into his mouth. But the water just dribbled around his lips.

An uneasy feeling swept over her. The hand holding up Eirik's head felt warm. She set him down gently and placed a hand over his forehead. The skin was unnaturally hot. Fever had already set in.

19

"The attackers were indeed Jarl Thorsten's men."

A ripple of unease went through those gathering in the longhouse at Gunvald's words.

Grimar's father held up his hand for silence. "We will, of course, not let this attack go unanswered."

While some families huddled together, muffling their cries, several warriors sent up a rumble of furious agreement.

"Though we lost many brave warriors, Jarl Thorsten's men suffered for their cowardly night attack. They have been beaten back, and two of their longships are now ours."

The words satisfied the soot- and blood-covered fighters but did little to comfort those who'd lost loved ones or their homes. Grimar drummed his fingers impatiently on the back of the Jarl's large chair. He stood at his father's side as a show of support both to the Jarl and to the frightened villagers. Gunvald had assured him that his presence, along with Eirik's absence, would go a long way in securing Grimar's place as a leader in the villagers' minds.

It was all Grimar could do not to roll his eyes at the solemn tone his father took, or at the weeping women and children. His people were growing soft. Those who'd died were already dining in Valhalla with Odin. These emotional displays were an embarrassment.

Just then the bitch Madrena stepped forward. Her eyes flickered to Grimar for a moment, the light of defiance shining in them.

"I think you should know who was responsible for alerting the village of the attack, Jarl."

Grimar jerked in surprise at Madrena's boldness. What game was she playing, drawing attention to herself in a council meeting?

Gunvald waved her on.

"It was Laurel, the utlending thrall in Eirik's keeping." Again, the bitch's eyes flicked to Grimar to watch his reaction.

It was all Grimar could do not to curse aloud. His fingers dug into the wood of the back of the Jarl's chair, his knuckles turning white.

A shocked murmur rippled through the crowd. Even his father, normally so cool and composed, sat forward in his chair with a start.

"While we all slept, she ran from Eirik's cottage to sound the alarm," Alaric, the bitch's twin, said, stepping to her side.

Gunvald cleared his throat, likely to buy himself

time to formulate a response. "And where is the girl now?"

"She is tending to your nephew, who received a very minor wound in the attack," Alaric said, his eyes just as sharp as his sister's.

His father cleared his throat again. But before he could speak, he had to bang his fist against the arm of his chair several times to quiet the villagers. Even from the dais, Grimar could clearly make out their murmurs.

They were actually *praising* the thrall! Some whispered that she was more Northlander than utlending, while others openly commended her bravery.

"Then she is finally behaving as any thrall should," his father said loudly. "For from the beginning she ought to have seen to her master's needs and looked after the village's interests."

Their Jarl's less than subtle attempt to remind them of a thrall's proper role quieted some of the villagers. Yet even still others continued to whisper praise for the girl.

"Go," Gunvald said authoritatively even as his control over the council meeting slipped. "See to your kin and your homes. Before the first frost of fall, we will exact revenge on Jarl Thorsten!"

An angry cheer rose at his father's last words, but there was little energy left for celebrating their impending attack. The weary, overwhelmed villagers filed out of the longhouse and into the bright sunlight.

They needed less subtle maneuvering and more clear-cut action, Grimar thought with disdain as he watched them shuffle like sheep from the longhouse. His eyes fell on the back of his father's gray-white head, and he had to repress a sneer.

Once the longhouse was empty, Gunvald stood and motioned for Grimar to follow him into his attached private chambers.

"I warned you that the thrall girl was getting too comfortable here!" Grimar snapped as soon as the thick wooden door closed behind him.

Gunvald rounded on him. "Did you have something to do with this attack? Because if you did, by the gods, son or nei—"

"Nei, of course not," Grimar replied quickly. This was to be his village to rule over, so to outward appearances, it wouldn't make sense for him to have a hand in the attack. "But it is telling, father, that your mind would jump to such a conclusion."

Grimar narrowed his gaze on his father. Gunvald's face remained still, yet apprehension flickered in his pale eyes.

"I know what lust for power can lead men to do," Gunvald said carefully. "As do you."

"And look what it has gotten you—the Jarlship, just as you wished. Now *I* want it." He took a step toward his father.

Gunvald's hand twitched toward his belt, where his seax hung. "Is that a threat?"

"Nei, father. Not all of us will resort to killing kin for the Jarlship," Grimar said casually.

Gunvald's pale blue eyes widened. "I told you never to speak of that out loud. *Never.*" His lips trembled as he spoke, but Grimar wasn't sure if it was from rage or fear.

Grimar gestured around the small chamber. "No one is here to hear the story of how you stabbed your own brother in the back for the Jarlship, father."

This time, Gunvald actually drew his seax and leveled it at Grimar. Grimar only grinned.

"Finally, you *act*," he said. "I was wondering what it would take to get you to *do* something rather than just plot and plan."

"Do not toy with me, boy," his father said lowly, re-sheathing his seax. "You'd not be in the position you are today without me, and you damned well won't hold the Jarlship without my help."

Grimar dropped the grin from his face, yet he smiled inwardly. He'd made his move. He'd subtly challenged his father, threatening him with the knowledge that he had been the one to kill Arud the Steady—and it had worked. Grimar now knew that he could hold the information over his father, and that Gunvald would be forced to fear and respect him.

"Regarding the girl," Grimar said calmly, taking a seat in one of the chamber's large wooden chairs. "We should have acted already. Eirik has clearly grown attached to her, but now apparently so has the rest of the village."

Gunvald hesitated, his eyes wary on Grimar. Finally, he sat across from him. "We must proceed as planned. It will undercut my authority to do aught else other than sell the girl at the market in a few sennights' time."

Grimar almost shouted that he cared little about

undercutting his father's authority, for soon enough he would be Jarl. He bit back the exclamation, however. If he had learned anything from his father, it was that one must always have plans of one's own, plans that would remain secret.

"And what of Eirik?" Grimar said instead, clenching his teeth against his temper. "How can you be sure that taking the girl away from him will encourage him to return his attention to raiding in the west? What if the girl is the last thread preventing him from challenging you?"

Gunvald shook his head, but his brow wrinkled deeply. "He'll forget her soon enough. Once she is gone, he'll grow restless and wish to return to the quest for new lands."

Grimar snorted. "You haven't seen them together. You should heed my words more carefully."

Gunvald exhaled and let his gaze scan the thatched ceiling in thought. After a long pause, he finally spoke. "If what you say of his growing attachment to the girl is true, then taking her away from him will be a blow. It will weaken him, not strengthen his drive for the Jarlship."

Grimar ran his tongue over his teeth in thought. "Mayhap," he relented. Though his father's conniving ways usually bored him, he had to give Gunvald credit for his skill. "But why must we ignore the obvious solution? Eirik is my competition, not the girl."

Gunvald looked around nervously despite the fact that they were alone. "I've told you already. It would be more than coincidence if both Arud and Eirik met with accidents. You'd draw suspicion onto both of us. Heed me, Grimar," he said, leaning forward. "I know what it is to rule in the shadow of a dead man. You won't find the comparisons between you and the tragic hero Eirik would become in death very favorable."

Grimar cursed. His own father thought Eirik would make a better Jarl than he. Yet Gunvald made a good point that if Eirik were to die now, suspicion would fall on Grimar—which was why Grimar had been careful in the plan he'd put in motion a sennight ago. Grimar leapt to his feet and began pacing the length of the small chamber. He was tired of waiting—he wanted to act.

"We are so close, my son," Gunvald said quietly from his chair. "We only have to wait a few more sennights before the thrall girl is out of our hair. In the meantime, you must capitalize on the fact that Eirik isn't here to help rebuild the village. You must work day and night rethatching rooves, building funeral pyres for the dead—whatever it takes to place you in the hearts of the villagers. Show yourself to be a leader."

"And who knows," Grimar said, suppressing an inward smile. "Mayhap Eirik's wounds are worse than we know."

20

Laurel mopped Eirik's brow with a cool cloth, but his skin still raged with fever.

The burning had come on quickly and ran hot. For a while, Eirik had thrashed in delirium. He'd shouted at ghosts and flailed violently. It had taken all three of them to hold him down to prevent himself from re-opening his wounds. But now he lay still and quiet, which was so much worse.

Laurel shuddered as she turned her attention to his bare shoulder. She dabbed the cloth as gently as she could around the red, angry gash in his flesh. After it was clear that the wounds had festered, Alaric had held his seax over the kitchen fire, then pressed the glowing-hot blade into Eirik's shoulder and leg wounds. But the wounds festered again. Each of the last three mornings, they'd had to scrape away the pus and fiery scabs and re-cauterize the wounds.

Bright light flooded the hut and Laurel squinted toward the door. Madrena stepped inside, her face grim.

"Any change?"

"Nei," Laurel replied in Madrena's language. "The fever still racks him."

Madrena's head dropped for a moment, and she whispered something Laurel didn't understand.

"Sit, Madrena," Laurel said. "I'll make you something to eat."

Laurel began to rise to her feet next to Eirik's large bed. They'd managed to move him that first day from the table to the bed, but now she feared he would never again rise from the large, down-filled mattress.

"Nei," Madrena said, quickly crossing the hut to place a hand on Laurel's shoulder. "Don't bother over me. I'll see to myself. Besides, you need rest and sustenance more than I."

Laurel sank back down next to the bed, the cloth once again finding Eirik's fevered skin. She wasn't sure that she'd slept more than a few hours in the last four nights. Time passed eerily alongside the sickbed. It didn't help that they only had a few hours of half-darkness each night. And she would have forgotten to eat completely if Alaric and Madrena didn't alternate pressing food on her.

Madrena stood over the bed, her hand still resting on Laurel's shoulder. Laurel looked up to find her gazing at Eirik, her nigh-colorless eyes shimmering in the light of the kitchen fire.

"I didn't think it would come to this," she whispered, "but it is time."

Madrena drew the seax that hung at the belt around her hips.

"What are you doing?" Laurel choked out, struggling to put herself between Eirik and Madrena's drawn blade.

"What goes on?" The cottage door opened once more, blinding Laurel with the brightness outside. She barely comprehended Alaric's question for her eyes were fixed on the blade in Madrena's hand.

"'Tis time that he had this," Madrena said over her shoulder to Alaric.

To Laurel's horror, Alaric lowered his head and nodded solemnly.

"What in the name of God are you doing?" Laurel shrieked, her lack of understanding turning to hysteria. She doubted she could stop either one of them, let alone both of them, yet she wouldn't let any harm befall Eirik.

Madrena flipped the seax in her hand so that she held the blade between her fingers. She extended the hilt toward Eirik and lifted his uninjured arm with one hand. Then she wrapped his limp fingers around the seax's hilt and gently set his hand down so that the blade rested in his loose grasp.

Laurel looked between the two Viking warrior twins in utter confusion. "I...I don't understand."

"When a warrior dies in battle, if he fought well and honorably, he goes to Valhalla," Madrena began, her voice pinched.

Laurel nodded. "Eirik told me something of that."

"There is another place the dead can go," Madrena went on. "If a warrior is not killed in battle, or dies a less worthy death, he will go to Helheimr, home of the goddess Hel."

Laurel gasped and clutched her throat. "You mean if Eirik…if he dies…he will endure eternal damnation? Just because he wasn't on the battlefield?"

Alaric approached the bed and looked down at his friend. "From what Eirik told me of your religion, Hel's home is not the same as your underworld inferno. Helheimr is the resting place for the old and the sick. It is not damnation—but the glories of Valhalla will never be his."

"Then why did you put a seax in his hand?" Laurel asked. Though she'd learned much from Eirik over the last several sennights, so much of the Northmen's ways were still mysterious and confusing to her.

Madrena grinned faintly, though her eyes were tight with unspoken sadness. "Sometimes you can trick the Valkyries into thinking that a death occurred in battle. When—if—they come down to this hut, they'll see the blade in his hand and take him to Valhalla where he belongs."

Alaric turned to Madrena. "I brought a sheep. We'd best make a sacrifice to Eir."

"Eir?" Laurel said, already struggling against the limits of her understanding.

"The goddess of healing. If there is aught left that can be done, Eir will see to it. If not, the seax will guide the Valkyries to him."

As the words sank in, Laurel realized that both Madrena and Alaric thought Eirik was close to death—close enough to make a sacrifice to the goddess of healing, close enough that he needed the seax in his hand, and close enough that they thought the Valkyries might come down at any moment.

Laurel felt her heart crack open as a whoosh of air left her lungs. *Nay!* she screamed inside. *Nay, he cannot die!* She dropped the useless damp cloth and clasped her hands before her on the bed. Her knees ached against the stone floor of the hut, but she didn't care.

She prayed as tears began streaming down her cheeks. Her mind flitted back to her first memory of Eirik. His nasal helm had obscured most of his face, but when he'd stepped between her and Grimar and halted Grimar's raised fist, his bright blue eyes had locked on her. She shivered at the memory. She'd never seen a man so powerful, so captivating, before.

Yet he was also kind and gentle even when he could have used brute force against her. The memories of his compassion toward her on the Drakkar, how he saved her from both the ocean's cold grip and Grimar's, and that first, soft kiss surged through her. And heat flooded her to remember his barely restrained passion at the lake and in this very bed only four nights ago.

She'd never imagined she would be enthralled by a Viking warrior. Yet even more shocking, she'd grown to care for him. She had resisted her own feelings for too long. And now that she finally accepted that her heart had been captivated by the man lying unconscious before her, it was too late.

Madrena gave her shoulder a little squeeze of reassurance, but Laurel was lost in her thoughts and prayers. She was barely aware of Madrena and Alaric quietly exiting the cottage a moment later. Laurel didn't understand the Vikings' practice of sacrifice, and as a Christian, she was expected to shun it as heathenry and pagan barbarism. Yet on her knees next to Eirik, she was too humbled to judge their method of prayer. They all cared for him, and they would all fight for him in their own ways.

Laurel lost herself to her prayers as the tears continued to stream down her cheeks.

21

Light and darkness swirled together. Voices swam around him and he saw figures, but they were drowned out by searing, white-hot pain.

He saw his father. He was younger, the way he remembered him as a boy, before the terrible, mysterious accident that had taken him away. Arud the Steady's eyes were bright and laughing, his hair as golden as the midsummer sun.

"You think hiding will solve your problems?"

Eirik had lost his shield long ago, and his wooden practice sword had just split in two. He'd bolted behind the longhouse to evade his father's wooden sword.

"You can come out and face your fate like a man, or you can hide back there," his father called, laughter in his voice. "Either way, the gods will see you."

Eirik clenched his small fists. His father stood nearly twice as tall as him, but Eirik had begged him not to go easy on him in this practice match. And now here he was cowering because he'd lost his sword and shield, which had been nigh useless in his thin arms anyway.

He pulled himself to his feet behind the longhouse where his father ruled as Jarl of Dalgaard. Stepping around the corner, he faced Arud.

Arud gave him a little nod of respect, a smile playing around his mouth. Then he motioned Eirik forward with the tip of his practice sword.

Eirik strode back to the site of their mock battle, but on the way he snatched up one half of his splintered sword. With a vicious battle cry, he sprang at his father.

Arud easily sidestepped and blocked, but Eirik launched another attack, then another.

"Good," his father said as he worked backward, deflecting and evading Eirik's attacks. But then he bound Eirik's half-sword, twisting it so that the wooden hilt flew out of his hands.

Eirik was once again weaponless and squaring off against his far superior opponent.

"What now?" Arud asked calmly. He lifted his practice sword over his head to deal what would be a death blow in a real battle.

Without thinking, Eirik threw himself forward in a low tumble. He rolled right through his father's spread legs to pop up behind him. He gave a swift kick to the back of his father's knees, causing his legs to crumple. Arud fell forward, landing in a heap. The wooden sword slipped from his grip to spin in the dirt. Arud quickly rolled over, but by the time he was face-up on his back, Eirik had the practice sword in his hand and poised over his father's neck.

"Never give up," his father panted, his face breaking into a wide smile. "Whatever you do, just remember—keep fighting. You are destined for great things, my son."

Suddenly the familiar scent of juniper berry soap surrounded him, and his father's smiling face began to fade. He inhaled, and an image of Laurel's beautiful features floated before his eyes. Her dark hair framed her delicate face, the cream-colored skin flawless and softer than down. Her depthless eyes were close enough to see the little flecks of gold that sparkled in them. Her brows were pulled together in concern, and he tried to tell her not to worry. Those soft, rosy lips were moving, but he couldn't understand what she was saying.

He attempted to lift his hand to brush along her cheek, but fiery pain shot through his arm. He groaned and blinked, more of the hazy fog clearing from his mind.

"Madrena! Alaric!" Laurel was shouting to his friends, but she never took those dark eyes from him.

Light exploded around them, and he squinted against the painful brightness. Then he heard both Madrena and Alaric thank the gods. Their faces appeared over him, next to Laurel's, and he looked between the three of them. Why was everyone acting so strange? And why couldn't he move his left arm?

He tried to sit up but only made it halfway before three sets of hands pushed him back down. Even if they hadn't, his head had spun so violently that he would have fallen backward anyway. He opened his mouth to speak and instead spiraled into a dry coughing fit. Each jerk of his body sent blazing pain through his left arm and right leg.

Laurel held a cup to his lips and he drank several

sips of cool water. "What happened?" he finally managed to croak.

"The village was attacked. You were hit by two arrows," Alaric said.

Eirik tried to sit up again and managed to get to his elbows. "I must get to the battle then. Why are you and Madrena here and not fighting?"

Madrena gave him a strange look. "You've been unconscious for nigh five days, Eirik," she said. "A fever took you, and we all feared you wouldn't pull through."

Eirik exhaled. "Five days?"

Laurel nodded. Was his sight deceiving him, or were her eyes shimmering with emotion?

"And the village?"

"Safe and still mostly intact, thanks to Laurel," Alaric replied.

Eirik tilted his head to look at her more fully. "What does that mean?"

"I hid you in the underbrush after you were shot," she said, her eyes locked with his. "Then I ran into the village and raised the alarm."

"She can't wield a weapon to save her life, but she's braver than most warriors I know," Madrena said with a wry smile.

His heart twisted in a not entirely painful way at the revelation of Laurel's bravery. His most recent memories began drifting back to him. He'd been running to the village to alert them of an attack from three approaching longships when he'd been shot. Before that, he'd shared the bed he now lay in with Laurel, touching and tasting and leaving so much more pleasure to be savored. Because he'd asked her to marry him.

He exhaled again and slumped back on the bed, allowing the three of them to fuss over him. Alaric moved to stoke the fire while Madrena fetched more water and Laurel pressed a cool cloth to his brow.

She was still his thrall. Gunvald was still going to sell her in—it couldn't be more than a few sennights now. And he'd wanted to protect her, to secure her freedom through a marriage to him.

But nei, it was more than that. He wasn't simply acting honorably for her benefit, nor was he merely proposing marriage as a way to sidestep his uncle's authority as Jarl.

He looked up into Laurel's beautiful face. He raised his good arm and ran his thumb along the little crease between her delicately arched brows. He would die for this woman. But he wanted naught more than to live for her.

"You never answered me," he said low enough for her ears only.

"What?"

"You never answered me when I asked if you would marry me."

Her eyes widened and he feared he would drown in their dark depths.

"Aye," she breathed.

Now it was his turn to stare wide-eyed at her. He'd expected her to discuss it with him, to ask to think it over. But judging from the welling tears in her eyes and the small smile that was beginning to part those full, soft

lips, she'd done enough thinking already. She was sure—
he could see it in those dark, shimmering pools.

He cupped one of her downy-soft cheeks and pulled
her gently toward him. As her lips brushed his, he felt a
surge of pure energy jolt through him. How could he
have fought this for so long? The lust between them was
undeniable. But that lust had deepened to something
much more. He admired her strength, respected her
willingness to work hard, and was in awe of her
quick mind.

He parted his lips slightly and deepened their kiss.
His tongue caressed hers slowly, savoring the feeling of
life coursing through his veins once more. Was it possible? Did he love Laurel?

He'd never used the word for his encounters with
other women. Those times were always enjoyable,
comforting even, but not based on deeper emotion. Of
course he loved his father, Alaric and Madrena, the gods
—but this utlending woman, his thrall by law?

He shifted his hand to the nape of her neck, letting
his fingers slide through her chestnut hair. Her mouth
was so warm and wet, her tongue and lips so soft. She
sighed against his mouth, her scent, of juniper berries
and her intoxicating, warm skin, surrounding him.

He loved her.

Alaric coughed loudly on the other side of his
cottage, shattering their dreamlike moment.

"You should probably rest, Eirik," Alaric said. Eirik
shot him a dark look over Laurel's shoulder, which
brought a raised eyebrow and a quirked grin to his
friend's face.

"Madrena," Eirik said loudly. "Would you mind opening the chest at the foot of the bed for me?"

Madrena set down the half-full bucket of water she'd been pouring into the cauldron over the fire. She gave Eirik a quizzical look as she made her way to the foot of the bed.

"What do you need?"

"At the bottom, there is a small package wrapped in cloth."

Laurel pulled back a little and searched his face as Madrena dug through the wooden chest.

"This?" Madrena held up the cloth bundle in one hand.

"Ja. Bring it here." It was an effort to keep his face calm, for keen anticipation pounded in his veins.

Madrena approached the side of the bed where Laurel was perched and handed him the little bundle. He had to release his hold on Laurel's nape and hair to fumble one-handed with the linen wrapping.

As the linen slid away, the firelight fell on the contents inside.

Madrena gasped as she looked down at the finely wrought brooch as it emerged from the wrapping. It was actually more of an elaborate pin, with a circle of gold the size of his palm and a delicate little lance piercing through it to hold it in place against the cloth. The gold flickered in the low light from the kitchen fire. The inlaid pieces of amber along the rim of the circle and in the pin almost glowed.

Alaric strode to the bedside at Madrena's inhale. He too took in the sight of the brooch resting in Eirik's hand, and his bright green eyes shifted to Laurel, widening.

"Your mother's brooch..." Alaric began.

"Then you...you two are to be...married?" Madrena's voice was breathless with shock.

His eyes locked on Madrena and Alaric, waiting for any hint of their reaction beyond simple surprise. Though their condemnation of the union wouldn't stop him, they were the closest thing he had to family—even counting his cousin and uncle. He longed for their approval.

"That's...that's..." Madrena struggled to speak. Eirik held his breath, watching as her brows knit and tears filled her eyes. "That's *wonderful!*"

She fell to Laurel's side and threw an arm around both of them, careful of Eirik's left shoulder. Alaric whooped and slapped his hands together in joy. At their reaction, a strange weight lifted from Eirik's chest. He hadn't realized how much he'd wanted their support, but to have it now made Laurel's acceptance of him that much sweeter.

"Let us share a drink!" Alaric said as he strode to the small wooden cabinet above the cooking area. He removed a clay jug that Eirik recognized as the stock of his finest mead.

With a grunt, he managed to prop himself up to a half-seated position on the bed. He lifted the brooch and held it out to Laurel.

"This was your mother's?" she said quietly as Madrena and Alaric rummaged in the corner for more wooden cups.

"Ja," he replied. "I never knew her, for she died when I was just a babe. But my father gave this to her when he asked to marry her. He always said that she wore it every day from then on. It would have been sent with her to the gods when she died, but she asked my father to keep it until I was ready to pass it on."

His voice grew thicker as he spoke. He hadn't given the brooch much thought in the years that had passed since his father died and left it in his keeping. Now he sent silent thanks to both his mother and father for allowing him to give it to Laurel. This moment was a gift from them and the gods.

She took the brooch into her small hands and traced it with one finger. "'Tis beautiful," she whispered, her voice choked with emotion as well. "I'll wear it forever."

She removed the little pin and held the circle of gold against her chest. Then she threaded the pin through the material of her dress so that it was securely fastened right over her heart.

His heart swelled and his throat grew tight as he gazed at her in the firelight, his family's brooch glinting on her chest.

"To Eirik and Laurel," Alaric said, two cups in his hands as he halted at the bedside. He handed one to Laurel. Madrena also bore a cup, but as Eirik reached for it, she swatted his wrist.

"No mead for you. You get broth until you recover more of your strength." She handed him a steaming bowl that admittedly smelled wonderful.

"I hope you'll at least leave me a drop or two of my own jug. That mead is some of the best in the Northlands," he grumbled as he brought the bowl of broth to his lips.

"We'll make sure to enjoy it for you," Alaric said mischievously. "Besides, I deserve an extra cup or two, since it was my idea that you two should wed."

"Alaric——" Eirik gave a swift jerk of his head to silence his friend.

"What is it?" Laurel asked, looking back and forth between them over the rim of her cup.

Alaric's eyes flickered in understanding. "'Tis only that Eirik was being a blind, stubborn fool. It was clear as day that you two wanted each other," he replied smoothly.

Eirik exhaled slowly. Thank the gods his friend hadn't accidentally told Laurel that a marriage was in some ways strategic. Even though the thought of marriage had originally started as a way to evade Gunvald's decision to sell her, how could he explain now that his reasons were much deeper than that? It was a conversation he wasn't looking forward to, but one that he would need to have—soon. Once the threat of Laurel being sold in Jutland was completely removed, he would tell her. He didn't want to frighten her unnecessarily.

"Clear to an equally blind fool?" Madrena snorted. "What do you know of such matters, brother?"

"More than you, you old piece of leather," Alaric shot back. Madrena punched him hard in the arm. It was true that she wasn't like most other young women her age, Eirik thought as he watched the twins bicker. She'd been slow to take to Laurel, and yet now Madrena seemed protective and even…warm toward her. Apparently Laurel had the ability to soften more than one hardened warrior's heart.

Alaric refilled their cups and Eirik's bowl of broth as they settled into easy conversation. Eirik would have to talk to Alaric and Madrena later about how the village fared beyond their basic assurances that things were mostly intact. And he needed to discuss how his marriage with Laurel would go over with his uncle and cousin. He didn't need more trouble from Grimar, yet he couldn't imagine that he'd be happy. And Gunvald…

Eirik pushed the dark thoughts aside for the time being. He would mull over how his uncle might react to the circumvention of his ruling later. And even if, gods help him, Gunvald held fast in his command that Laurel be sold, Eirik would still marry her and find a way to save her from the slave market.

As the fire receded into coals, Alaric stood and pointedly looked at his sister. "I think we'd best be off," he said. "Eirik doesn't seem to need us anymore."

Madrena stood but shot a narrow-eyed look at both Eirik and Laurel. "I saw that kiss earlier. Don't even *think* about what you are both clearly thinking about. You need to rest, Eirik."

Laurel's dark eyes widened, and Eirik watched with amusement as a rosy blush came to her cheeks and neck. She'd been raised to disavow and look down on all pleasure. He'd have his work cut out for him in showing her just how right, just how wonderful, shared pleasure truly was. He felt a stirring in his blood at the thought. He would prove himself up to the task.

Alaric chuckled and took their cups and Eirik's bowl. Eirik gave Laurel a wink and entwined his fingers with hers, trying to convey the promise in his touch.

As Madrena continued to warn and scold, Alaric shuffled her toward the door.

Once they'd closed the door behind them, the cottage was quiet, yet tense energy vibrated in the air.

Laurel lowered her eyes to their entangled fingers. "What is your people's custom regarding marriage?" she asked softly. Her blush lingered, her skin cream and pink in contrast to the dark lashes resting against her cheeks.

"It is the tradition to have wedding ceremonies on Frigga's Day, which is only three days away, but we might not be able to bring in the *goði* by then." His mind suddenly churned with a combination of antici-pation and apprehension. There was much to do, yet the first step would be to confront his uncle to ensure that he would accept Eirik's plan to free and marry Laurel.

Laurel's eyes fluttered up to him, a look of confusion in her gaze.

"Forgive me," he said. "You have been speaking so well and learning so quickly that I forget sometimes that you are still an utlending. Frigga is the goddess of marriage. Frigga's Day falls once every sennight and is a good day to get married. A *goði* is like a priest. We don't have one in Dalgaard, but there is one only a day's journey from here. He is usually brought in for ceremonies."

"And what is involved in the ceremony?" She still eyed him cautiously, but he hoped with some explanation she would begin to feel more comfortable with the customs of the North.

"Well," Eirik began, thinking back to the last wedding celebration he'd attended. "The bride and groom begin their preparations early on Frigga's Day. They bathe and dress with care. Then they meet the *goði* in a field or under a bower of trees."

"Outdoors? It doesn't happen in a church or…or a temple of some sort?"

"Nei, for the couple wishes to be as close to the gods as possible, without rooves and walls getting in the way," Eirik said, brushing a strand of chestnut hair from her face and tucking it behind one ear. "A marriage union is about the joining of two lives, two families, and about creating a new family. We want the gods and goddesses of fertility, abundance, fair weather, and bounty to see us clearly."

She swallowed but nodded for him to go on.

"Then we will place both of our hands on my father's sword, which was his father's before him, and pledge in the sight of the priest and the gods that our lives are forever intertwined, that we will carry on the honor of our families and pass it to the next generation."

Her gaze faltered and she lowered her eyes once more. "I cannot speak to my family's honor or what I can pass down from them," she said quietly.

He took her chin in his hand and lifted it gently. "That is not so unusual, Laurel. In fact, some Northmen know their families quite well and exclude them from their marriage pledges intentionally. The most important thing is that we are forming a *new* union. The honor of the future can still be determined."

His eyes dropped to the brooch on her chest. It rose and fell gently with her breath. "I should have saved that as a morning-gift, but I was too impatient," he said with a soft smile.

"What is a morning-gift?" Her brief sadness seemed to be passing already. She truly was suited to the North-men's way of life.

"It is the gift that a new husband gives his new wife. It symbolizes their...physical union," he said, reaching up to trace the circled gold with one finger. "And it is the first of many gifts that passes between husband and wife."

Her eyes dipped to where his finger played along the brooch's edge. Then he grasped the pin between his thumb and forefinger and slid it out. He readjusted the pin so that it went through the center of the circle.

Her eyes widened and darted to his face. Though she was innocent, she apparently understood the sexual implication of the brooch, and of the practice of giving a morning-gift after a night of consummating the marriage. His blood stirred between his legs at the look of surprised comprehension she was giving him.

"I couldn't wait to see it on you," he breathed, his fingers still playing along the golden brooch. Her eyes slid closed and she leaned almost imperceptibly into his touch. He brought his hand closer so that as his fingers traced the brooch, his palm brushed against the swell of her breast.

Her soft lips parted on a little exhale at the contact.

His blood pounded hotter to know that even a light touch could bring such a passionate response from her. It was as if the gods had made them each perfectly suited for the other, so intense was their desire when they loosened the reins on their control.

He pressed his hand closer, making their contact more firm. She moved against his palm, already longing for more.

He attempted to raise his other hand to her breast, but a sharp twinge of pain in his left shoulder halted him. He gritted his teeth against a groan, but the sound escaped.

"Are you well? What is it?" Laurel said, her eyes flying open. The worried crease between her brows returned as she searched him.

"'Tis naught," he said, the pain already fading.

"Madrena was right," Laurel said as she stood. She looked down at where he lay half-propped against the wooden headboard. "You need to rest and heal. I am ashamed that I—"

He caught her wrist before she could spin away in embarrassment.

"Nei, Laurel, don't," he whispered. "I want you so badly. I've wanted you since the moment I saw you."

Her wrist stilled in his hand, though she remained half-turned away.

"I tried to keep myself from wanting you, first by reminding myself that you were Grimar's thrall, and then when you became my own thrall. Desiring you went against everything I believed in—it threw the matter of my honor in my face."

She tilted her head, listening.

"But I was weak. I let myself kiss you that first night after the council meeting. I told myself it would be just one kiss. But then at the lake, I wanted to take you, to make you *mine* as a woman, not as a thrall. I succumbed to my own weakness again. And before I was shot——"

He swallowed at the memory of her taste, her wetness, the sounds of her ecstasy as she writhed in pleasure under his fingers and tongue. "That night, I hoped you'd forgive my weakness and accept me anyway. So you see, I've always been weak around you. Tonight is no different, except that I only have to fight the pain in my limbs rather than the pain of wanting you so much and denying myself."

To his surprise, she turned on him with a small smile playing around the corners of her mouth. "That was a clever speech," she said. Then she sobered slightly. "But are you sure you're well enough to——"

He gave her wrist a sudden yank so that she tumbled down onto the bed next to him. "I'm still plenty strong," he said, rolling slightly so that he pressed into her. She squeaked in surprise, but then he captured her lips in a kiss. He kept it light so that she could turn away if she wished. But to his pleasure, she pulled his neck down so that their lips were molded together more firmly.

He propped himself up on his good arm so that his elbow took most of his weight. He inhaled and was rewarded with the intoxicating scent of her skin and hair mixed with the traditional Northland juniper soap.

He needed to taste her, to fill his senses with her until the dull pain in his shoulder and leg faded away. He flicked his tongue against her lips, asking entrance. She granted it with a sigh of pleasure that sent his cock pulsing. There was indeed plenty of strength and life left in him. In fact, the hot need coursing through his veins made his pain seem distant.

As his tongue came in contact with hers, he experimentally tried to lift his left arm again. Pain still stabbed him, but it was less now, and the stiffness in his shoulder was ebbing. He moved his hand so that it rested against her ribs, just below her breasts.

He could feel her breath growing shallow against his hand as their tongues swirled and caressed each other. He let his hand inch upward slowly, feeling each delicate rib on her inhalations. By the time the edge of his hand had reached the soft swell of one breast, she was panting against his lips.

He luxuriated in the contours of her breast, letting his fingers explore even while he kept his wounded shoulder relatively immobile. Even through the wool of her overdress and the linen of her shift, he could feel her nipple hardening into a bud as he moved. He remembered just how sensitive she was there, and he almost lost his patience and the silent vow he'd made to himself to make this first time between them, her first time ever, slow and memorable.

She arched against his hand, silently demanding more than simple exploration from his fingers. He moved up slightly to unfasten one of the silver pins holding the shoulder strap of her overdress. When the task was done, he pushed the woolen dress down so that only her shift stood between her breast and his hand.

As his fingers circled once more, this time with less material between them, she moaned into his mouth. Her nipple was a tight bead now, one that was shooting pleasure throughout her body, if her arching and soft moans were any indication. He realized with a start that he'd never seen her fully naked yet. That would be remedied this night.

At the thought, his cock throbbed nigh-painfully against his linen pants. Though someone, likely Alaric, had done him the favor of removing his torn and bloody clothes and re-dressing him in a fresh tunic and pants, Eirik nevertheless wanted to curse the act, for he wanted naught more than to be rid of his clothes. He longed to feel Laurel's bare skin against his, to feel their heat and sweat mingling, to bury himself deep within her.

Something that sounded close to a growl escaped his throat. His cock was now straining against his pants. Laurel's hip was nestled along his pelvis so that with each one of her little shifts and twitches, she rubbed his length in unconscious seduction.

He matched the motions of his tongue to how he had licked and caressed her sex five nights ago. She moaned again, and her leg drifted up to brush the outside of his left thigh in invitation. He moved his sore arm down so that he could cup her sex in his hand. He could feel how hot and wet it was even through her shift. She ground herself against his hand.

"Do you remember what my fingers felt like?" he breathed against her lips. She nodded, her eyes fluttering over him. They were almost black in the dim light from the embers.

"And do you remember what my tongue felt like?" She moaned as her eyes closed again and her body arched against his cupping hand.

"Do you want more?"

She sank her teeth into her bottom lip as her hips moved in a little circle, pressing into both his hand and his aching cock.

"Aye," she panted.

"I need to see you."

Her eyes fluttered open again, and a glimmer of confusion shone through the hungry desire. He tried to move his hurt arm across their bodies to undo her other shoulder strap, but he halted halfway, wincing in pain. She made a sound of understanding and gave him a little nudge backward so that he was partially propped up on the bed's headboard once more. Then she stood from the bed and gazed down at him.

With her eyes locked on his, she reached for the other pin holding her shoulder strap. She unfastened it and pulled the woolen overdress down the length of her body. As the fabric bunched and slid, he was treated to the view of first her curving breasts, then her narrow waist, and finally her gently flaring hips before the material fell lifeless to the floor.

With the still-smoldering embers behind her, he could faintly make out her rosy nipples and the dark hair between her legs as she stood before him in her shift. She bent for a moment to clasp the hem. Then slowly, one inch at a time, her skin was exposed to his eyes.

He held his breath as the shift brushed past her calves, then her knees. Her thighs glowed red-gold in the light of the embers. The hem hugged her shapely hips for a moment before sliding past them. His gaze was riveted on the apex of her legs for one breath, erotic thoughts of touching, tasting, delving into her there roaring through his mind.

Her arms drew over her head and her flat, smooth stomach came into view. Then the faint shadows underneath her breasts appeared. The linen shift whispered over the swells of her breasts, snagging for the briefest moment on her hard nipples. Suddenly her hair cascaded down around her shoulders as her head came free of the shift.

Eirik's head spun as he gazed at her hungrily. He was greedy for the sight of her. Every inch of her pale skin, warmed by the light of the dying fire, captivated him. His stomach clenched in anticipation of what they were about to share.

He reached for his tunic but had to stop when his left shoulder twinged in pain. "Will you help me?"

She stepped forward and leaned over him, her breasts coming closer to his face. Her hair spilled over one shoulder and tickled his chest. Her fingers reached for his tunic and brushed his swollen cock. He sucked in a breath at the contact.

"Did I hurt you?" she asked, freezing.

"Nei," he bit out. "Well, ja, actually. You torture me with your beauty, Laurel. And your touch is driving me to the brink of madness."

She blinked at him, but then a little smile played at the corners of her mouth. "That sounds terrible. Do you wish me to stop?"

"Nei," he groaned. Leave it to the ever-serious Laurel to tease and find humor in a moment like this. As she eased his tunic up his torso and over his good shoulder, he added, "You, too, know something of this wondrous torture, don't you?"

She blushed and the smile spread on her face. "Aye, I am feeling it now."

She slipped the tunic over his head and then carefully worked it down his injured shoulder and arm. She stood back for a moment, her dark eyes riveted on his bare chest. His cock pulsed under her gaze. He was glad his form gave her as much pleasure as hers gave him.

Her hands skimmed over his chest and along his ridged stomach. He held his breath and gritted his teeth at her feather-light touch. He wanted more contact, but he had to give her time to explore and test her instincts.

Her fingers stopped at the top of his linen pants, and he had to bite back a curse at the proximity to his needy cock. She slowly undid the tie there and parted the material slightly. As she eased the pants down his hips, he clenched his jaw, his cock rubbing against the linen.

Suddenly his cock sprang free and she gasped as he groaned at the abrupt freedom. But then his eyes flickered down to her and the ache deepened, for her gaze was locked on his manhood, her lips parted in surprise. She unconsciously licked her lips, and he wondered for the first time in his life if it was possible for a man to lose his seed without even being touched.

There was so much he wanted to do with her, so much he wanted to show her. But they had time, he reminded himself. This was only the first of many nights of pleasure.

"Lift, please," she said as the pants got stuck against the bed. Using his good leg as a support, he thrust his hips upward. It didn't help him maintain his hold on the need pounding through his veins in the least.

She eased the linen over his wounded leg and he had to hold his breath again to keep the pain at bay. All this moving was difficult, even with the haze of lust settled over his limbs. He felt his first flicker of doubt about whether he should be engaging in these intimacies with Laurel. What if the pain was too great? Could he even move properly to bring them both pleasure?

Then a new idea came to him, filling his mind with erotic images.

"I don't think I can...take you on your back," he said.

Her gaze flickered between his eyes and his rigid cock, which was standing up from between his legs.

Her eyes widened. "But how else..." Even in the low light, her deep blush was visible.

He took her wrist and gently drew her back down so that she sat on the edge of the bed facing him. He let his hands skim over her skin, brushing her shoulders and down her arms, feathering his fingers along her back. She shivered and closed her eyes.

"There are many ways, Laurel," he breathed, his palms sweeping against her nipples. He moved lower to trace his fingertips down her stomach. Then he wrapped his hands around her hips. He lifted her slightly and guided her over him. To accommodate his movement, she had to lift one of her legs over his hips to avoid his wounded thigh.

"Oh," she gasped as it became clear to her what he was doing. She now straddled him, with his erect cock jutting between them.

Before she could blush in embarrassment again, he reached between her legs and brushed the damp seam of her sex. She gasped again at the contact and unconsciously parted her legs a little more around his hips.

"You're so wet for me," he gritted. He parted her folds and found that pulsing spot of a woman's pleasure. She moaned and her head fell back. To keep herself upright, she propped her hands on his chest. As he slowly circled his finger against her clitoris, her hands turned into talons, clawing at his chest and stomach. He reveled in the sensation, knowing that his touch drove her mindless with pleasure.

He doubted she realized it, but her hips were beginning to twitch and shift. Clenching his stomach, he pulled himself close enough to flick his tongue over one beaded nipple. She jerked and arched at the contact. He licked again and this time was rewarded with a roll of her hips against his hand.

"That's it," he breathed. She was finding her rhythm, letting her instincts drive her toward pleasure. Given how she was raised, he was awe-struck by the well of passion deep within her. It was as if they had been meant to share their bodies, their desires, their pleasures, all along.

He lowered himself back so that he was half-propped against the headboard once more. He returned his hands to her hips, grasping her hard, letting his fingers dig into her yielding flesh. He shifted her slightly forward so that her sex pinned his manhood to his lower stomach. Then he slid her wet folds up the length of his cock.

This time he didn't manage to repress the curse that rose to his lips. The feel of her warm sex, its wetness gliding along him, the sight of her straddling him—it was all too much. He nearly lost himself after that one touch.

He guided her down and back up his length, feasting his eyes on her high, round breasts, her spread legs, and the folds of her sex as they slid along his cock.

She was panting hard, her hips beginning to move of their own accord. He couldn't take any more of this exquisite agony.

"I need you—now," he growled. He clutched her hips and lifted her off his length long enough to position his cock at the entrance of her sex. She inhaled as the tip of his manhood found her opening. He froze, his fingers digging into her hips.

Laurel's eyes fluttered open and found his at his sudden halt. Though their dark depths were hazy with passion, he saw a flicker of clarity cross them. She gave him a little nod.

With all his control, he moved an inch inside her. He clenched his teeth against the nigh-overpowering urge to thrust all the way in. Her wetness allowed him to glide another hair's breadth, but she was so tight. This was going to hurt her, but he swore to himself that he would give her pleasure once the necessary pain had passed.

In one swift movement, he pulled down on her hips, thrusting himself fully inside her. He heard himself groan in ecstasy, but the noise was drowned out by her own cry. He forced himself to loosen his grip on her hips so that she could pull back slightly to ease the pain.

"I'm sorry, Laurel," he bit out. "The pain will soon be gone."

He thrust into her once more, the tightness nearly driving him mad. She slumped forward over his chest, her arms going limp. A sound that was a cross between a moan of pleasure and a whimper escaped her. He strained his neck forward so that he could capture one of her nipples in his mouth, laving it.

Her hips twitched slightly, so he withdrew and re-entered her again. This time, with his cock buried inside her and his tongue laving her nipple, the sound she made was more pleasure than pain. With each one of his slow thrusts and flicks of his tongue, her breathing increased and her back arched a little more.

At last, he felt the telltale roll of her hips. She wanted more. She began matching his rhythm, meeting his thrusts and arching into him. He struggled not to lose himself. Not yet. Not until he heard her cries of pleasure, felt her pulse around him.

He moved his mouth to her other breast, giving it the same attention as the first. Now her fingers were once again digging into his flesh as their bodies pulsed and drove together. Her dark hair spilled all around him like a veil, surrounding him with her scent.

He wasn't going to make it. It was all too much. Just as

he felt his control slipping, her breath hitched and caught in her throat. Her fingers flexed and clawed reflexively and her back arched even more. A wordless cry of ecstasy rose from her throat, and she squeezed around his cock.

His last thread of control shredded in an instant. He bellowed out his own pleasure as wave upon wave of sensation crashed over him. He felt himself erupt deep within her, spending himself. As he spiraled down through the pleasure, their breaths mingled.

He slowed their rhythm but stayed buried within her until the last quakes of ecstasy had finally faded. She slumped all the way down onto his chest, fully spent. He gently eased her to his side so that he could tuck her under his good shoulder.

"I am no longer a maiden," Laurel said quietly after a long silence, her voice unreadable.

"Nei, you are not." He looked down at her for a hint of her emotions, but her face was obscured against his chest.

"I am going to be a wife."

"Does that please you, Laurel?" he asked, suddenly fearing that she was having regrets. "Do...do *I* please you?"

She lifted her head so that he could fully see her face. Tears shone in her eyes, but they were tears of happiness.

"Oh, aye," she said, her face splitting into a smile more radiant than the sun.

He pulled her to him and kissed her until they were both laughing against the other's lips. She settled her head back onto his chest and sighed contentedly. Soon her breaths fell into the easy rhythm of sleep.

Eirik forced himself to stay awake. Though sleep called, he didn't want to miss any of this moment. He was going to be married to the strong, smart, good woman lying next to him. And it wasn't an arranged marriage, as he'd always expected to be wrangled into some day. This was a marriage of—was there any other word for it than love? Nei, he loved Laurel. A powerful surge went through him at the acknowledgment. When she woke, he'd tell her. Then he'd speak with his uncle and make sure Laurel's fate was safe. After that he'd have to see about getting the *goði* down from the mountains by Frigga's Day.

His mind swirled with the happy tasks ahead of him. Finally, he'd found a way to free her from thralldom, protect her from the schemes of Grimar and Gunvald, and do right by his sense of honor. He could rest at last.

22

Grimar stumbled out of the longhouse and toward a clump of nearby shrubs. He fumbled impatiently with the ties on his pants. He'd already drunk several horns of ale, and the liquid was nigh bursting inside him.

As he finished relieving himself in the shrubs, he heard a pair of voices coming toward him. He stuffed himself back into his pants and quickly retied them. As he listened, he could make out the voices of a man and a woman. Had he fallen upon a nighttime tryst, perhaps? If the lovers wanted darkness, they'd only have another hour or so of blue light before the sun rose again.

He listened closer from the cover of the shrubs.

"...surprised you're as happy as you are, sister," the man said.

Grimar cursed under his breath. No illicit love-making to spy on after all. Just a brother and sister.

"I know I was against it at first, but she's more than proven herself worthy," the woman replied.

Grimar's mood darkened further. Not just any brother and sister pair. Those voices belonged to Alaric and Madrena, his cousin's favorite toadies.

"Ja, she has. Mayhap this will finally put an end to Eirik's strange behavior of late," Alaric said. The two were almost level with the shrubs behind which Grimar crouched.

Madrena snorted. "Mayhap. Though I doubt he'll want to return to his old ways once he's married."

A cold stone sank in Grimar's stomach. Married? Eirik? They couldn't be speaking of anyone else other than the thrall girl, either. He had to bring a fist to his mouth to keep himself from cursing.

"Ja, you may be right. With Laurel under his roof, he may never want to leave again." Dimly, Grimar recognized the notes of sadness and frustration in Alaric's voice, but he couldn't think on that now. His head swirled with a mixture of ale and this new information.

Eirik was going to marry Laurel. Grimar forced his mind to reason out why. If Eirik married Laurel, she would no longer be a thrall. So Eirik was trying to defy his father's ruling that the girl be sold.

But if she stayed in the village—and especially if she became his wife—Eirik would remain here, too. As those cursed twins had said, he would no longer be distracted by the desire to explore and raid in the lands to the west.

So much for Gunvald's plan to remove Eirik's distraction and return things to the way they had been before their voyage westward—with Grimar poised for the Jarlship and Eirik preoccupied. His father was a fool. Thank the gods Grimar had taken matters into his own hands.

Worse, though, if Eirik were willing to circumvent Gunvald on his decision to have Laurel sold, what else— or *who* else—would he challenge?

Madrena and Alaric's voices faded as they passed the longhouse and moved deeper into the village. As Grimar rose from his crouch, he felt the tip of a blade press into his back. He sucked in his breath as the blade nudged slightly deeper into his cloak.

"Jarl Thorsten still awaits payment."

The voice behind him was little more than a whisper, but Grimar spun and clamped a hand over the man's mouth.

"Do you wish to draw attention to yourself, fool?" Grimar hissed at Thorsten's henchman. He grabbed the man's arm and dragged him farther away from the longhouse and into the shadowy trees closer to the rocky mountain walls.

Once they were fully concealed and well out of earshot of anyone in the village, Grimar rounded on the man. "And why does Jarl Thorsten think he still deserves payment after failing in the task I gave him? My cousin lives!"

"We attacked as you asked," the man replied, his eyes narrowing on Grimar. "We spotted the solitary hut further up the fjord and even saw a figure emerge from it. One of our archers sent two arrows into him. We saw him fall. If the man you wished to have killed still lives, perhaps the fault is yours, not Jarl Thorsten's."

Grimar had to clench his fists to prevent from striking the man for his insolence. Nevertheless, the warrior before him was taller and broader and still held a seax in his hand. He needed to cool his temper lest he do something foolish.

"Are you going to pay, or do I need to extract payment from you?" the man said lowly. The seax glinted in the bluish light.

Grimar suppressed a wince. He'd skimmed several dozen gold coins from his father's store of loot, but it still wasn't enough to pay Jarl Thorsten their agreed amount for killing Eirik and covering it with the appearance of a feuding neighbor's raid.

Like a bolt of lightning, a thought struck Grimar.

"I can give you something of far more value than the price I promised your Jarl," he said, the idea taking hold.

The man eyed him. "The Jarl did not authorize me to negotiate, only to collect what was agreed upon."

"But what I am offering is far better," Grimar replied, a smile spreading on his face. "There is a thrall sheltered not far from here. She is young and innocent. She'll fetch triple the price I owe Jarl Thorsten at the slave market in Jutland, if not more—unless your Jarl decides to keep her for himself."

The hulking man grazed his thumb along the sharp edge of his seax. Grimar held his breath, praying to the gods that his plan would work. Finally, the warrior nodded.

"Where is she?"

"I'll take you to her. She's in my cousin's remote hut. Don't enter, for I am still not sure what his condition is, and you'll not want to face him lest he overpower you."

The warrior stiffened and bared his teeth, but Grimar rushed on. "Besides, it will be best for you to remain unseen. Simply wait for her to emerge from the hut and take her."

The man nodded and motioned for Grimar to lead the way. As he wound his way toward the path leading to Eirik's hut, he had to press his lips together to prevent from laughing in glee.

In one fell swoop, he would rid himself of the thrall girl and pay Jarl Thorsten. No connection could be made to him, either for the attack on Dalgaard or Laurel's disappearance. And he would thwart his cousin's effort to circumvent the decision to sell the girl on the slave market.

With the girl gone and Eirik wounded, no one, not even his father, could stop him from taking the Jarlship now.

23

Laurel stirred and blinked her eyes open. Her head still rested on Eirik's chest, which rose and fell peacefully. She lifted her head, careful not to disturb him, and glanced around the cottage. The fire had now completely gone out, but sunlight streamed in around the edges of the furs covering the windows. It was hard to tell what time it was this far north, but she guessed that it had only been a few hours since she'd fallen asleep.

The memories of what she and Eirik had just shared came flooding back. Her skin heated, but not in embarrassment. Nay, their union had been powerful, emotional, and passionate, but not shameful.

And now she was to become his wife, and he her husband. She felt the last threads of her old life, the one filled with loneliness, self-denial, and shame snap and fall away. She no longer had to listen to Abbess Hilda call her very existence a sin and punishment. She no longer had to duck her head and bite her tongue. For she would now truly be free. Free to love Eirik, free to learn and work and hold her head level.

She sat up and felt a twinge between her legs. It was yet another reminder that her old self was gone. She stood quietly and scooped up her shift. As she slipped it down her body, she gazed at Eirik. He was still naked, with only a fur pulled loosely across half his body. His wounds were no longer an angry red color, but instead were scabbed over and dry. His body was so strong, hewn from a lifetime of battles and hard work. She shivered at the memories of both his gentle touches and his rough need when he'd taken her.

As she moved to step over her crumpled dress, the brooch caught her eye. She unfastened it from the dress and studied it again. Never had she seen anything so beautiful. Longing to keep it close, she grabbed a cloak from a peg by the door and pinned the brooch to the inside of it. As the cloak settled around her shoulders, the brooch pressed against her heart, concealed from view. She smiled at the feel of the cool metal through her shift.

She stepped outside quickly, trying to keep the slanting early light from waking Eirik. He needed his rest. Once the door was closed quietly behind her, she went around the cottage to the stream. The water rippled and gurgled happily, matching her mood.

Once she'd seen to her needs in the nearby bushes, she splashed water over her hands and face. The stream water was cold even in midsummer. The air was fresh and full of the scent of plant life, a faint whiff of salty air coming from the fjord behind her. She sighed contentedly, her ears filled with the sounds of the stream.

Suddenly a hand clapped over her mouth while another yanked her head back by her hair. She screamed, but the hand muffled the noise. Her neck twisted painfully, struggling against the hand gripping her hair.

She clawed at her attacker and won a curse from him, but his hold didn't loosen. She raised her heel and brought it down as hard as she could on the top of the man's foot. Then she kicked at his shins.

He lifted her straight up so that her feet flailed in naught but air. Then just as suddenly, he dropped her. She landed on the hard-packed dirt with a whoosh of air. She struggled to inhale even as she tried to scramble to her feet. But the hip and shoulder she'd landed on ached deeply and wouldn't cooperate with her efforts to flee.

Before she could draw a full breath, a rag was thrust into her mouth. She screamed against it but made even less noise than she had with a hand over her mouth. Her attacker tied the gag in place with another rag, then wrenched her arms behind her back. The bite of more bindings cut into her wrists.

She was hoisted in the air once more, this time over her attacker's shoulder. As she was bent and lifted, she caught sight of his unfamiliar face, twisted in a triumphant sneer.

Her mind reeled and she tried to scream again, to flail and dislodge herself from his grip. But it was no use.

Where was this barbarian taking her, and why? Her attacker strode farther away from the cottage, going in the opposite direction from the village. She lifted her head and watched as the cottage and Eirik grew farther and farther away.

∽

Eirik's hand reached for Laurel, but all he found was an empty span of bed next to him. He lifted his head to scan the small cottage for her. She wasn't there.

She must be seeing to her needs outside. He let his head fall back on the bed as he savored the memories from a few hours ago. He was the luckiest man in all the Northlands—nei, in all the lands beyond as well. His eyes trailed lazily along the thatched roof as he waited for her to return. Perhaps she would be naked.

Nei, she was too modest to venture out of the cottage in naught but her skin, despite the fact that they were isolated and away from the village. But mayhap she only wore her shift.

He eased himself up so that he could peer over the edge of the bed. Sure enough, he saw her crumped overdress, but no sign remained of her shift. He smiled, relishing the anticipation of seeing her come back through the cottage's door. Perhaps the early morning light would stream in behind her so that she might as well be naked.

He propped himself up on his good arm. It had been quite a while since he'd noticed her absence. It was strange that she wasn't back yet. His eye caught on the rumpled dress on the floor again. He reached for it and shook it out. But the brooch that had been there the night before was missing.

Something was wrong. He sat up fully but had to pause while his head spun. He hadn't been upright in five days. When his vision cleared, he scanned the cottage once more. Naught was amiss, yet fear snaked through his innards. One of the cloaks by the door was gone as well. Where could she have gone? And why wasn't she back yet?

A dark thought stole over his mind. Nei, she wouldn't have tried to escape. She'd made no effort to do so thus far, and she seemed resigned to her new life here. She was more than resigned—Eirik had thought she was genuinely happy.

"Laurel!" he bellowed, hoping she was nearby enough to hear. But silence was his only answer.

He pressed himself to his feet and immediately fell back to the bed, his wounded thigh stabbing with pain. He cursed his own weakness and stood again, gritting his teeth against the piercing pain radiating from the wound. He dressed quickly and hobbled to the door, barely putting any weight on the bad leg. As he yanked open the door, bright light streamed into the cottage.

He called her name again but got no response. He saw what he thought might be her footprint in the dust along the path leading to the stream, so he dragged his bad leg that way. The stream gurgled cheerily, but Laurel's complete disappearance sent an eerie shadow over the scene.

His gaze swept the area. Naught indicated her presence. Then he glanced down and his heart lurched into his throat.

At his feet in the mud along the stream were two sets of footprints. One was small—clearly Laurel's. But the other was large enough to be a man's. The mud along the stream's bank was churned up as if a struggle had occurred. Then only one set of footprints made a path away from the stream—the man's.

Eirik tried to bolt after the trail of tracks but immediately collapsed. He struggled to his feet once more using his one good leg and arm. He had to reach her somehow. His leg and shoulder screamed at him, but he didn't listen. He hobbled around the front of the cottage and scanned the narrow sliver of land between the mountainsides and the fjord.

In desperation, he turned his gaze in the opposite direction of the tracks, back toward the village. His eyes locked on a flicker of movement on the path.

"You! Halt!" he bellowed, hobbling in the direction of the village. The figure ahead of him froze, but he couldn't make out who it was.

After a long moment, the figure started moving toward him on the path. As he drew closer, Eirik inhaled sharply in recognition.

"Grimar! What are you doing here?"

His cousin's gaze swept over him in assessment. "I was coming to check on you. Your friends told me that your injuries weren't serious, but now I see that they were trying to be kind."

Eirik waved away Grimar's apparent concern. "I can't find Laurel. Have you seen her?"

Grimar's eyes widened and he shook his head slowly. "Nei, cousin, I haven't. She wasn't in the village when I left a few moments ago, and she hasn't passed me on the path."

Eirik cursed and swung his head back in the direction of his hut. "I fear...I fear something has happened. There is a set of large footprints leading away from my cottage."

"Are you sure," Grimar began delicately, "that the girl didn't simply...leave?"

"Nei, she wouldn't do that," Eirik bit out, the memories of her tear-filled eyes as she'd agreed to marry him swirling in his mind.

Eirik exhaled and shoved his hair back with his fingers. He was wasting time. If Grimar said she wasn't in the village, then there was clearly only one other direction to search for her. He needed to find her—now. She was clearly in some sort of danger.

"I'm going after her," he said, racking his brain for a plan.

"Alone?" Grimar said, his brow lowering. "That doesn't seem wise, especially in your condition." Again, his cousin's calculating eyes swept over his nigh-useless shoulder and the leg on which Eirik could barely put any weight.

"I can't wait to form a search party!" Eirik barked. His insides were beginning to coil in panic. The longer he stood here, the farther away Laurel likely was.

"Let me help you, cousin," Grimar said softly, his eyes scanning the ground in thought. "We can leave right now if you wish."

Eirik nodded and turned to head back in the direction of the tracks, but then paused. "Why, Grimar?" he said, glancing over his shoulder at his cousin. "Why are you offering to help me now?"

Grimar hesitated for a heartbeat but then shrugged. "You are kin," he began falteringly. He searched for words for another moment. "Besides, my father said that we would split the profit from selling the girl," he went on more steadily. "If she is gone, then I won't get my cut of the profits from our raid in the west."

Eirik barely suppressed a growl at Grimar's answer. It was like his cousin to only think of profits when Laurel's life was in danger. But he would take any help he could get without having to waste more time going into the village and organizing a party of warriors.

"Come," Grimar urged, taking Eirik's good arm to help him walk faster. "We're wasting time."

Eirik let Grimar help him hobble back toward his hut. He pushed aside the foreboding curling in his innards at Grimar's eagerness to help. He couldn't let himself become distracted. Laurel's life was hanging in the balance.

24

Laurel twisted against the bindings on her wrist to no avail. Her hands ached, both from how tight her assailant had tied the binds and from her struggles against them.

Her eyes scanned the deeper part of the fjord one last time as they sailed out of its mouth and into more open waters. The coastline was still visible to their left, but on the right spanned naught but unfathomable water.

She shivered despite the warm mid-morning sun beating down on their little boat. Her attacker had carried her for what felt like miles but was probably only a few moments' walk away from Eirik's cottage before he cut in toward the fjord. There he'd dumped her into the wooden hull of this small boat and pushed off. The craft was sized to be sailed by only one or two men and was small enough that if she were to stretch out her legs, she'd almost touch his feet where he stood by the tiller.

Other than handling her roughly, he hadn't made any moves to harm her—yet. She silently sent up a prayer for her safekeeping. Mostly he seemed thoroughly occupied in the sailing of their small vessel.

She cursed herself for the thought, for at that moment, he fastened the sail in place and crouched before her. She withdrew her knees into her chest defensively and scooted all the way back into the prow, which was less than a foot behind her.

The man scrutinized her with hazel eyes. His dirty blond hair was braided back from his face and pulled into the topknot that so many Viking warriors seemed to wear. The sides of his head were shaved, giving him an even more imposing appearance.

He was enormous even in a squatted position. He was both tall and broad, built like Eirik, except perhaps even wider and thicker. He wore a seax on his belt and two axes crisscrossed his back.

At least he didn't wear a nasal helm or a heavy coat of chainmail, she thought, trying to calm her terror-stricken mind. Otherwise he'd be not only more intimidating, but nigh impossible to attack should she managed to formulate a plan of escape.

Even as she forced the thought of escape to the front of her mind, her clenched stomach sank in utter dejection. She was in the middle of open waters on a boat with a hulking Viking warrior with no one else in sight. It was hopeless.

The man reached toward her and she flinched back, but her head hit the unyielding wood of the prow.

"Pretty thrall," he said hoarsely. He pinched some of

her hair between his fingers and eyed it. "Pure. And long hair, too. Unusual. You'll fetch a good price at the market, indeed. Unless the Jarl wants you."

Her cries of confusion and outrage were muffled by the gag in her mouth. He sneered at her, but then snorted. "You want to talk, pretty one? We have a long sail ahead of us. I could use the distraction."

He roughly yanked the strip of cloth holding the gag in her mouth from her face. She spat out the filthy rag and coughed, trying to rid the taste from her tongue.

"Why do you have long hair, thrall?" the man asked with a frown.

"My…my master wished it so," she croaked. If this Viking was like the other Northerners in the village, he wouldn't take kindly to the idea that Eirik treated her like a freewoman.

"Humph. But your master left you innocent?" The man's brow furrowed in confusion.

Her mind reeled. Who had told this man that she was a virgin? And what was the correct response to such a question? If she said that she was still an innocent, would she raise his suspicions? A darker fear stabbed through her. Would he see her virginity as an enticement and try to take her himself? Or if she admitted that she was no longer a maiden, would he think that there was no harm in having her as well?

Her thoughts raced back to what he'd said a moment ago—something about how her virginity would fetch a higher price at market. If that was so, then he'd have a reason not to touch her.

"Ja, he did," she said, fumbling for words. "He

was…he was saving me. As a gift. To one of his friends."
For the first time, Eirik's kind and decent treatment of
her was a liability, for she had limited knowledge of how
most Northmen dealt with thralls.

The man nodded dismissively and she had to bite
back a sigh of relief. "Your master's delay is to my Jarl's
benefit," he said with a smirk.

"And…and who is your Jarl?" How much information would she be able to glean from this warrior? She
had to tread cautiously so as not to alert him to what she
was doing.

"You don't recognize the sail?" he said, pointing
upward. She glanced at the pattern of blood-red
diamonds against the white sail and shook her head.
The diamonds looked familiar, but she couldn't place
them in her jumbled mind.

He gave her a quizzical look. "You must be an
utlending. I thought you talked funny as well."

"Ja, I was captured by my master in a faraway land,"
she said diminutively. Perhaps she could lull him into
giving her more information.

The man eyed her skeptically but then nodded. "I
overheard Grimar the Raven boast to Jarl Thorsten of
the lands to the west. Now even the Jarl has caught the
wanderlust and hopes to sail there as well."

Laurel couldn't stop her eyes from widening and her
jaw from growing slack. "Did…did you say *Grimar*? And
Jarl Thorsten?" The Jarl's name drifted back to her from
memory. Madrena had told Alaric that the attack on
Dalgaard had likely come from Thorsten's men. But
Grimar? What was his connection?

Her captor laughed in her face at her dumbfounded expression. "Though you speak our language well, perhaps you are simple-minded," he sneered. "Grimar the Raven requested that we attack your little village. You are the payment to my Jarl for the attack."

Her mind lurched at this revelation. Grimar was in league with their attackers. He was responsible for countless deaths, as well as Eirik's injuries.

"But why?" she breathed aloud. "Why would Grimar wish to attack his own people?"

The man shrugged and leaned back on his heels. "The attack was just a distraction. I overheard him tell my Jarl that he wanted to get rid of some kin of his, someone getting in his way."

Laurel swallowed the cry of horror rising in her throat and forced herself to keep breathing. Grimar had meant for Eirik to be killed. And he'd passed her off into the hands of another Jarl as payment. Her racing mind snagged on the memory of Madrena warning her about Grimar. She'd said that he probably wasn't dangerous, just far too interested in Eirik's health. Now Laurel knew the truth—Grimar was more than dangerous. He was set on murdering his own cousin.

"How...interesting," she managed to choke through her tight throat.

Just then, a flicker of movement caught her eye over the man's shoulder. In the distance behind them, skimming out of the mouth of the fjord, was a small ship. She forced her eyes away and back onto her captor so as not to rouse his suspicion. But another quick glance told her that there was indeed a ship behind them, and it looked to be drawing closer.

Her heart leapt into her throat. Could it be Eirik? She couldn't let herself hope. But if there was any chance of escaping before she was delivered to Jarl Thorsten and either sold or kept as his slave, this was it.

But she had to keep her captor distracted somehow to ensure that he wouldn't turn around and spot the boat's sail as it approached.

"Your Jarl must be a very wise man to look to the west for exploration and raiding," she began.

Something was digging into her back where it pressed against the boat's wooden prow. She shifted slightly to alleviate the pain.

"Ja, he is a great man—far more powerful than the weakling Jarl Gunvald in your master's village," he smirked.

"The lands to the west would certainly reward your Jarl for his efforts," she went on. Her fingers brushed against a jutting piece of iron. Perhaps it was an exposed rivet poking from one of the wooden planks behind her. She ran her fingers around it tentatively and found a rough patch on one of its surfaces.

The man eyed her, and she froze. "What kind of rewards?" he said skeptically.

She relaxed a hair's breadth. "There are many unprotected places called monasteries along the coast in my homeland of Northumbria," she said. She sent up a silent prayer for forgiveness for what she was saying, but if she managed to escape, the Viking before her would

never be able to use the information against her homeland or its people.

"These monasteries are places of worship," she went
on. As she spoke, she eased her hands over the exposed
rivet so that her cloth bindings rested against its raw
edge. "They are filled with treasures reserved for our
God. I'm sure Grimar mentioned all this to Jarl
Thorsten." Ever so slowly, she rubbed the bindings over
the rough-edged rivet.

Her captor snorted. "Grimar the Raven boasted so
much that we laughed at him."

She remembered Grimar's reaction to being
laughed at on the Drakkar. It had almost cost her her
life. "What he spoke of is true," she said, widening her
eyes for effect. "In my land, we believe that God is
praised through the giving of our wealth. Monasteries
like the one I lived in are filled with gold, silver, and
jewels."

She kept her wrists moving ever so slightly back and
forth over the rivet while she spoke. She was rewarded
with the feel of the snapping of a few threads of cloth.
Her eyes fluttered over her captor's shoulder. Without a
doubt, the other ship was gaining on them.

"And are there more treasures like you locked away
in these monasteries," the man said huskily, his eyes
openly perusing her body.

She swallowed hard. She'd thought she was safe
from the lust that now flared in her captor's hazel eyes.
But somehow she'd stumbled into dangerous territory.

"There are women in every land, are there not?" she
said falteringly.

"Pure women? Women for the taking?" He reached out and fingered her hair once more.

"Indeed," she breathed, trying to lean away from his touch while also keeping her wrists in position over the rivet. Another few threads snapped. "Women like me —*valuable* women."

She held her breath, praying that her words reminded the man that he could not touch her. The approaching boat drew closer by the moment. It was almost within shouting distance.

"Ja, valuable." her captor said, leaning back once more with a dark look on his face. But then a sickening smile tugged at his lips. "But we can have a little fun without harming your value, can we not?"

Her stomach squeezed nauseatingly as he reached for her. With one hand, he flicked aside her cloak to expose her shift-clad body more fully. As he did, Eirik's brooch, which was still pinned to the inside of the cloak, brushed against her chest.

His eyes hungrily stared at her. As his other hand moved toward her, the last of the threads holding her wrist bindings popped.

GRIMAR HAD BEEN sure that his plan had crumbled and that he was done in when he'd heard Eirik calling him on the trail back to the village. He'd led Jarl Thorsten's henchman to Eirik's cottage and waited with him in behind a screen of shrubs until the girl had emerged.

He should have left then, but he'd enjoyed watching

the girl struggle uselessly against the giant warrior. He let himself imagine that he was the one yanking her hair, tossing her to the ground, and then throwing her over his shoulder, as he had when he'd first laid eyes on her.

Once he'd watched Thorsten's man and the girl move out of sight, he'd nonchalantly walked along the path back toward the village. Thank the gods Eirik had been so distracted by Laurel's absence and his own wounds that he hadn't questioned Grimar more or challenged the tale that he was merely coming to check on him. Eirik was blinded and made a fool by his attachment to the girl. He deserved the fate Grimar had planned for him.

Though he'd initially wanted to escape Eirik's presence as fast as possible, a plan had begun to form at witnessing just how desperate and impatient Eirik was to find Laurel.

Gunvald had been right to caution Grimar against taking any action against Eirik in the village. The villagers would never believe that Eirik, strong, steady, and capable warrior that he was, would simply meet with an accident in his own cottage. Even Grimar's plan to stage an attack from a neighboring village that left Eirik dead was risky. If Jarl Thorsten ever blabbed about Grimar's hand in arranging the attack, he'd have far worse than mere suspicion to deal with.

Yet Eirik himself provided Grimar the perfect opportunity to end his inconvenient life.

They'd followed the henchman's tracks to a rocky beach along the fjord not far from Eirik's hut. It was clear that Laurel had been taken by water. So Grimar had guided Eirik to a *skute* moored not far from them in the fjord.

Though Grimar couldn't be sure, he'd stake gold on the fact that the *skute* would be faster than whatever craft Thorsten's man had used. For one, the henchman only had himself to sail his boat, while Grimar and Eirik could both maneuver the *skute*. Besides, the *skute* was the lightest, fastest type of ship in all the Northlands, even with one of its sailors hobbled by injuries.

Eirik was only half paying attention to the rigging in his hands, his eyes continually scanning the fjord waters. Grimar smiled inwardly. This was going to be too easy. Even still, he'd decided to wait to kill Eirik until they reached Thorsten's henchman. He'd underestimated his cousin once already. Two arrows hadn't put him down, and he couldn't risk Eirik surviving yet again.

He'd wait until the Jarl's man could help him dispose of Eirik. Then they'd sail on to Jarl Thorsten's holding and Grimar would present the thrall girl as payment himself. Depending on the Jarl's mood, he might even request a portion of her worth in return, considering how much more valuable she was than the debt he owed.

"I see something!" Eirik shouted over his shoulder. He pointed toward a fleck of red against the sea. It could be none other than the henchman's boat.

The two of them fell into motion tying the sail and repositioning the tiller. As the distance between the two ships closed, they worked fluidly side by side. For the briefest of moments, Grimar felt a wistful longing to share more times like these with his cousin.

Grimar inhaled the salty air deeply. "This is how it should be, isn't it, cousin? The two of us out on the sea, ready to kill, to recapture the treasure that is rightfully ours?"

Eirik rounded on him, his face dark with fury. "You relish the fact that Laurel has likely been taken by some spineless attacker? She is not some toy to be passed around, nor is she yours at all. I *love* her."

Grimar's innards twisted in revulsion, but he managed to keep his face placid—barely. His cousin had truly grown weak. He should be ashamed to call himself a Viking. The last traces of consideration for his kin vanished. Eirik had to die—just as his father had.

They were almost on top of the little boat now. Grimar could make out the broad back and shoulders of Jarl Thorsten's man. He returned his gaze to his cousin once more and gave him a little smile.

Bringing his fingers to his lips, he whistled loudly, the sound cutting through the air. The Jarl's henchman spun around and stood, taking in the sight of their *skute* only a stone's throw away from his boat.

"What are you doing?" Eirik bellowed. "We had the element of surprise."

"Oh, cousin," Grimar said with a grin. "You're so like your father. So noble. So trusting."

Grimar nodded toward the henchman. "When we are alongside you, jump onto my boat and help me deal with him," he shouted. The hulking man nodded his comprehension.

"Like your father, you will die a pathetic death at the

hands of your own kin," Grimar went on, turning back to Eirik.

Eirik bared his teeth in a snarl of rage and reached for his hip, but he wore no seax, so rushed had been their departure.

"And like Arud the Steady, you'll die weaponless," Grimar grinned. "Never to reach Valhalla, and never to see Dalgaard again."

Grimar drew his seax. The blade flashed in the sun as it descended toward Eirik's heart.

25

Just as her captor's hand closed on one of her breasts, a loud whistle cut through the air. He jerked his hand away and stood so that he towered over her. He looked down on her for a moment with a leer before turning to the other boat, which was nearly on top of them.

Her breath left her in a whoosh. Her relief at her captor's distraction swelled through her even as her heart crumpled. She'd pinned her hopes on keeping the presence of the other boat from him, praying that it was someone—anyone—willing to help and who would catch her captor off-guard.

But then a familiar voice floated to her ears. If she'd been breathless a moment ago, now her lungs and heart froze in her chest completely.

Grimar.

Through ringing ears, she vaguely comprehended that Grimar was ordering her captor to board the newly arrived boat and help him deal with something. Nay, not something—*someone*.

She glanced up from her cowering position in the prow. Her captor's back was still to her as he waited for the boat to draw nearer. He'd all but forgotten her, discarding her as a nonthreat.

Slowly, she eased her aching hands from behind her back. The shredded bindings fell away, but her hands were stiff and slightly discolored. She squeezed them into fists and released them over and over until she could trust that she would be able to use them.

She glanced around the small boat, but there was naught she could use against her captor. Her cloak shifted around her shoulders and the brooch brushed her chest.

Before the idea was fully formed, she unfastened the little lance holding the gold circle to the inside of her cloak. She caught the circle as it slipped from the material and placed it silently on the wooden boards below her.

Just as silently, she stood and stepped closer to her captor's back, the long pin clenched in one aching hand. Around his hulking frame, she caught sight of the other boat. It was nearly alongside them now. Her captor put one foot on the gunwale, preparing to launch himself onto Grimar's vessel.

But then her eyes fell on the other person in the boat beside Grimar. It was Eirik. Before she had time to scream a warning, Grimar unsheathed the seax at his belt and raised it over Eirik.

Eirik twisted out of the way just in time to avoid the

blade sinking into his chest. But the seax nevertheless glanced across his left arm, just below his already wounded shoulder. He roared in pain and rage.

"Help me with him!" Grimar shouted to her captor as he raised the seax once again.

Without thinking, Laurel drew back her hand and drove the brooch's pin as hard as she could into the side of her captor's neck.

The man twitched at the impact and reached a hand to his neck in confusion. As he withdrew the little golden lance, a fountain of blood erupted from his neck. He bellowed and rounded on her. One hand clutched wildly at the gash in his neck while he brought his other hand back and swung at Laurel.

He leveled her with a powerful blow to her head. The force of it sent her flying. Her legs rammed into the boat's side and she went tumbling over the gunwale and into the water.

The cold water was like a second blow. She hadn't had time to take a breath before flying overboard, and now she struggled and flailed toward the surface. The old panic surged through her at being stranded and helpless in the vast waters beyond the fjord. She clawed and fought against the water's icy fingers, which drew her down even as her lungs screamed for air.

Somewhere deep in her mind, she heard Eirik's voice, calm and reassuring.

If you fight the water, it will fight you.

She brought her clawing fingers together to form an oar-like shape, as Eirik had taught her. Kicking with

278

both her legs and stroking with her arms, she drove herself toward the surface. As she broke into the air and took a huge breath, she kept her legs kicking and her arms and hands slicing through the water like paddles.

She looked up and saw the two boats several feet away. They were now touching, but her captor still remained on his original vessel. Blood was everywhere. The hand clutching his neck was almost invisible beneath the waterfall of blood pouring from his wound. He stumbled and tried to right himself but only tripped on his own feet. His knees caught the gunwale, and he went tumbling overboard into the water next to her.

She stroked and kicked frantically away from where he went splashing into the water, but a moment later his head emerged mere feet away from her. He sputtered and thrashed as he tried to keep his head above water, but he seemed to be losing control of his limbs as the blood continued to spurt from his neck and into the water.

He gurgled something incomprehensible and reached for her even as his head dipped below the surface. His arms grazed her and she screamed in terror. She threw herself out of his grasp as he continued to sink.

But just when she thought she was safe, a yank on her cloak dragged her underwater. Her captor clutched the bottom of her cloak even as he drifted deeper. She surged up with all her might, but she would never be able to pull both her weight and his up to reach the surface again.

Her hands, aching and stiff from the bindings and the icy water, fumbled with the cloak's ties at her neck. The water drew even colder as she continued to be dragged down. With her last remaining strength, she pulled as hard as she could on the ties. As they popped, she instantly felt the weight of her captor vanish. She floated, suspended deep in the cold water.

She pushed her arms up and drew them to her sides as she kicked her burning legs. She let the water buoy her even as she paddled toward the surface. Dark spots swam before her closed eyes. The last of her breath escaped in bubbles past her face.

Suddenly she erupted through the water's surface and into the life-saving air. She inhaled hard as if it were the first breath she'd ever taken.

"Laurel!" Eirik's desperate cry came from Grimar's boat. God be praised, he was still alive!

"Eirik!" she sputtered between gulps of precious air.

"Hang on!"

She still couldn't see him, but she had to trust that he would survive and pull her to safety. Both boats' sides rose too high out of the water for her to climb up them herself. He would make it, she told herself over and over again as she kept her head above water. He would make it.

Just then a scream of pain tore the air. Her own terrified cry joined it. "Eirik!"

BLOOD DRIPPED down his left arm from Grimar's first

stab. If Eirik hadn't thrown himself sideways at the last moment, he'd have Grimar's seax buried deep in his chest now. Eirik backed away from Grimar's blade, but all too soon his heels bumped into the small boat's prow. He was cornered.

"Help me with him!" Grimar shouted to the man in the other boat.

Eirik's eyes jerked to the large warrior, but a flicker of movement behind the man drew his attention. Before he could shout a warning to Laurel, she stabbed the giant in the neck. A second later, he heard her scream and splash into the water.

He turned his attention back to Grimar, begging the gods to aid Laurel while he was locked in combat with his cousin.

Grimar's eyes darted from Eirik to his henchman, who was stumbling wildly and bleeding profusely. The giant warrior tumbled overboard, giving Eirik the briefest moment of distraction he needed.

He lunged at Grimar, planting his good shoulder into his chest. At the impact, the seax clattered to the boat's deck. The two of them landed in a heap, with Grimar's body absorbing most of the impact. Eirik pinned him with his weight, fumbling to secure his arms.

But Grimar evaded him and fisted one of his hands, driving it into Eirik's wounded shoulder. Eirik bellowed in pain and was forced to roll off to the side.

Grimar scrambled past where he lay prone and clawed his way toward the seax. Weapon in hand once more, Grimar spun and began stalking toward Eirik.

Through the haze of pain blurring his thoughts,

Eirik remembered the Hnefatafl game he used to play with his father and that he now played with Alaric. He'd been outnumbered, but Laurel had leveled the odds, giving him a chance. He was outarmed, with naught to use against Grimar's seax other than his own two hands. But he was not outmaneuvered.

He dragged himself to his feet and scrambled the few steps to the thick wooden mast in the middle of the boat. He positioned himself so that the mast stood between him and Grimar. Grimar smiled faintly as he bore down on him. When he was within striking distance, Grimar thrust the seax at his good shoulder, knowing he couldn't defend himself with his wounded left arm.

But Eirik ducked around the mast just in time to evade the stab. Grimar quickly thrust again, this time on the other side. Eirik was ready for him. He grabbed Grimar's wrist with both hands and spun around so that he had Grimar's arm pinned against the mast. With one quick shove, Eirik heard the snap and Grimar's anguished scream, letting him know he'd broken the arm.

The seax fell to the deck once more, but this time, as Grimar scrambled back, holding his broken arm, Eirik leaned down and retrieved the weapon. Grimar's eyes widened as Eirik pointed the blade toward him. With a flick of the wrist, Eirik tossed the seax into the water.

"You're an even greater fool than I thought," Grimar breathed, still clutching his arm.

"Nei," Eirik panted. "I am a man of honor. And no

matter what happens to me in this lifetime, the gods see everything."

Grimar's pale eyes flickered with something close to fear, but it was quickly replaced with bloodlust. He bellowed a war cry and lunged at Eirik, slamming into him. Grimar drove Eirik all the way into the boat's high siding. Eirik's back rammed into the gunwale and the breath was forced from his lungs. Grimar clamped a hand over Eirik's neck, squeezing as hard as he could.

The strength in Grimar's grip wrenched Eirik's head and neck backward over the water. His back arched over the gunwale, sending shooting pain through his whole body.

Just then Eirik heard a splash and desperate gasps on the other side of the boat.

"Laurel!" he rasped, using some of the precious air he had left.

She called to him frantically. "Hang on!" he wheezed, using the last of his air.

He'd been trying to pry Grimar's hand away with his own, to no avail. In that moment, he released his hold on Grimar and jammed both of his thumbs in Grimar's cold, pale eyes. Grimar screamed in agony as blood swelled around Eirik's thumbs.

Grimar's grip loosened as he fell backward. But Eirik held fast to his head, his thumbs still burrowing into Grimar's eye sockets. When Grimar was fully laid out on the deck, Eirik released him and took hold of his neck. Grimar gurgled and thrashed against Eirik's hold, but Eirik's weight was too much. He tried once more to strike Eirik's wounds, but his flailing limbs couldn't find purchase.

Eirik leaned into his hold on Grimar's neck with his weight and all his remaining strength. His cousin thrashed with the force of a dying man desperate for air, yet Eirik's grip was unrelenting. He poured his rage into the hands that squeezed Grimar's neck—rage for his father's death, for Laurel's kidnapping, and for Grimar's treachery and attempt to kill him.

His vision narrowed until all he could see were Grimar's bloody, unseeing eye sockets. He could hear naught but the increasingly faint gurgles coming from his cousin's mouth. And he felt naught other than pure, white-hot rage as he took his cousin's life slowly and sent him to his reckoning with the gods.

Grimar had long ago gone still, yet Eirik could not release his hold on his neck. Dimly, in the back of his mind, he registered splashing noises.

Laurel.

His grip finally eased. It was over. Grimar, his cousin, his childhood companion, his would-be murderer, was dead.

He stood on shaking legs and turned from the body. As his eyes refocused and he shifted his gaze to the water, his heart lurched.

Laurel was struggling to keep her head above water, yet she treaded bravely. As she caught sight of him, she cried out wordlessly. He unwound a length of rope from the rigging and tossed it to her. She clung desperately to it as he hauled her in toward the boat with his one good arm. When she was to the boat's side, it took both of their remaining strength to get her over the gunwale.

She tumbled over the gunwale and onto the deck, completely exhausted. He fell to her side and dragged her into his arms. She was shivering uncontrollably.

They didn't speak for a long moment, both too spent to do more than cling to each other. Her body was so cold and small pressed against him. He pulled her closer, giving her his warmth.

Finally, she lifted her head and looked along the deck toward Grimar's still form.

"Is he...?"

"Ja," Eirik choked out. "He is dead. I killed him. I killed my kin."

She took his face in her icy hands. "You did the right thing, Eirik," she said through quivering lips. "Grimar was behind the attack on the village. He was giving me as payment to Jarl Thorsten for killing his own people."

The words barely penetrated the numbness descending all around him, but they smothered the lingering shame Eirik felt at killing his kin.

"He told me something else. He told me that my uncle killed my father," Eirik said flatly, staring at Laurel's beautiful, worried face.

She inhaled sharply and pulled him to her in a fierce embrace.

"My father was robbed of a warrior's death, robbed of Valhalla." he went on, feeling the stirrings of hot rage in his chest and throat once again.

"Nay," Laurel whispered against his neck. She took a breath but paused before going on. "I don't know what you believe about your gods, but my God sees all. He knows what is in men's hearts. He knows your father was a good and honorable man, and a warrior. I believe he has found his proper resting place in the afterlife."

Her words cut him to the core. He dug his fingers into her hair, longing to drag her impossibly closer, to never let her go. Suddenly he realized that he'd been so focused on his own struggle over killing his cousin that he hadn't even ensured Laurel's wellbeing.

"Are you all right?" he asked, his voice filled with alarm. He pulled back slightly to look at her face. "Did he hurt you?"

She swallowed and her eyes filled with tears. "Nay, he didn't hurt me. I will be all right. But Eirik—"

He froze, desperate to do anything for this woman, his love.

"I want to go home. To Dalgaard."

His heart squeezed nigh-painfully at her words. "I love you," he said, holding her gaze.

She blinked, surprise flitting across her dark eyes. Then her eyes grew even fuller with tears until they overflowed down her cheeks. "I love you, too."

He took her mouth in a raw, desperate kiss. He clung to her wet and shivering form, and she gripped him with just as much intensity. He would never be whole again without her.

Finally, he pulled back to let them both catch their breath.

"Forgive me," he said, turning serious once more. "But there is one thing I must do before we can return home."

286

"What is it?" she asked.

The fog of numbness and shock was finally starting to lift, and Eirik knew he needed to take care of the mess Grimar had made.

"We must sail a little farther. I have a message to deliver to Jarl Thorsten."

26

"Where are we going?"

"Just a little farther," Eirik replied, shifting the tiller slightly in his hand.

Eirik had lashed the two boats together, with her captor's boat trailing behind the slightly larger vessel in which Eirik and Grimar had arrived.

She had to swallow hard as Grimar's name came to mind, followed swiftly by the image seared into her memory of his blood-filled, empty eye sockets staring lifelessly at nothing. Eirik had dragged his body to the other boat and laid him down on the small deck.

"There," Eirik said, pointing. "See that opening?"

Laurel followed Eirik's finger to an inlet off the open waters in which they sailed. It was wide at the mouth but narrowed the deeper it went.

"Another fjord?" Laurel asked.

"Ja. Jarl Thorsten's village lies farther in." He turned so that they began sailing into the fjord.

"We aren't...we aren't going to go see him, are we?" she asked, suddenly uneasy. The last thing she wanted was to face this mysterious enemy with both of them exhausted and Eirik wounded.

"Nei, but I have something for him," Eirik said darkly. He moved from the tiller to the mast and lowered the sail. Their brisk clip suddenly changed to a slow drift.

Once the sail was down, Eirik moved to the stern and hoisted himself over the gunwale and onto the other boat with a grunt.

She watched as he hobbled toward where he'd laid out Grimar's body. When he dragged the body up into his embrace, she gasped. "What are you doing?"

He didn't respond. Instead, he propped Grimar's body against the boat's mast and began lashing him to it. By the time he was done. Grimar's lifeless frame was securely tied to the mast so that it looked like he stood upright. His dead, bloody sockets stared out eerily.

Laurel had to put a hand over her mouth and turn away from Grimar's unseeing gaze. She heard the sail of the smaller boat unfurling, then their boat shifted slightly as Eirik's weight rejoined hers.

As he unfastened the ropes holding the two boats together, her mind began to piece together what he intended.

"You are sending Grimar's body as a warning to Jarl Thorsten?"

"Ja. Now he'll know that we've discovered Grimar's treachery, as well as his own part in raiding the village. The Jarl has lost his ally and gained a new enemy."

As the last of the ropes between the boats fell away, the smaller vessel caught the wind and immediately darted past them.

"There will still be a reckoning for the lives the Jarl's men took in Dalgaard. But Thorsten won't soon forget such a message," Eirik said grimly, his eyes following the boat as it made its way deeper into the fjord.

Laurel's thin shift ruffled in the light breeze. She'd dried and warmed quickly in the fresh air and warm sun. She crossed her arms over her chest as she watched the small boat sail away.

Her hands brushed against her chest and a terrible sinking feeling stole over her. "The brooch," she whispered.

"What?" Eirik began raising their sail once more.

"The brooch you gave me," she went on, her eyes filling with tears. "I left the circle on the deck of the other boat. I used the pin to stab that man. I think he dropped it somewhere on the deck as well. 'Tis gone."

"You mean this brooch?" Eirik said, stepping to her side. He extended his hand and in his palm lay both the circle and the pin. The pin was crusted in dried blood but still intact.

Her eyes went wide, first on the brooch and then on his face. "How did you…"

"I saw them just now as I was…dealing with the body," Eirik replied. "I thought you might want them back."

She nodded vigorously, and he unfastened the little lance from its circle. He rubbed the bloodied pin against his tunic as best he could, but his clothes were so tattered and blood-soaked as well that the pin remained reddish. He leaned forward and secured the brooch to her shift, right above her heart.

"Let's go home," he said, his voice thick with emotion.

She could only nod, her own throat already choked with tears.

BY THE TIME they neared the docks jutting out from Dalgaard, Laurel's body had grown stiff from the traumas of the day. Between her capture, her daring attack on her captor, all the swimming, and helping Eirik sail the boat back to the village, she was nigh shaking with exhaustion.

She could only imagine how Eirik felt. He hobbled on his good leg, barely able to put any weight on his wounded right thigh, and he'd completely given up the use of his left arm. His left sleeve was covered in blood, and red marks showed around his throat as well. She feared what collection of smaller cuts and bruises she would find once they got to his cottage and removed his tunic.

As they approached the village, Laurel made out two figures hurrying to the end of the dock. The pale and sandy blond heads of Madrena and Alaric grew increasingly distinct.

"Where have you been? Alaric and I went to check on you several hours ago, only to find your cottage deserted," Madrena set in as their small boat bumped against the dock. Her eyes locked on the two of them and her eyes widened. "What has happened to you two?"

"Gather everyone in the village square," Eirik ordered. He tried to ease himself over the gunwale and onto the dock, but he had to stop, cursing in pain. Alaric bolted to his side and helped him onto the dock. He propped himself under Eirik's good shoulder, taking much of his weight.

Laurel would have landed on the dock in a heap of wobbly limbs as well if Madrena hadn't rushed to her side and helped her. Taking in the fact that Laurel only wore a wrinkled and salt-crusted shift, Madrena unfastened the lightweight cloak she wore and spun it around Laurel's shoulders.

With one arm steadying her, Madrena brought her free hand to her mouth and whistled loudly. Those seeing to their business around the village froze, and several heads began popping out from doors and windows.

"Everyone to the square!" Madrena barked, with Alaric echoing her order in his loud, deep voice.

"Take me to the longhouse," Eirik gritted through his obvious pain.

They staggered across the square, which was quickly filling with curious villagers. They must have been quite the sight. A worried murmur rose around them as they made their way toward the longhouse.

Inside, the longhouse was just as dim as the first time Laurel had set foot in it.

"Jarl Gunvald!" Eirik shouted, shattering the silence of the empty longhouse. "I challenge your Jarlship!"

Both Madrena and Alaric inhaled sharply and exchanged a wide-eyed glance. After a long moment, Gunvald's white-gray head emerged from a door leading to his private chambers. Even from this distance, Laurel could see his pale eyes, so much like his son's, go round in fear.

Without a word, Gunvald stepped from his chambers and slowly made his way across the empty longhouse.

"May I choose the weapon?" Gunvald asked quietly when he reached their little group.

"I do not challenge you to a physical contest," Eirik bit out, his eyes riveted on his uncle. "But rather a challenge based on the laws of this land regarding the bonds of kinship."

If Laurel had thought Gunvald's eyes had been wide before, now they nearly bulged out of his head. He swallowed thickly and glanced between the four of them, as if assessing his ability to escape.

"The villagers gather in the square as we speak," Alaric said coolly. "We'd best join them."

Eirik nodded for Gunvald to go ahead of them. Reluctantly, the Jarl stepped around them and toward the door leading to the square. Throngs of villagers now lined the square, waiting expectantly to learn what was afoot.

As the Jarl emerged from the longhouse and shuffled into the middle of the square, the crowds fell into a hushed silence. Eirik shrugged off Alaric's help and stepped forward.

"Jarl Gunvald, brother of Jarl Arud the Steady, father of Grimar the Raven, and my uncle," Eirik said in a loud, clear voice. "I challenge you for the Jarlship."

A ripple of surprise went through those gathered.

"On what grounds do you challenge the Jarl, Eirik, son of Arud?" someone from the crowd shouted.

Eirik leveled Gunvald with a hate-filled stare. "On the grounds that he murdered my father."

27

A shocked cry from the collected villagers exploded in the air. Even Laurel gasped at hearing Eirik so publicly and baldly accuse his uncle. Yet she knew he spoke the truth, and anyone who looked at him now could see that his eyes burned with conviction.

Laurel felt Madrena stiffen in outrage next to her. Alaric actually bared his teeth in fury. In the Northlands, violence was the way of life, but acting without honor—especially toward one's kin—was the worst sin.

Gunvald's eyes flew around the crowd wildly, searching for any ally. Finally, he faced Eirik.

"Who told you something so despicable?" he asked, trying to draw himself up.

"Your son, my cousin, confessed it to me," Eirik said. His words drew another gasp of shock from those gathered.

Gunvald's lips turned white as he clenched his teeth. "And where is my son now?"

Eirik's mouth curved down in disdain. "I cannot speak to where his spirit resides, for I doubt any of the gods would take him in," he said flatly. "But his lifeless body is sailing into Jarl Thorsten's harbor as we speak."

Pandemonium erupted. Villagers shouted in confusion and outrage. Gunvald bared his teeth and took several steps toward Eirik. Alaric and Madrena instantly jumped in front of him, each drawing the seaxes at their belts.

Eirik held up his fist. "Silence!" he bellowed over the noise of the crowd. Slowly, the villagers lowered their voices from shouts to murmurs.

He suddenly turned his intense eyes on Laurel. "I will let this woman explain why Grimar, my cousin, is dead and in the hands of our enemy."

"But she's an utlending!" someone yelled.

"She's a thrall! She cannot speak here!"

"She warned the village of Jarl Thorsten's attack!" Madrena shouted over the crowd. "If it weren't for this utlending thrall, we'd all have died in our beds!"

The crowd fell into a stunned silence at Madrena's words. Several nodded in agreement. Then Laurel felt the weight of all their eyes shift to her. She started to shrink back, but Madrena nudged her forward into the open space in the middle of the square.

"What Eirik says is true," she began in their language. "Grimar is dead, at Eirik's hand."

The murmur of discontent once again swelled, but she went on in her loudest voice. "I was kidnapped in the early hours of this day by one of Jarl Thorsten's men. He told me that he knew Grimar well, for Grimar was in league with the Jarl. He arranged for the Jarl's men to attack the village."

Gasps of astonishment filled the otherwise taut silence. After a long moment, Gunvald found his voice.

"Grimar would never do such a thing. He longed to be Jarl of Dalgaard. He would never endanger the village or its people."

"The attack was meant for a specific purpose," Laurel said for all to hear. "Grimar wanted Eirik dead."

"Nei!" Gunvald shouted. His pale eyes flared with rage as he glared at Laurel.

"Then why did he draw his seax on me and try to kill me?" Eirik said, his voice icy cold. "He knew Laurel's abductor and asked him to help finish me off."

"Where is this man who is supposedly in league with my son?" Gunvald asked, appealing to the crowd. But the villagers remained silent.

"Laurel killed him," Eirik replied.

Madrena turned her clear eyes on Laurel, a look of admiration in them.

Gunvald snorted. "You expect us to believe that this little girl killed one of Jarl Thorsten's men? And that Grimar, who loved this village and wanted nothing more than to lead it, was working with our enemy to organize an attack? And for what? To kill you, nephew?"

"Ja," Eirik said evenly. "For I would never make such claims lightly, and I would never harm my kin. Yet as Grimar raised his blade against me, he confessed that he was only doing as his father had done to steal the Jarl-ship." Eirik's eyes flashed a challenge as he pinned Gunvald with his stare. "Do you accuse me of lying?"

The villagers went still as they watched Gunvald. Something seemed to shift in the air at that moment. Eirik was unquestionably beloved and trusted by all in the village—it was plainly written in the expressions Laurel saw as she looked around.

Gunvald scanned the faces of those gathered, once more looking for an ally. But his son was dead and his secret had been revealed. Gunvald turned his pale eyes on Eirik for a long moment, assessing him.

"I killed my brother, Arud the Steady," Gunvald said quietly. "I beg for mercy."

The entire crowd seemed to exhale all at once. Eirik's eyes hardened on his uncle. Laurel's stomach twisted. Would Eirik grant mercy to Gunvald after all he'd done? She knew it wasn't her place, and she was an outsider, but she silently prayed for honor and justice to guide Eirik's actions, whatever he chose to do.

"How did you do it?" Eirik bit out through clenched teeth.

Gunvald swallowed hard before speaking again. "As you know, he died while we were raiding to the east. But we got separated from the main battle. His back was to me, so I...I struck."

"Why?" Eirik whispered. "Why would you kill your own brother?"

"I considered myself his advisor of sorts," Gunvald replied, holding Eirik's stare. It was as if the crowd had fallen away and they spoke only to each other. "But as Jarl, he had all the power. I was always in his shadow."

A look of horror crossed Gunvald's face. "Yet I have learned that even with Arud dead, his shadow still hangs over me. The memory of his rule is more beloved than mine." He turned his frightened gaze on the villagers. "Even in death, you love him more than you love me!"

The crowd began to rumble in disdain. Some villagers spat toward where Gunvald stood alone in the middle of the square. Others called for him to face the gods for his dishonor.

Eirik held up a hand and the crowd instantly fell silent. Some invisible shift in power had taken place right before Laurel's eyes, for the entire village now followed Eirik's lead.

"And so you raised Grimar on such poison," Eirik said, his eyes riveted on his uncle. "You wanted him to follow your Jarlship with his own, even if it meant killing kin."

"Nei!" Gunvald said. "Please, you must believe me! Ja, I wanted Grimar to be Jarl, but I forbade him from touching you. But the boy was too wild, too uncontrollable. He…he got away from me." Gunvald dropped his white-gray head into his hands, as if fully realizing for the first time that his son was dead.

After a long moment, he lifted his head. His pale eyes were red-rimmed. "I didn't know that he was in league with Jarl Thorsten, or that he planned to kill you. I warned him what would happen if he harmed you— that suspicion and comparisons would shadow his rule forever, as it has mine."

He struggled for a moment before going on, his voice barely above a whisper. "You are so like your father, Eirik. Whenever I see you, I fear that Arud has come back from the dead to haunt me."

Eirik didn't speak, but he continued to look hard at his uncle.

Gunvald fell to his knees. "I beg of you, nephew, you must believe me and have mercy on me. I only wished to distract you from the Jarlship, not hurt you. That is why I ordered the utlending thrall girl to be sold at the slave market in Jutland by summer's end. I didn't want you to have a reason to stay in Dalgaard. You must believe me —that was the extent of my involvement in this."

Laurel inhaled sharply. Jutland. The man who'd kidnapped her had said something about selling her in Jutland as well. But what did Gunvald mean when he said he'd *ordered* her to be sold at the slave market?

Eirik's head snapped to her, his bright eyes going wide. Her mind spun. Had that been the plan all along? Had that been Gunvald's initial decision the first day she'd arrived in Dalgaard?

"Laurel, I'll explain everything—later," Eirik said, his tone firm but his blue eyes pleading.

"Cut out his innards!" someone from the crowd shouted.

"Feed him to the dogs!"

Eirik's attention was tugged back to Gunvald as the villagers began hurling insults and threats at their former Jarl. She saw Eirik's face pinch slightly at the task before him. He was now the village's leader—it was up to him to dole out the punishment to his uncle.

"I declare myself Jarl of Dalgaard!" Eirik shouted over the crowd. "Does anyone challenge me?"

Those gathered immediately fell silent. The air was still and laden with anticipation. Even Gunvald seemed to be holding his breath where he knelt in the middle of the square.

"I have made a decision about the fate of my uncle," he began in a level tone, though Laurel detected the tightness in his voice.

Murmurs rippled through the crowd once more, calling for Gunvald's death in a dozen ways.

"Gunvald will be…banished."

A collective gasp rose from the villagers. "What does that mean?" Laurel whispered urgently to Madrena. But before Madrena could reply, Eirik turned to her. He spoke loud enough for everyone to hear.

"It means that Gunvald will forevermore live outside the protections of the law and community. It means that he is unfeedable, unferriable, and unfit for all help and shelter. It is worse than death, for he cannot ask the gods to take pity on him. He is the living dead now."

"Ja, he is not one of us!" someone shouted.

"His dishonor will follow him for the rest of his life!"

"Be gone! You are dead to us!"

Gunvald looked desperately around him, rising slowly to his feet. Laurel couldn't tell if he was in any way relieved not to be put to death, for his face was transfixed with fear. Several villagers closed in around him and began shoving him toward the docks. He tried to call something to Eirik, his voice pleading, but the words were swallowed up by the swelling crowd.

Laurel's feet felt rooted in place, yet her eyes followed the strange procession to the docks. One of the villagers gave Gunvald a swift push into one of the small boats Laurel had seen used for fishing within the fjord.

"Never return!" the villagers were shouting as they shoved Gunvald's little boat into the fjord. With fumbling hands, Gunvald unfurled the small sail in the middle of the boat. The wind was with him, for he began moving swiftly toward the mouth of the fjord. The villagers' disdainful cries followed the little vessel until it was merely a speck on the horizon.

At long last, the villagers began trudging back to the square where Eirik, Madrena, Alaric, and Laurel stood silently.

Alaric moved to Eirik's side and wordlessly clasped forearms with him. A look passed between the two men. Alaric's green eyes shone with admiration as Eirik gave him a little nod that they both seemed to understand.

Then Madrena stepped next to Eirik and turned to those gathered. "Long rule Jarl Eirik, son of Arud the Steady!"

The villagers roared their approval. Someone shouted "Jarl Eirik the Steady!" and the crowd soon took up the chant. Laurel watched Eirik in awe. His bright blue eyes were dimmed somewhat with moisture as the villagers repeated his given name with his father's earned name.

Finally he held up a hand and the crowd grew quiet.

"My first ruling as your Jarl was to banish my uncle. My second is that I declare this woman free."

Laurel suddenly felt the weight of not only Eirik's eyes on her, but the penetrating gaze of the villagers. She winced at the silence that followed Eirik's proclamation, but slowly, those gathered began to nod. Then someone in the back started to cheer, and the rest took up the sound, making their approval known.

Eirik strode to her side. "We will feast tonight to honor Laurel, and to acknowledge the changing of the Jarlship." At that, the crowd gave one more cheer and began to disperse to ready themselves for the celebration.

Eirik exhaled and slumped over. He'd been so rigid, so commanding, that Laurel had almost forgotten that he was still recovering from the two arrow wounds, as well as the injuries Grimar had inflicted.

Alaric rushed to his side and propped him up under his good shoulder again.

"To my cottage," Eirik said, his voice strained with pain. "We can at least have a few hours' rest before the celebration this evening."

As they walked along the faint path toward Eirik's hut, Eirik and Laurel explained all that had transpired to Madrena and Alaric. When Eirik told of Laurel's bravery in attacking her captor, Madrena pounded Laurel on the back so hard that the air was knocked from her lungs. Yet when they reached the cottage, a somber mood fell over the group.

"Jarl Thorsten will not soon forget your delivery of Grimar's body," Alaric said darkly. "But many in the village will want to deal the Jarl a greater blow in retribution for the lives lost."

"We'll hit his holding before the first frost of the year," Eirik vowed.

Both Alaric and Madrena nodded grimly before departing down the path toward the village.

Laurel helped Eirik into the cottage and to his bed. He eased himself down with a groan.

"I was to be sold at a slave market?" Laurel blurted out, too tired to measure her tone.

Eirik winced, though she guessed it wasn't entirely from his physical pain.

"Ja. That first day, Gunvald ordered that by the end of the summer, you'd be taken to the market in Jutland and sold. Grimar and I were to split the price you brought. It was his idea of a fair resolution to Grimar's and my claims to you."

Several emotions surged through her so quickly that she had to pause to sort them out. She felt relief that Gunvald's ruling would never be carried out. The thought of being sold at an open market sent shivers of horror through her. Yet her mind flitted back to that first night when Eirik had told her that she would remain his thrall indefinitely.

"And you didn't tell me. You lied to me."

He caught her hands and pulled her down so that she sat on the edge of the bed. His eyes locked on her. All traces of weariness vanished, yet they were filled with a deeper pain.

"Ja, I did. I thought I was doing the right thing by keeping the information from you. I knew from the second Gunvald passed down his ruling that I would find a way to protect you from such a fate. I didn't want to frighten you with the thought of being sold, because I was going to do whatever it took to make sure that never happened."

She eyed him cautiously. "What were you going to

do? How would you have avoided your uncle's decision?"

He swallowed, and for the first time, Eirik looked genuinely afraid. Laurel felt herself holding her breath as she waited for him to speak.

"The only solution I could come up with was to…to marry you."

Laurel's stomach dropped and her chest squeezed painfully. "That's why you proposed that we wed?" She snatched her hands back from his.

"That was how it started," Eirik said, his voice filled with desperation. "By marrying you, you would be made a freewoman, and then you couldn't be sold. But it has gone far beyond that, Laurel. You must believe me. I love you."

He reached for her. She hesitated, letting him wrap his hands around her waist. "Is there aught else?" she said, trying to sort her swirling thoughts and emotions. She didn't doubt his love, nor hers. Yet it stung once again to be reminded that when she'd first arrived in Dalgaard, her fate hadn't been her own.

"I must say something more," he said quietly. "In truth, I could have simply challenged Gunvald's ruling, and thereby his Jarlship, several sennights ago. By Odin, Madrena and Alaric have been encouraging me to do so for years. But I thought marrying you would be a better course of action."

He paused but she remained silent, so he went on. "I was too cowardly to challenge Gunvald then. I didn't want to face my responsibility to lead this village, to fulfill my father's belief that I was bound for great things. But it was more than that. Even then, my love for you had taken root in my heart. I was a coward twice over, for I didn't want to admit it to myself or you, but I longed to join our lives together, to wake up next to you every day, to stand by your side in awe of your bravery and intelligence."

He lowered his eyes, but his hands squeezed her waist. "I wanted you, but I couldn't find the courage to admit it. My approach was wrong, but you must know that my love for you guided me."

She reached out and took his face in her hands, drawing his eyes up to meet hers. The sennight-old stubble on his jawline and cheeks tickled her palms. His dark-gold brows were drawn together over his blue eyes, brighter than the midsummer sky.

What did *she* want? She was so tired of her fate not being her own. Yet this was the man who, even when she was considered his property, gave her a choice and treated her with dignity. She thought back to her life in Whitby Abbey under the thumb of the cruel Abbess Hilda and vulnerable to Brother Egbert's lecherous desires. She shivered at the memory of her brief but horrifying days as Grimar's thrall. And then she thought of her life with Eirik—his commitment to honor, the way he treated her as an equal, and the passion between them.

She wanted to marry this man, but more than that, she wanted to make the decision for herself. She wanted this union to be on her terms as well as his.

"I know you acted as you did to protect me," she began, holding his gaze. "But I hope I have proven that

I no longer simply need your protection. I need your trust, your respect, and your openness. We cannot have any more lies or secrets between us."

He nodded solemnly, his eyes searching hers.

"I understand your desire to protect me, for I desire to protect you, too," she went on.

"You saved my life by attacking that man, Laurel," he said, his eyes bright with emotion.

"Just as you saved mine," she replied, her throat growing thick. "I love you. Can we still be married this Frigga's Day?"

His eyes widened at her words, but then he pulled her to him in a rough embrace. When he finally eased his hold on her, he chuckled.

"Unfortunately, I doubt we'd be able to fetch the *goði* in time. We'll have to wait a sennight."

He sobered quickly as he pulled back so that he could lock eyes with her. "You'll still have me?"

"Ja," she replied with a little smile.

He pulled her under his good arm and leaned back onto the bed, drawing her down beside him. As she nestled her head onto his chest, she looked up at his face. His eyes were closed and his mouth turned up in contentment.

"Frigga's Day cannot come soon enough," he said just before he dropped off into an exhausted sleep.

EPILOGUE

"Repeat the vows again to me." Madrena was fumbling with the shoulder straps at the front of Laurel's dress. Despite the woman's brusque tone, her fingers shook slightly.

"I'll remember them. And if I don't, I'll just look to you to remind me. Everyone knows I'm an utlending," Laurel said.

"Ja, but every day you become more and more like one of us," Madrena said, a crease forming between her light brows as she tugged on the strands of beads draping between the two pins on Laurel's dress. "We don't want to draw everyone's attention to the fact that you are an utlending."

Laurel only laughed and patted Madrena's shoulder. Even in her softened behavior toward Laurel, the woman was still a hard-edged warrior who was used to getting her way. Madrena only snorted and muttered under her breath, but she went about fastening the brooch Eirik had given Laurel to her chest. "You should have had someone who's actually been through this ceremony to help you," Madrena said.

"But none of them would be you," Laurel replied simply. For her kind words, she got an eye roll from Madrena, but the woman's lips curved up slightly.

"We'd best be on our way. There's just one more thing." Madrena turned and retrieved the crown of flowers that several of the village women had made for the occasion. As Madrena set the crown on top of her head, Laurel was surrounded by the delicate scents of wildflowers.

"Come on! We'll be late!" Madrena grabbed Laurel's hand and pulled her out the door of Eirik's cottage. Several hours ago, Alaric had fetched Eirik to help him with his own preparations for the occasion.

Laurel hurried to keep up with Madrena's long-legged stride as she made her way to the village. The buildings were unusually quiet and the square was empty as they strode by. Madrena pulled her toward the mountainsides and the narrow path to the practice fields. Before Laurel could catch her breath enough to ask Madrena where they were going, they reached the clearing.

The meadow, normally filled with warriors hacking away at each other, was now nigh overflowing with villagers dressed in their best. Most of the women and even a few men had flowers woven into their hair or held little bouquets.

Madrena motioned for Laurel to step forward, and slowly the villagers began to part, creating a path to the back of the meadow. As she passed, women approached and handed her a blossom or two until her hands were overflowing with wildflowers.

So overwhelmed was she that she didn't notice until she'd almost reached the far end of the meadow that the path the villagers were clearing for her was leading her directly to Eirik. She inhaled as she took in the sight of him.

His golden hair was braided back from his face along the sides of his head, but otherwise it fell in waves around his neck and shoulders. He wore a simple, clean tunic, but with an elaborate leather belt and scabbard around his waist. He'd shaved his face, and she could make out the hard contours of his jaw.

He stood under a tall wooden bower that was intricately carved and painted in a multitude of colors. Atop the bower lay several leafy tree branches, providing dappled shade from the late summer sun. A man she'd never seen before stood next to Eirik garbed in pale linen robes. He must be the priest.

As she stepped to Eirik's side under the bower, she locked eyes with him. All of Madrena's drilling and training in how to conduct herself in a Viking wedding flew from her mind as his bright blue eyes pierced her.

She went through the motions as if in a dream. The priest said several words to those gathered as well as to her and Eirik. Then Eirik drew the sword at his hip and presented it to Laurel. She had to set down her bouquet of flowers to receive the sword.

"I place my family's sword in your keeping," Eirik

intoned loudly. "To be given to our sons when the time comes."

Madrena had told her this would happen but hadn't warned her just how emotional it would be. Eirik's eyes misted as he passed the sword, which had belonged to his father, into Laurel's hands. She felt her own throat grow thick at the future that lay ahead of them—one filled with many happy children, if God granted her wish.

Then the priest instructed both of them to put their hands on the sword's hilt. "Eirik the Steady and Laurel the Brave are now united in the eyes of the gods and mortals alike," the priest said. The villagers cheered heartily, but shock made Laurel almost deaf to them.

"'The Brave'?" she said to Eirik over the noise.

"Ja. Since you don't have a family name, we decided to give you one," he said, his eyes twinkling with merriment. Before the priest could instruct them to do so, Laurel planted a kiss on his smiling lips, much to the amusement of those gathered.

The villagers began to file out of the clearing and make their way to the longhouse for the start of a three-day long feast and celebration of the union. Madrena had assured Laurel, though, that they wouldn't have to be present the entire time. In fact, the woman had smiled conspiratorially at Laurel and said that after the first evening of feasting, Laurel and Eirik would be excused from the rest of the celebration.

Eirik sheathed his father's sword as she scooped up her wildflower bouquet. Then he took her hand in his and followed the trail of villagers toward the longhouse.

By the time they reached it, villagers had already begun to make merry, both inside and in the square.

As they approached the doorway to the longhouse, all eyes seemed to fall on them. Eirik drew his father's sword and laid it across the door's threshold. Then he moved to physically bar her from crossing through the doorway.

Laurel gave him a little bow of acknowledgement. Madrena had explained this custom and she knew her role. If she were to trip or stumble as she stepped through the door, it would portend bad luck for their marriage. Eirik was to take her hand and guide her safely across the threshold.

She extended her hand for him to take, but at the last moment, he scooped her up in both his arms. She shrieked in surprise as he carried her over the doorstep, to the pleased roars from those watching. When they were inside, he set her down and retrieved his sword. She swatted him on his good shoulder, though his still-healing wounds did not seem to bother him after a sennight of rest.

With a grin, he led her to the raised dais, where two large chairs and a table awaited them. As they took their seats, servers began delivering trays of smoked meats, apples and berries, bowls of vegetable stew, and fresh flatbread. Ale and mead were already circulating, but a special pitcher of mead and two cups sat on their table.

As the celebration wore on, musicians began to play drums and flutes, and several rounds of singing and dancing erupted in the longhouse. Eirik's hand found hers under the table and he intertwined their fingers as they watched the merriment.

"Earlier today Madrena and Alaric asked if you might be willing to teach them your language this winter," Eirik said, leaning in to be heard over the music and singing.

She turned fully toward him, not hiding her surprise. "Why?"

Eirik shrugged. "They are both gripped by wanderlust," he replied. "They want to return to your land and see more of it for themselves."

"To raid?" Fear suddenly pinched her stomach, cutting through her happiness. Though this was her home now, she couldn't condone—or aid in—the raiding and pillaging of her homeland.

"Nei," Eirik said, his eyes soft. "To settle."

She felt her eyes go wide as he went on. "For the benefit of our people, my hope is that we can find new lands to grow into, and to live peacefully alongside the present inhabitants. We can trade, teach them some of our ways, and learn some of theirs."

Laurel chewed on his words. She couldn't imagine Viking warriors settling down to farm or raise livestock in Northumbria, nor could she imagine people like Abbess Hilda welcoming pagan barbarians in any way. And yet, she and Eirik were proof that the two sides could come together in peace.

Then another thought struck her, and she once again felt the twist of fear in her stomach.

"And will...will you be joining them on these voyages?"

He untwined their fingers and lifted his hand so that he could caress her cheek with his thumb. "Nei, Laurel. My duties as Jarl will keep me in Dalgaard. And besides," he said, his eyes penetrating her, "all I could ever want is here."

She closed her eyes for a moment, savoring his words and his touch.

"Eventually we'll have to move, of course, but only into the chambers off the longhouse," he said once her eyes had fluttered open again. "It is the rightful place of the Jarl and his wife."

Even though the sweet honey taste of the mead filled her with warmth, she felt her heart sink slightly.

"We'll have to leave your cottage?" she said. "I've grown quite…fond of it."

A slow smile spread across his face, his eyes pinning her with a heated look. The day they'd held the celebration to honor Laurel's freedom and Eirik's Jarlship, they'd both been so exhausted from the trials they'd survived that they'd fallen into bed and slept like the dead. But every night since then, and sometimes in the mornings as well, they'd explored each other's bodies, finding their pleasures and passions together.

"Well," Eirik said, considering her, with that sensuous look that held a promise in it, "I suppose we can stay there for our honey-moon."

"Honey-moon? What is that?" Madrena hadn't said anything about such a thing.

Eirik leaned in even closer until his lips brushed her ear. "We have a full moon cycle from this day—two fort-nights—where we will be expected to retreat from the responsibilities of daily life, drink as much honeyed mead as we please, and simply…enjoy each other's company." His hot breath tickled her ear, causing a shiver to race over her skin.

"Did I hear you say honey-moon?" Alaric stepped onto the dais, holding something behind his back. After a pause to make sure he had their attention, he produced an enormous clay jug from behind him.

"Since we drank so much of your mead, we thought we'd better replenish your stock," Madrena said, coming to stand next to Alaric with a rare smile on her face. "Besides, we can't have you running out before your honey-moon is over. Speaking of which…"

Madrena motioned to several villagers near the dais. Eirik groaned and began protesting, but the longhouse grew quiet as the villagers turned their gaze on them. The air was thick with excitement and anticipation, as if everyone knew that something was about to happen. Laurel looked between Madrena, Eirik, and Alaric in confusion, but Eirik was too busy grumbling, while Alaric and Madrena both had wide, mischievous grins on their faces.

The villagers whom Madrena had indicated grabbed torches and lit them in the large central fire. A ripple of gaiety swelled among those gathered.

"I think it is time our Jarl and his bride went to bed!" Alaric said loudly. The crowd cheered and shouted ribald jokes, some of which brought heat to Laurel's cheeks. Alaric grabbed Eirik by one arm, the jug of mead in the other. Madrena took hold of Laurel and guided them both out of the longhouse.

"What is this?" Laurel asked Madrena over the cheers and merriment of the villagers.

"Just another Viking tradition," Madrena said, her eyes flashing with laughter in the torchlight.

Alaric and Madrena took the lead with Eirik and Laurel in tow. The villagers holding the torches fell in beside them, with the others streaming behind, singing and shouting gaily.

By the time they'd reached Eirik's hut, Laurel's skin burned in a hot blush at all the attention and bawdy humor around them. She shot at glance at Eirik, and even though he looked uncomfortable as well, he was smiling good-naturedly.

"Off to bed, you two!" Alaric shouted, thrusting the jug of mead into Eirik's hands. He opened the cottage door and hustled them inside, but to Laurel's relief, the door closed behind them, leaving them alone in the dim hut.

Songs and jokes drifted outside, but the villagers were now making their way back to the longhouse for more celebrating. Soon the only sound was their own breathing.

"I have been thinking about this moment since I saw you in the meadow." His voice held the same promise as his sensuous stare had earlier that evening in the longhouse.

He set down the jug of mead and stepped toward her. Leaning down, he inhaled against her hair and the crown of wildflowers she wore. He sighed contentedly, then gently removed the crown and set it aside. Next he let his hand slip along the strings of beads hanging between the two pins holding the shoulder straps of her dress. His hand brushed over first one breast and then the other, sending ripples of awareness through her.

She would have been nervous about her wedding night and the consummation of their marriage had she still been a maiden. Yet she had learned over the last sennight spent with Eirik that there was naught to fear, and so much pleasure to be had. She'd never known that she was so passionate, but she was now coming to trust in and revere the beauty and rightness of the physical expression of their love.

Slowly, he unfastened the pins holding her dress over her shoulders. The overdress slipped along her shift and down her body. Meanwhile, her fingers worked on his belt. She lifted the belt and scabbard, sword and all, away from his body, setting them aside.

He leaned in and kissed her, but it wasn't the jubilant press of lips they'd shared earlier at their wedding ceremony. This kiss was slow, soft at first but deepening, communicating the assured pleasures they were about to share.

She reveled in the tantalizing caresses of his tongue. Her mind flitted to all the things he could do with that tongue, and the coil of heat in her belly flared to life.

He pulled her against his chest, bringing new awareness and sensation to her breasts where they pressed against every hard ridge and plane of him. She could feel the stiff column of his manhood solidly grinding into her belly.

Suddenly he stooped and scooped her up with a hand behind each of her knees. She squealed in surprise and clung to his neck as he secured her legs around his hips and strode toward the wooden table against the wall.

He set her down on the table but held her legs around him, circling his hips against her to show her how much he wanted her. She dropped her arms from around his neck and leaned back, propping herself up with her hands. She let her head fall back as a moan escaped her. His hardness rubbed against her most sensitive spot, both a tease and a promise of what was to come.

He released his hold on her legs, and she drew them up slightly so that her heels rested on the table. He skimmed his hands down her front, over both hard-tipped breasts and across her belly. The touch was so light and fleeting that it caused her to shiver, but his hands returned soon enough, this time more firmly. They found each one of her breasts, his thumbs circling her nipples.

Without realizing it, her hips were beginning to writhe and swirl against his to the rhythm of his hands. Her breathing had grown ragged and she didn't bother to suppress the sighs and moans passing her lips.

He jerked away from her, and she raised her head to protest the sudden absence of contact, but then he gripped her thighs. He yanked her shift up past her hips and knelt between her spread legs.

She let her head fall back onto the table at the first flick of his tongue. This kind of pleasure, this level of closeness, was almost too much. But instead of shying away from the intimacy, she spread her legs wider, beckoning him on.

He flicked and laved, sucked and swirled, until she was arching in pleasure and crying out his name. Ecstasy stole over her, flooding her with light and sensation.

When the throbbing pleasure began to ebb, he stood and tore off his tunic to reveal all the hard lines, ridges, and valleys of his torso. He pulled her up to him, and she could feel the warmth of his skin even through her shift.

Just as he started to lift her toward the bed, she wriggled from his hold and spun around so that she now pinned him against the table. Her hands found the ties on his pants and she gave him a wicked smile as her fingers worked.

His blue eyes, already hazy with passion, flared with renewed heat as her intent became clear. As his pants slid down his muscular legs, she knelt before him. She'd already learned in their sennight of exploring and loving each other with their bodies that she could wreak the same pleasurable torture on him with her mouth as he did on her.

He watched as she flicked her tongue over his swollen cock, teasing him. When she circled the head with the tip of her tongue, he cursed, his whole body tensing. And when she took him into her mouth, he clutched the edge of the table, his knuckles turning white as if he were holding on for dear life.

She gave him the same torturous treatment he'd given her. She ran her fingernails up the insides of his thighs and he shivered, biting off a curse and a groan.

As her fingers brushed against the sack hanging between his legs, he jerked and pulled her back by the shoulders.

Without a word, he drew her up and moved toward the bed—*their* bed. He lifted her shift over her head so that they were both naked, then eased her back onto the down mattress.

She readily opened her legs to him as he lowered himself on top of her. Giving him pleasure had stirred her own desire once more, fanning the flames of passion burning within her. She felt his rigid cock nudging at her entrance and lifted her hips, begging him on.

With one swift, hard thrust, he entered her. Their cries of pleasure mingled as she adjusted to his size and length.

Even though both of their skin was enflamed from their desire, she felt a shiver steal through her. This joining was somehow different, somehow deeper, for they had not simply joined their bodies, but also their lives, forever.

He began moving in and out of her. She locked eyes with him, silently sharing all her pleasure, all her emotions as they slid apart and plunged together. She was his, body, mind, and spirit, as he was hers.

Another wave of ecstasy swelled within her, lifting her up toward the heavens. She dug her fingers into his back, the surge and pulse of pleasure rising and rising impossibly high until suddenly the wave broke over her, flooding her, sweeping her away. Distantly, she heard him reach his own release as they clung to each other, riding out the wave.

As they spiraled back down to the soft bed, he

remained inside her, their bodies pulsing, their panting breaths mingling.

They were bound together inextricably. Laurel didn't know if it was some twist of fate or an act by her God, but her life had changed irrevocably the moment she'd laid eyes on Eirik. And now they were one, stronger together than as individuals, entangled in the sweet ecstasy of life.

The End

AUTHOR'S NOTE

On June 8, 793, Vikings landed on the small island of Lindisfarne off the coast of Northumbria, an ancient kingdom in what is now northeast England. They raided the undefended monastery they found there, killing some monks on the spot, drowning some from their ships, and keeping some as slaves. Thus is said to be the start of the Viking Age.

The Vikings who made landfall on Lindisfarne were likely surprised to find so many unprotected riches. Word spread through the lands we would eventually come to call Scandinavia, and within a few years, more Vikings raided other Christian holy sites in Ireland, Scotland, and southern England.

Monasteries, often located on islands or other remote locations to avoid interference by the outside world, were hit especially hard. Fear of the raiders from the north spread quickly, with Vikings being called "wolves among sheep" for their merciless and swift attacks, and their superior seafaring and battle capabilities.

One such monastery to fall to Viking raids was Whitby Abbey. South of Lindisfarne along the Northumbrian coast, Whitby was founded in 657 A.D. under the name Streoneshalh. It was laid waste by Danish Vikings between 867 and 870 A.D. Though Whitby Abbey is real, I have taken liberties with it in this story—first in having a raid occur earlier, in 806, second in calling it Whitby rather than Streoneshalh, and third in having the raiders be from an area that would become Norway rather than Denmark. The history of the Abbey is fascinating, however, and seemed too rich not to include. (Fun literary crossover tidbit: the ruins of Whitby Abbey inspired Bram Stoker in writing *Dracula*. In the novel, Dracula comes ashore at the Abbey resembling a large dog!)

Whitby Abbey was indeed what was called a "double monastery." It housed both nuns and monks, who lived separately but worshipped together. Double monasteries could have both an abbot and an abbess, but in an unusual quirk of history, abbesses were more common, and their authority was to be obeyed absolutely.

The character of Abbess Hilda in this tale is a slight nod to the historical figure St. Hilda of Whitby, though the resemblance is little more than a shared name. The real Hilda was born nearly two hundred years before this story takes place. She was the founding abbess of Whitby Abbey, then known as Streoneshalh. She was renowned for her wisdom, energy, and skills as a teacher and leader (unlike the fictitious Abbess Hilda). She is considered one of the patron saints of learning and culture, and the feast day of St. Hilda is celebrated on November 17, 18, or 19 (depending on the church).

The Second Council of Nicaea declared in 787 that double monasteries were henceforth forbidden, in part because men and women "living together gives occasion for incontinence." In other words, pregnant nuns became a problem. The Council decision meant that no new double monasteries could be formed, and the ones already in existence couldn't admit new members, thus ensuring that double monasteries would die out on their own (as we see happening by 806 in this story). But the Council's decision was almost unnecessary, for when Vikings began raiding monasteries, many fell into obscurity on their own.

In light of the Vikings' overpowering abilities against such monasteries, it is understandable that their victims painted them as savages, barbarians, and ruthless heathens. This is the image of Vikings that has been passed down through history (along with horned helmets). The reason for this is because while Vikings didn't have a system of written language (besides runes used sparingly), those they attacked did. While normally the victors get to be the writers of history, in this case the victims wrote it—because they could write!

But today a new story of Vikings and their way of life is emerging. Though Vikings did indeed raid and pillage across the British Isles, Western Europe, Eastern

Europe, and as far as North America, North Africa, and the Middle East, they also settled, traded, farmed, and lived peacefully in these lands.

As portrayed in this story, in the early 800s, Jutland (part of modern-day Denmark) was centralizing its power, while other areas of Scandinavia remained isolated by physical barriers and scattered power. Many historians now believe that Vikings began raiding not simply to grab wealth and land, but to escape the limited resources and farmland of Scandinavia. Some also argue that Vikings were subjected to cruel practices under expanding Christianity and wished to retaliate.

Whatever their reasons for expansion, Vikings had complex social and legal systems based on a strong code of honor. From the Vikings we get the precursor to the game to chess (called Hnefatafl), shipbuilding advancements, and countless words that made their way into the English language. But we also get such concepts as outlawry—literally being banished to live outside the protection of the law and community. (Special thanks to Robert Wernick's *The Vikings* for the phrase "unfeedable, unferriable, and unfit for all help and shelter" regarding one who is banished.) It was a harsh time, but also a time of law, culture, and society.

Though this is a work of romantic fiction, I aimed to capture some of the struggles, complexities, and pleasures of the Vikings' way of life. I hope you enjoyed traveling back to the Viking Age with me! Thank you!

Make sure to sign up for my newsletter to hear about all my sales, giveaways, and new releases.

Plus, get exclusive content like stories, excerpts, cover reveals, and more. Sign up at www.EmmaPrinceBooks.com

THANK YOU!

Thank you for taking the time to read *Enthralled* (Viking Lore, Book 1)!

And thank you in advance for sharing your enjoyment of this book (or my other books) with fellow readers by leaving a review on Amazon. Long or short, detailed or to the point, I read all reviews and greatly appreciate you for writing one!

I love connecting with readers! Sign up for my newsletter and be the first to hear about my latest book news, flash sales, giveaways, and more—signing up is free and easy at www.EmmaPrinceBooks.com.

You also can join me on Twitter at:
@EmmaPrinceBooks.

Or keep up on Facebook at:
https://www.facebook.com/EmmaPrinceBooks.

TEASERS

FOR EMMA PRINCE'S BOOKS

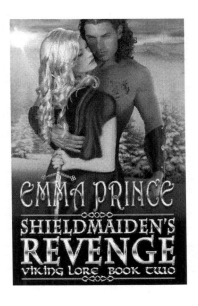

Madrena burns hot for revenge against the man who attacked her village and shattered her life five years ago. When a dark-haired stranger named Rúnin washes ashore in her village, he promises to be her guide in exchange for his freedom. Though Rúnin knows the man Madrena seeks, his life depends on keeping her at a distance, lest her sharp gray eyes discover the secret he must protect at all costs.

Despite the danger, Madrena risks trusting Rúnin. The two travel deep into the Northland wilds, only to be entangled in a world of secrets and peril. Even as they resist the heat that crackles between them, the fires of desire rival those for vengeance. But when Madrena's plans are threatened, will the fierce shieldmaiden choose love over war? And can Rúnin save them both from their pasts?

Taste the sweetness of a blooming first love in *The Bride Prize* (**Viking Lore Novella, Book 2.5**)!

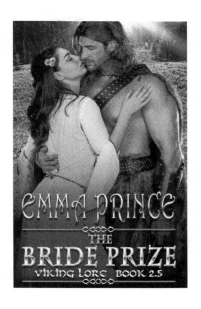

With his family lost to illness, Tarr leaves the only home he's ever known with nothing but a dream—to sail across the North Sea to the mysterious lands in the west. In order to earn a spot on his Jarl's voyage, he must compete against his fellow Northmen in games of strength and skill. But when he learns that the prize for winning the competition is the hand of the dark-haired beauty he met only days ago, will he be forced to choose between his dreams and his heart?

Eyva wants nothing more than to train as a shieldmaiden, but her parents refuse, hoping to yoke her to their Northland farm forever. When they put her up as the bride prize for their village's festivities, she fears she will never escape the fate of a grueling life on her parents' farm. But Tarr's longing gaze and soft kisses just might give her the courage to fight for herself—and for their budding love.

Get swept away by the passionate tale of the Vikings' encounter with the Picts in *Desire's Hostage* (**Viking Lore, Book 3**)!

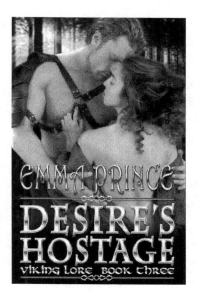

She is his hostage...

As the daughter of a proud Pict chieftain, Elisead's duty is to make a marriage alliance for the betterment of her people. Yet the forest spirits whisper to her, calling her into the woods to carve in stone the long forgotten markings of the old ways. But when she witnesses a terrifying band of Northmen land on the shores of her village, she senses that her fate lies with the golden leader who entrances her with his dancing emerald eyes and claims her with his forbidden touch.

Desire binds them together...

Alaric sets sail from the Northlands with the weighty responsibility of making a permanent settlement in Pictland. To build an alliance with a local Pict chieftain, Alaric agrees to exchange hostages—and claims the chieftain's daughter as his leverage. Now, his greatest challenge is to resist Elisead, the auburn-haired beauty who captivates him completely. When the fragile negotiations turn deadly, Alaric must choose between his mission and his desire to protect Elisead from the mysterious forces working against peace between their peoples.

Highland Bodyguards Series:

The Lady's Protector, the thrilling start to the Highland Bodyguards series, is available now on Amazon!

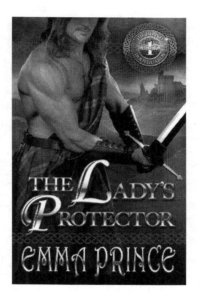

The Battle of Bannockburn may be over, but the war is far from won.

Her Protector...

Ansel Sutherland is charged with a mission from King Robert the Bruce to protect the illegitimate son of a powerful English Earl. Though Ansel bristles at aiding an Englishman, the nature of the war for Scottish independence is changing, and he is honor-bound to serve as a bodyguard. He arrives in England to fulfill his assignment, only to meet the beautiful but secretive Lady Isolda, who refuses to tell him where his ward is. When a mysterious attacker threatens Isolda's life, Ansel realizes he is the only thing standing between her and deadly peril.

His Lady...

Lady Isolda harbors dark secrets—secrets she refuses to reveal to the rugged Highland rogue who arrives at her castle demanding answers. But Ansel's dark eyes cut through all her defenses, threatening to undo her resolve. To protect her past, she cannot submit to the white-hot desire that burns between them. As the threat to her life spirals out of control, she has no choice but to trust Ansel to whisk her to safety deep in the heart of the Highlands...

The Sinclair Brothers Trilogy:

Love braw Highlanders as much as rugged Vikings? Let Robert and Alwin's story capture your heart in **_Highlander's Ransom_**, Book One of the Sinclair Brothers Trilogy. Available now on Amazon!

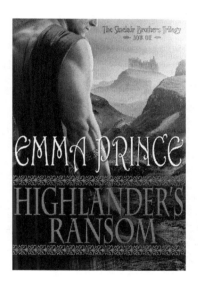

He was out for revenge...

Laird Robert Sinclair would stop at nothing to exact revenge on Lord Raef Warren, the English scoundrel who had brought war to his doorstep and razed his lands and people. Leaving his clan in the Highlands to conduct covert attacks in the Borderlands, Robert lives to be a thorn in Warren's side. So when he finds a beautiful English lass on her way to marry Warren, he whisks her away to the Highlands with a plan to ransom her back to her dastardly fiancé.

She would not be controlled...

Lady Alwin Hewett had no idea when she left her father's manor to marry a man she'd never met that she would instead be kidnapped by a Highland rogue out for vengeance. But she refuses to be a pawn in any man's game. So when she learns that Robert has had them secretly wed, she will stop at nothing to regain her freedom. But her heart may have other plans...

ABOUT THE AUTHOR

Emma Prince is the Bestselling and Amazon All-Star Author of steamy historical romances jam-packed with adventure, conflict, and of course love!

Emma grew up in drizzly Seattle, but traded her rain boots for sunglasses when she and her husband moved to the eastern slopes of the Sierra Nevada. Emma spent several years in academia, both as a graduate student and an instructor of college-level English and Humanities courses. She always savored her "fun books"—normally historical romances—on breaks or vacations. But as she began looking for the next chapter in her life, she wondered if perhaps her passion could turn into a career. Ever since then, she's been reading and writing books that celebrate happily ever afters!

Visit Emma's website, www.EmmaPrinceBooks.com, for updates on new books, future projects, her newsletter sign-up, book extras, and more!

You can follow Emma on Twitter at:

@EmmaPrinceBooks.

Or join her on Facebook at:

www.facebook.com/EmmaPrinceBooks.

Made in the USA
San Bernardino, CA
03 March 2018